As We Amongst the Sleeping Swans

BFJ MULLEN

As We Sat Amongst the Sleeping Swans

This is a work of fiction. Names, characters, businesses, places, events and incidents are either the products of the authors imagination or used in a fictitious manner. Any resemblance to actual persons, living or dead, or actual events is purely coincidental.

As We Sat Amongst the Sleeping Swans

CHAPTER 1

I had been ready for two hours before I heard my father leave the house. I waited until I heard his van exit onto the road before I knew it would be safe to leave with my bags, no questions asked. My mother had arrived home two hours before, after her shift as a night nurse in the local hospital. She wouldn't get up for another hour to get the twins ready for school. The coast would be clear now.

I got up and out of my room without putting the light on, the less noise I made the better. Before descending the stairs with my hastily packed bags, I couldn't resist a quick visit to the twin's room. Stephen and Claire lay sleeping peacefully in their bunk beds, Stephen on the bottom and Claire, the boss between them, on the top. I tiptoed carefully to their beds and tenderly kissed them both. Having just entered their teenage years they would have been mortified to have their older brother show them such a form of affection, but I couldn't have left without seeing them. Both blissfully unaware, slept and dreamt on. I stood there for a moment longer, trying to hold back the tears, as I knew it could be the last time I ever saw them. I turned on my heels and left the room quickly and quietly, the lump in my throat increasing by the second.

My mother was a light sleeper, so I carefully descended the stairs, avoiding all the creaky spots I had grown accustomed to since I was a child. I didn't feel like breakfast, didn't have the stomach for it, so I headed straight for the door and quietly slipped out.

It was 6.30 am, and the sun was struggling to rise over the sleepy blanket of sky. It was cold, damn cold. Frost lay on the ground and I walked quickly down the country road, my footing not the steadiest on the glassy surface. It was about a mile to the bus-stop from our house, the bus leaving at 7.15, so I had plenty of time. I usually got on the 8.15 bus to go to tech, so few of my friends would be on the earlier bus, the less suspicions raised about my overnight bag, the better. Luckily for me, Lisnaderry was scarcely populated and the traffic at that time of the morning virtually non-existent. After a brisk walk, I arrived at the bus-stop, pulled out my packet of ten and lit a cigarette, the steam from my breath and the smoke producing a cloud around me. I inhaled deeply and let the smoke medicate my frayed nerves.

The bus arrived a few minutes late, as usual, and I took a seat about half-way up. The warmth thawed me a little and I sat, rubbing the window, looking out upon the early morning countryside, the landscape speckled in frost with all its Christmas postcard beauty.

It hit me then how much I would miss it all. A country boy through and through, I didn't know how I was supposed to survive the city. It was the first time I had truly thought about what I was planning to do, and nausea rose in me. I took my mind elsewhere to help swallow it down.

As We Sat Amongst the Sleeping Swans

The bus slowed down, and the doors swished open. Caroline Johnson, a girl who went to the Protestant school in town, got on and sat a few seats up from me. Carrying her files and wearing her school blazer, she really was a class act, a notch above all the other girls from the area. Of course, she hadn't even looked at me when she put her files and bag on the rack, not interested in some wee bollocks, who had barely turned eighteen. A girl like that needed a man, mid-twenties, with a job and a car...I knew I didn't stand a chance. I had an urge to get up and go sit beside her though, spin her a few chat-up lines and chance my arm, see what would happen. "God loves a tryer", my dad would always say. What did it matter if she told me to get lost, she would never see me again anyway. Typical of the eighteen-year-old wee bollocks I was, I began to sweat, struggling to breath at the thought of getting up to do such a thing. So, I sat where I was and daydreamed about a day when I *would* have the balls to do it.

I sat further, relishing the journey. The bus was quiet, and my mind drifted to where I was going. I wouldn't let myself think about what happened the night before...I couldn't. If I didn't think about it, then it didn't happen. I resolved to concentrate on the future, not the past.

Dublin was to be my destination. Belfast had been considered, but Dublin prevailed because it was bigger, and I knew less people in it. A lot of people from the area had went to Belfast to study in university, so Dublin would give me greater anonymity. Dublin scared me, but Belfast scared *the shit* out of me.

As We Sat Amongst the Sleeping Swans

The bus reached its destination and I waited for everyone to get up before I did, relishing Caroline Johnson's curves on the way out. The town was busy enough for a Thursday morning and again I felt self-conscious walking around with my bags, feeling they would rouse suspicion in anyone who knew me. I checked the timetable to see when the next bus to Dublin was and cursed under my breath when I saw the options available. There was a bus at nine, but I couldn't get it as I had to go to the Credit Union in town to lift some money. The Credit Union didn't open until ten, and the next bus wasn't until midday. A surge of anger rose in me. What the hell was I going to do, I wondered. It wasn't even 8 o'clock yet, so I had two hours to kill before I could get to the Credit Union, four hours before I could get on the bus. It was freezing, I couldn't be hanging around Dunbay until 12 o'clock as I'm sure my mother would be in town at some stage before that. If she, or anyone who knew me saw me hanging around like a lost soul, instead of being in tech, I could end up being in deep shit. Besides, the news would have broken around the whole country by that stage, and I'm sure everyone would be looking for me, looking to see what I knew about it all. When I found my mind racing back, I nipped it in the bud immediately and decided to head to Tony Parker's flat.

Tony (Nosey) Parker was a stoner Frankie had introduced me to a few months before. He was older than us, perhaps mid to late twenties and perpetually unemployed, though his flat was decked out to the nines and he had a social life that rivalled the rich and famous. He was from a rich family, the reason for his unmerited affluence.

As We Sat Amongst the Sleeping Swans

Before I knew it, I had arrived at his flat, as I had walked briskly to warm myself up and avoid getting noticed. I knew Nosey's place would be a safehouse as he wouldn't ask too many questions, and nobody would expect me to be there.

I rang his doorbell and waited for a moment or two before rapping on his front window. A surge of panic arose in me as it only occurred to me then, that he might not have been in. Luckily, after about thirty seconds I seen the curtain twitch and his red, stoned eyes peer out from behind them. I could hear him scuffling around and pictured him putting on some clothes, as he had probably been sitting around in his pants. He opened the door and grunted something inaudible at me, his charmless welcome as much a tonic to me as if he had rolled out the red carpet and put a glass of champagne in my hand. He walked back into his flat and I followed, invitation pending. A haze of smoke wafted from his living room, unsurprisingly, and I followed him towards it. A pretty girl sat cross legged on a chair in the room. She wore a pair of knee length leather boots, but made them look stylish, not slutty- a rare talent indeed.

"Nikki, this is JP. JP, this is Nikki.", Nosey introduced us to one another whilst walking past her, accepting her offer of the joint. I smiled shyly, her beauty intimidating.

"Hiya JP", she replied, her manner friendly, a suggestion of an accent, Belfast perhaps. "What does JP stand for?", she asked, her eyes filled with an innocent curiosity. I couldn't work out whether her beautiful doe-eyed expression was natural or because she was very stoned.

"John-Paul", I replied.

She sat still for a moment before a thought dawned on her confused, stoned features.

"Were your parent's big Beatles fans?"

It was my turn to be confused.

"What?", I replied, "Beatles fans?"

"John and Paul. Lennon and McCartney?"

I laughed.

"I never thought of that. I'll use that in the future, that's good."

She looked more confused than before; "So, why are you called that? Why do you have two names?"

"Well, I was born in 1979, the year Pope John-Paul came to visit Ireland. A lot of boys my age are called John-Paul because of that."

Nosey, lying on the sofa watching morning television, let out a little chuckle of laughter. "I'd be careful what you say, JP. Nikki's a Protestant from East Belfast."

"I don't care. Nikki, I couldn't care less about any of that and I couldn't care less about the Pope. Nosey, do you mind if I make a cup of tea?", I asked.

"Work away man. But only if you make us some too."

As We Sat Amongst the Sleeping Swans

I went to the kitchen and put the kettle on. I made a pot and brought it in to them. I poured the tea and Nosey offered me the joint. I declined; it was far too early for that.

We sat drinking the tea, watching tv in silence. Nosey was stoned, so stoned he didn't ask me why I was there so early in the morning and why Frankie wasn't with me. I had never visited before without Frankie, him being the one who introduced us. I always thought Nosey was great craic, only realising then how much of a dull stoner he really was. It was Frankie who had always kept the craic going, cajoling and slagging, stimulating humorous reactions from people. He could extract sweet fun and laughter from even the sourest of pusses.

Nikki smiled at me and asked what I did for a living. I think she fancied me, but I couldn't care less, the numbness of my soul all-consuming at that time. Nosey obviously picked up the vibe she was sending out and answered quickly; "What does he do for a living? Goes to school, Nikki. He's only a baby, hahaha."

"Fuck up, ballbag.", I replied, against my better judgement, continuing; "And what do you do? Lie up gettin' stoned on your aul boy's money all day."

Nosey's father was Mick Parker, a very wealthy architect who reportedly owned (and designed) half of Dunbay. I shouldn't have reacted so harshly, as I ran the risk of getting kicked out onto the street for the next few hours. Outwardly I remained calm, but inwardly I was a mess, any little thing would push me over the edge.

As We Sat Amongst the Sleeping Swans

"*Excuse me*", Nosey very patronisingly replied; "Do you want to get knocked the fuck out? Coming in here insulting me in my own home."

"Any day you're fit, Nosey.", I laughed, trying to diffuse the situation a little. It didn't work as he sat glaring at me, obviously awaiting an apology.

"Sorry. I just had a...rough night".

I had to stop myself there in case I divulged anything further. They would find out soon enough, hopefully when I was fully immersed in the city of Dublin and miles away from it all.

Luckily, he didn't ask me to explain, simply shaking his head and telling Nikki I obviously had my period the night before. She didn't laugh. I felt myself liking her more by the minute.

"Some toast?", I asked, knowing both wouldn't be able to resist. Both nodded without taking their eyes off the television. I escaped to the kitchen and took my time making it.

I brought the toast in and both ate with gusto.

"Lovely toast", Nikki complemented; "Are you not having any?"

"Nah, I had breakfast already.", I lied.

"Party last night, Nosey?", I asked, trying to make conversation. I felt awkward around him without Frankie in our company. He nodded without saying anything further.

"Just a group of friends and a few drinks, JP", Nikki answered on his behalf. "We haven't been to bed yet. We did a little poetry reading and had a bit of a sing-song."

Pretentious pricks. I wanted to tell Nosey what I thought but knowing a statement like that would lead to certain exclusion from his flat, I reigned myself in and just nodded in response.

"Maybe we should head to bed now, Nikki? Been a long night.", Nosey asked suddenly out of the blue.

Perhaps a little embarrassed at Nosey's directness, Nikki replied, "What about JP? We can't just leave him..."

"Don't worry about JP. He can let himself out when he needs to...right JP?", he asked, turning to me, winking.

"Uh, yeah...yeah, no problem.", I replied.

With that, Nikki got up, bid me farewell and retired to the bedroom, Nosey following her like a hungry wolf. Nosey always had the reputation of being a ladies man. He certainly proved it then in the way he skilfully lured Nikki to bed in one fell swoop. I could only dream of one day having such moves.

Left alone in the room, I lay on the sofa and tried to doze off for a while, it was going to be a long day. Every time I closed my eyes, his face came to me...that look in his eyes. I pushed the vision to one side in my mind and looked at my watch. It was only 9.15. I would hang around until after 11, go to the Credit Union, lift some money, then head for the bus-stop. I went to the kitchen to make coffee and regretted it immediately, hearing the mumbled voice of Nosey and the giggles of Nikki coming from the bedroom.

"Lucky bastard Parker.", I muttered under my breath, my spirits arising in the hope *I* would maybe get some action in Dublin. I decided to concentrate on the adventure aspect of my journey, rather than viewing it exclusively as an escape exercise. It would be a one-off adventure. I was young, relatively good looking and had a bit of money in my pocket, what could go wrong?

I returned to the living room and almost found myself getting a little stoned from the smoke that lingered in it. I drank the coffee and enjoyed the bolt of alertness it afforded me. Outside the room, the world was fully awake. The world went on regardless, no matter what tragedies visited its people.

The television blared in the background. The programme was about white, middle classed, smug fuckers buying and selling white middle classed suburban homes. Once more, I missed Frankie. If he was watching the show, he would have been giving a running commentary, mocking, and impersonating the smug pricks. I would have been rolling around laughing, Nosey and Nikki wouldn't be in bed and Nikki would be eating out of the palm of his hand.

Life would be a lot duller without him.

I would be a lot duller without him.

The television was terribly bland, usual daytime TV fayre. Even after drinking the coffee I could feel my eyes rolling in my head from tiredness and boredom. Seemingly seconds later, I jolted awake and looked at my watch. Shit, it was 11.30. I had slept for over two hours. Immediately I panicked, bolted from the sofa, and spilt cold coffee all over my jeans in the act. I grabbed my bags and rushed out of the room, out the front door and onto the street. I began to jog towards the Credit Union. It would be a fifteen-minute run, at a good enough pace, made even tougher by carrying the bags and trying to remain incongruous. Luckily, I was fit, and running had never been a problem.

I arrived in twelve minutes, a little hot, sweaty, and out of breath. There was a queue of mostly old fuckers who hadn't much else to do in front of me and I swore under my breath. The queue moved slowly, and I checked my watch to see it was nearly ten to twelve. My heart soared when an irritated looking aul biddy emerged from the back office, taking her seat at the kiosk, beckoning one of the old guys up to her. I was now third in the queue and my heart soared further when an old man dropped out and left without saying a word. The lady in front of me was called and I was now top of the queue. After what seemed an eternity, the old man in booth two finally turned and shuffled out of the building. I strode up to the booth and could see the teller was pissed off that she didn't get to call me. I handed her my book.

"Yes", she hissed.

These fuckers. You would have thought it was their own money they were giving out.

"I want to take it all out please.", I replied.

Her eyebrows raised, and she muttered that she would have to check if they had enough cash in the till before giving it to me.

It was only just over a grand. From her reaction you'd have thought I'd asked to take out a million. One thousand, forty-two pounds and sixty-four pence to be exact. My poor aul granda had died four years previously and had left all five of his grandchildren a grand each. After having taken out the odd score and putting a little back in myself with money I had earned from doing odd jobs for the farmers around Lisnaderry, I had just over a grand to my name. I didn't want to empty the account, but knew I would need every penny of it, if I were to set up a life in Dublin and beyond.

She rifled through the till and pulled a pile of notes from it, counting it as she went. Then she put it to one side and seemed to count the pounds and pennies even more carefully than she had the notes. She counted it twice and went to recount for the third time when I looked at the clock behind her to see it was now five minutes from twelve. My heart raced and I almost told her to keep the change herself, before she slid it under the glass to me.

"Thanks", I muttered before turning on my heels, trying to restrain myself from sprinting out the door. As soon as I got out onto the street, I put my head down and sprinted for the bus station. When I arrived, the bus was reversing out onto the road. I frantically wagged the driver down and was met by another irritated expression.

As We Sat Amongst the Sleeping Swans

The fuck was it with these irritated assholes today, I wondered.

He reluctantly swished the doors open for me.

"Eight-ten", were his only words. I gave him a tenner and he muttered something about correct change under his breath whilst making a big deal about trying to find some change for me. I looked back over my shoulder, nervously checking no-one who knew me was watching, knowing I had been careless sprinting up the street in full view of everyone in the town. There was no-one around, but I still wanted to board the bus quickly and get my head down. I almost told him to stick his change but bit my tongue, knowing many of the bus drivers were cranky, power crazed little shits who would relish the chance to refuse someone entry. I had seen them do it before. To my great relief, he printed my ticket and gave me the change before closing the doors behind me.

The bus was almost empty apart from a few old timers heading on a daytrip to Dublin on their free bus-passes. I made my way to the back seat, put my bag in the rack and lay down, keeping my head down below the window.

The driver backed out onto the road, put the bus into gear and headed on the road to Dublin. A wave of relief washed over me and with-it, tiredness. I closed my eyes and sweet sleep transported me on the way to the metropolis.

As We Sat Amongst the Sleeping Swans

CHAPTER 2

I had always been an average kid.

In school, I had never been bullied, nor been a bully. I had never been a popular kid, nor was I unpopular. I gave my parents very little problems, but didn't give them much to brag about either, unlike my other siblings.

There were two types of young men who grew up in Lisnaderry. Those who were mad into football and those mad into farming.

I fell into neither camp.

Sure, I had passed myself on both the football and agricultural fields, but neither excelled nor obsessed about either.

My passion was music. I played the drums my parents bought me for my 10th birthday in one of the sheds out the back of our house. Again, even though I loved playing them, I was distinctively average. I had joined a few different bands with some of the "townies" I had gone to school with but didn't feel I was quite good enough. Much like playing football, I preferred to lark around at home, getting lost in my own world, rather than having the pressure of having to perform in front of a critical crowd. In our back yard, I played in front of 80,000 adoring fans, scoring winning goal after winning goal. In our shed I was Keith Moon on the drums, playing to a sold-out Wembley stadium. I couldn't perform though. I labelled myself a dreamer though realistically I was a bottler, fear of failure crippling any ambitions I had.

You can see why I was nervous around girls.

In my head I was Don Juan. In reality, I was more Coronation Street's Don Brennan!

Even though I grew up in a family of four children, I was the middle child. My elder sister, Susan, was three years older than I, and the twins, Stephen and Claire were five years younger. I displayed classic middle child traits. I was average in every sense, and strangely happy to be so.

Susan was in University in Belfast studying law. She breezed through exams and seemed to make everything look effortless and easy...a hard act to follow. Claire was Miss Popular in school. She was a funny little thing and was the apple in my father's eye. Stephen was the boy I wished I had been. Star footballer, tough guy, good looks and all the charisma and humour his sister had. God only knew what he would grow up to be- film star, athlete...President? Also, the little shit shared the exact name of my hero. Stephen Patrick Morrissey.

The Morrissey.

I loved all my siblings equally. They were all more talented, popular, and smarter than I was, but I didn't care. I had my little average niche, my middle-child seclusion and was happy with my lot.

My father, like most men from the country was a part time farmer. We had a small farm of around forty acres, and he would graze cattle on it during the summer and house them in the silo in the winter. He did it for the enjoyment more than anything else, as he certainly didn't make much money from it. His main income came from his job as an electrician. My mother was a nurse who worked mostly nights. We were a solid, working class family. Our parents were proud of us and we were proud of them. Sometimes my father wouldn't be home from work by the time my mother had to leave for her job, so I had to baby-sit the twins. My father wouldn't be home some nights until around nine or ten which meant I had to get the twins ready for bed. I didn't mind though, always willing to help where I could.

My parents wanted me to become a teacher. I had no interest in becoming a teacher. I studied English, History and Art for my A-Levels and probably could have studied either subject at degree level if I wanted, such was the interest and talent I had for them. I probably could have gone on to teach either one of them too…but I didn't want to. Teaching would be too boring, and strait laced for me. Even though I could have been perceived as boring and strait laced myself, perfectly suited to such a stable and noble profession, I had delusions of grandeur or "notions" as the people of the country would say. I wanted to be an artist, a writer, a rock-star, a Fleet street journalist or even a historian. I wanted to be anything that meant I could live in a big city and have cool, unconventional trendy friends. The last thing I wanted was to teach at the local school and settle down in Lisnaderry with a local girl and start a conventional life and family.

Deep down though I knew I would do exactly that.

As We Sat Amongst the Sleeping Swans

The greatness of youth, as I had always been told, was being afforded the luxury of dreams.

I certainly was a dreamer.

My middle of the road personality was mirrored by where I sat on the school bus. I didn't sit at the back with the tough, cool kids, nor did I sit at the front with the "nerds". Right in the middle I sat, and I could speak equally to both demographics. I had many acquaintances, but no real friends. It never bothered me either. Some kids desperately latched onto others, entering friendships with others they didn't even like in an attempt not to be alone. I couldn't give two fucks either way. As I said, I was a dreamer and enjoyed my own company, lost in my thoughts and dreams.

All that changed the day I met Frankie Harris.

It was a Monday evening in September, at the beginning of term. I was coming home from the local Technical college where I had recently begun my A-Levels. The bus was packed as usual on the way home, as it dropped students off to all the neighbouring townlands and villages around Dunbay on the road to Lisnaderry. There had always been a few "townies" who got on the bus, getting off just outside the town-a nasty little clique who kept to themselves and sat near the back of the bus. No one on the bus liked them, as the rest of the kids on the bus were all from the country...country boys and townies rarely mixing in any social situation.

As We Sat Amongst the Sleeping Swans

On that day, the four of them were particularly rowdy and a few missiles had been launched down the aisle. A few of the younger boys who had been hit with the objects sat ignoring them, not wanting any further hassle-it would after all be a few minutes until the thugs got off at their stop. The missiles had been harmless enough, a few paper balls, the odd pencil, and a rubber eraser or two.

Just then, a heavy looking wooden hanger was launched down the aisle. That was going to hurt I thought, thanking God it had avoided me. It landed on the lap of a boy I had never seen before. He sat a few seats up from me, near the front. He had dirty fair, spiky hair and wore a green wax coat, something the likes of Jack Sugden from Emmerdale would wear, though he looked nothing like a farmer. He stood up and gazed down the bus, seeking out the culprit.

"The bus is going that way.", one of the townies Paul Dowds shouted. Dowds was a hard fucker who few would have messed with. The boy wearing the wax coat smiled and sat back down in his seat. No one thought anything more of it, no one was going to mess around with Dowds and his gang...no one in their right mind anyway.

Five minutes later, the bus pulled over to let the townies off at their stop. I gazed out the window, daydreaming, when suddenly I heard a loud crack. I jolted from my daydream, frantically looking around to see what drama had suddenly unfolded. It took me a second or so to see the new boy towering over the crouching figure of Paul Dowds. He held the remnants of the wooden coat hanger, Dowds almost cowering in front of him, rubbing the top of his head.

"Have some of that, ye fucker!", the new boy said in a very cool and calm tone. Dowds looked up at him, no fight in him whatsoever, so completely shocked and taken aback he was.

"And there's plenty more of that if ye fancy it", the new boy continued, half grinning.

Dowds and his cronies got off the bus, slinking away with their tails between their legs, the bus erupting in a chorus of cheers. The new boy theatrically bowed to his newfound fans, milking the adulation for all it was worth.

The bus had coronated its new king.

When it came to my stop, about twenty minutes or so after the incident, I made my way to the front of the bus. As I walked past where the boy sat, he stood up.

I half-panicked, hoping he wasn't going to whack me with something too, until he put me at ease with a warm smile. We both walked to the front of the bus and got off at the same stop.

I wasn't used to having company at my stop. The only other person who got off with me was Stephen, when he would stay behind to get the later bus once a week after football training.

We walked in silence for a moment or so.

"Where do ye live?", he asked, a trace of a southern accent.

As We Sat Amongst the Sleeping Swans

"About a mile down the road here. I usually just walk. You?"

"I'm from Ballymoy. I just started in the Tech today. My ma's supposed to be picking me up. Hopefully she remembers, be a long walk if she doesn't.", he joked.

It was around five miles from Lisnaderry to Ballymoy.

Just as I was about to ask him about the hanger incident, a beaten-up Nissan pulled up in front of us. My eyes almost popped out of my head when I caught a glimpse of who was driving the car. It was one of the most beautiful women I had ever seen. Blonde, gorgeous, with a pair of breasts...whoa, I had never seen the likes. She looked like a living Barbie doll. I looked over at the boy. Yes, he was cool...very cool, and probably handsome from a female point of view, but he was punching well above his weight.

He must have read my thoughts as he turned to me, half smiling but with a threatening glint in his eye.

"Don't even think about it. Not one word."

Embarrassed that my reactions towards her had been so noticeable, I blushed and shrugged my shoulders.

"Sorry. But...well done, fair play to ye."

As he walked towards the car, he turned back towards me.

"Well done?", he laughed; "She's my *ma*, dickhead"

He had told me his mother was picking him up, but my brain must not have been able to comprehend this woman *was* his mother when I saw her. I presumed she would have been like *my* mother...middle aged and a bit frumpy.

"Ye want a lift?", he cheerily asked, any semblance of bad feeling from the mix-up gone.

I accepted and hopped into the back seat.

Loud heavy metal music played from the stereo system and the car was full of a thick smoke. The mother's cigarettes were sitting on the dashboard of the car and he picked them up, took one out of the packet and lit it. Seemingly forgetting his manners, he looked back over his shoulder and offered one to me. I took one, thinking how cool we all were, smoking in front of an adult...his own mother too.

"Ma, turn that shit down a second. I want to introduce you to my friend."

She turned the music down and he spoke; "Ma, this is...shit, I never got your name. What do they call you then?"

"John-Paul. JP for short.", I mumbled in reply.

"Ma, this is JP. JP, this is my ma...Charmaine."

"Ello", his mother replied in a very husky and sexy English accent.

"I'm Frankie, JP."

"Frankie...pleased to meet you.", I mumbled, and he laughed at my pathetic greeting.

As We Sat Amongst the Sleeping Swans

His mother didn't really speak. She looked a bit zonked out, like she was stoned or had taken some heavy medication. She was gorgeous, even under close inspection. Her complexion was flawless, pouting lips and a fantastic figure from what I could see from her seated position.

We sat in silence, smoking. When we came close to my house, I asked her to pull in. She pulled over without saying anything, just staring straight ahead. I threw my cigarette out the window, so my mother wouldn't see it.

"See you tomorrow JP", said Frankie over his shoulder.

"Yes", I replied as I hopped out of the car.

There began a friendship we would have for 18 months or so.

Before inevitably, I would fuck it up as only I could.

CHAPTER 3

I awoke just as we were entering the outskirts of Dublin. I sat up and wiped the drool from my mouth, self-consciously looking around to make sure no-one seen me. The bus was fuller than when I had boarded, though no-one sat near the back where I had been lying sleeping. Thank fuck for that as I had probably been snoring, farting and all sorts.

I hoped I hadn't been talking in my sleep.

I didn't really care if the people on the bus heard my snores and farts. To hear what my subconscious was revealing...well, that was a different story.

A quick glance around the bus assured me I hadn't been talking. The people around me looked tired and bored-they wouldn't have been if I had been revealing what was on my mind!

I stretched and yawned, realising only then the grogginess that had grown upon me, the type of lethargic haze that only an uncomfortable nap during the day brings.

A wave of panic suddenly crashed me into full alertness.

What was I doing? I had never spent a night away from home, apart from the rare school trip when I was younger, and then I was on strict orders to phone my mother at least twice before I went to bed. How was I going to cope on my own? I didn't know a soul in Dublin. No-one knew me either or would give a shit who I was.

As We Sat Amongst the Sleeping Swans

Did I have a plan?

Did I fuck.

I had to see out the week, lie low and get away from it all.

Then what?

I really hadn't thought this through.

Just as we entered the suburbs of Dublin, I noticed the life that existed around the place. People hustled and bustled around, living their lives.

What about *my* life?

What about *Frankie's* life? I had to stop myself, had to nip those thoughts in the bud.

Practicalities. I had to be more like my dad. The most practical man I knew. He wouldn't be dwelling on dead thoughts, thoughts that were counter-productive, he would be getting things done, making things happen.

The thought of my dad going about his normal days' work, only to come home that night to find me gone, almost made me break down in tears.

I simply couldn't think of my mother or the twins. It would be too much thinking about them and their reaction to my disappearance.

Where was I going to stay? What was I going to do? I had to get a job. The thousand pounds in my pocket wasn't going to last long in Dublin, dear hole that it was.

As We Sat Amongst the Sleeping Swans

Shit! I hadn't changed my sterling into punts. I would have to do it in Dublin. I would get screwed with the exchange rate. I could just imagine my dad's disgust at my absent mindedness.

"Fuck sake boy. Letting them free-state fuckers take your good sterling for nothing.", he would say, exasperated.

Although my dad was a staunch Nationalist, and most of his friends came from across the border, he loved nothing more than a good rant and rave about those "free-state fuckers."

The bus began to slow as we hit the heavy Dublin traffic. My heart began to rattle in my chest and a cold, clammy sweat came upon me.

Could I jump on the next bus home?

No-one would know about any of this.

I couldn't though. I had to get away...run.

Dublin, as scared as I was of her would be my sanctuary. Her vast bosom would ensconce me.

I had been in Dublin before for football matches, but it was different then. The games had been at the weekend, the city had been quiet. The people were from our county, or from the rival county we were playing. But the spirits had always been good, everyone was in good form. There was plenty of slagging and joviality and I knew lots of people from where I came from. They were times of celebration, whether our team won, lost, or drew.

As We Sat Amongst the Sleeping Swans

Dublin today was different. The people rushing around the streets and driving in their cars seemed isolated, self-interested, and cold. There were no team aspirations. The rat-race had taken over, some of the people resembled rats.

The rain began to fall outside, and I began to enjoy the bus journey. People rushed around in the streets, unfolding umbrellas, and trying to seek shelter. It was early March and the weather was predictably unpredictable. Just a moment before, the city had been doused in a sun that radiated no heat, now rain had taken over.

The lion or lamb that was supposed to "come in", seemed to be having some identity issues.

Typically, just as I was enjoying the cocoon the bus afforded me, we approached the station. I felt weak at the thought of having to get off and make my way. Sure, I had just turned eighteen, but at that moment I felt as helpless as an eight-year-old. Deep down I wanted my mother.

"Fuck sake, man-up, JP.", I whispered to myself.

I could imagine Frankie's response to my fear. Unlike most things he found funny, he wouldn't have found my irrational fear too funny. Disgust would have been his reaction, as he had to almost drag himself up in his life, unlike me and my sheltered upbringing.

The bus stopped, and I was the last to get off. Unlike the interior of the bus, the station was cold, loud, and busy...very busy. People rushed around like zombies. I came to Dublin for anonymity, but if the city was to be this self-interested and cold, I think I had misunderstood what anonymity meant.

I walked aimlessly around the station, trying to get my bearings but not knowing what my bearings were, or where they would take me. I walked into a shop in the station and picked up a can of Coke. My head swam, and my lips were dry, I hoped a sugary drink would cure me. I took it up to the sharp faced girl at the counter and produced a fiver.

"No sterling here, punts only", she responded, her Dublin brogue as sharp as her features.

Fuck. I hadn't converted the money yet.

"Is there a Bureau de Change around?", I asked her.

"A wha'?"

"A Bureau de Change", I repeated, feeling like a dick for saying "Bureau de Change", instead of simply asking for somewhere to change money.

She raised her hands in a very irritated and confused fashion, her sharpness lacerating my soul.

"A place to change money.", I finally submitted.

"Roun' the corner", she replied whilst ushering the next customer in the queue to her. *He* even looked at me irritably, and I sloped off to get my money changed.

I began to turn red at the thought of Frankie's reaction if he had witnessed the scene.

"Bureau de Change", he would mock...and rightfully so.

What a dick I was at times!

I found the counter and walked straight up to the bored looking man sitting behind the glass. A slow day for him perhaps, but the chances were everyday was slow for him, no-one stupid enough to convert their sterling to punts in Dublin...except me.

I had the grand rolled up with an elastic band and I handed it over to him. He counted it slowly and handed me back a stash of twenties.

"£1140", he declared, not even bothering to look at me. He probably couldn't look me in the eye after the daylight robbery he had just carried out. I don't think he really cared though; given the circumstances.

"£1140?", I asked, "What exchange rate are you giving me?", maths never being a strong point.

He looked up at me, as if a little disbelieving of my stupidity.

"One fourteen"

"One fourteen? For fuck sake, I can get one twenty-two, one twenty-five back home."

"Watch your language sonny.", he scolded, "If ye could get one twenty-five why didn't ye get it then?"

He made a valid point, to be fair. Reinforcing my naivety, I simply shook my head in disgust and sloped off.

As We Sat Amongst the Sleeping Swans

I quickly did the maths in my head as I walked. I reckoned I could have gotten £1250 if I'd changed the money before I boarded the bus. I'd been done £110 in one fell swoop. How many more days and nights could that have given me in the city?

Deciding not to dwell too much on the terrible exchange rate, I moved through the crowds and made my way onto the streets. Out on the street, the hustle and bustle overwhelmed me. I was a country boy. To me, Dunbay and Ballymoy were big towns, even though they were tiny compared to others.

Dublin was in a different league altogether.

As I mentioned, I had been in Dublin the odd time for matches, but those games had been on Sundays when the city slept and the fans of the two rival teams took over for the day. Dublin was fully awake now and from the mood of the place, it seemed to have gotten out of the wrong side of bed.

I put my head down and walked quickly. My geography and sense of direction had always been terrible. I had always associated Dublin with three places: Croke Park, Lansdowne Road, and O'Connell Street. As the first two were sporting venues, I was left with the only option of the O'Connell Street area for accommodation.

How would I get there?

I hadn't a clue.

The streets were buzzing with activity, but I didn't want to stop anyone to ask for directions. Where were the stereotypical friendly and approachable

As We Sat Amongst the Sleeping Swans

Dubliners? The people seemed cold and dull, unlike the warm and colourful characters I'd always heard of.

I walked for twenty minutes or so. At one stage I had seen the same office blocks twice and realised then I had been walking in circles, going nowhere quickly. I walked a further five minutes down a long street until I stumbled across a tourist information office. I asked the lady how far I was from O'Connell Street and she handed me a map and gave me a few directions. I thanked her and walked along the street, trying to observe the street names and landmarks of the city. After a lot of walking, I stumbled across my destination. To my disappointment, it was just a huge bustling area with no sign of any accommodation.

"Fuck sake", I muttered to myself as the rain began to fall once more. A light drizzle at first until the heavens predictably opened again. At that moment, I walked past a large record store and to escape the downpour I sloped inside. I hoked inside my rucksack and to my relief, found the Walkman. The tape inside was "The Best of The Smiths". I could easily listen to that on a continuous loop, but as I had a few quid in my pocket and needed some fresh entertainment, I browsed the store in search of something new.

"OK Computer" by Radiohead immediately jumped out at me, followed by "Urban Hymns" by The Verve. They were all I needed. I browsed further for the sake of staying indoors until the rain cleared. For the first time that day I had something to look forward to, listening to those new albums that evening.

As We Sat Amongst the Sleeping Swans

Outside, the rain had abided a little. I walked in search of accommodation, walking away from O'Connell Street. I walked for a further ten minutes or so. At one point, at a set of traffic lights where I stood waiting for the green light, a car pulled up, music blaring. I found my eyes drawn to the passengers of the car and my reaction to them must have been completely noticeable. Inside the vehicle were four black men. Nothing too strange, but for me, I had never seen a black person in the flesh before, now four of them sat in front of me. The two in the front looked at me. I didn't know how to react. I smiled and put my thumb up at them. What the fuck was I doing? The lights turned green for me to cross the road and I looked back at the car. The two black men smiled and gave me the thumbs up too.

I almost laughed. Maybe the city wasn't as scary as I'd anticipated. The men's responses were genuine, they weren't taking the piss, they seemed good natured.

Maybe I could seek out more black guys and "hang out" with them.

Maybe they would understand and "get me" better than "my own" people.

Maybe I could begin rapping...join a gang?

What the fuck was I thinking? Where was my mind?

Two minutes ago, I had never even seen a black person before. Now I was going to become adopted into their culture and join a gang.

As We Sat Amongst the Sleeping Swans

I hadn't slept nor ate the night before. I needed to get a room for the night... badly.

Finally, I stumbled along a street with many B&B's. To my annoyance, most had signs up saying there were no rooms available. I paced up and down the street...nothing. What would I do if I couldn't find a room?

A hotel, maybe?

How much would that cost though?

Panic began to set in. Panic always visited if things weren't going as I'd anticipated.

Just as I had given up, setting off for a hotel, I walked past a middle-aged lady, who stood, shaking a rug out onto the street.

"Do ye have any rooms at all, missus?", I asked, not really breaking my stride as I noticed the sign outside that said there wasn't.

"I have one. We had a cancellation. Do you want it?", she replied without ever looking at me.

"Yep, aye, I'll take it.", I replied, trying to contain my enthusiasm.

She finished shaking the rug and invited me in. She took a book out from behind the counter at the bottom of the hall and put her glasses on.

"Name?", she asked.

I panicked. Should I give a fake name? What if she found out? She would kick me out or probably phone the Gardaí because of her suspicions.

Fuck it.

"John-Paul Morrissey."

She wrote my name in her book and I suddenly broke out in a cold sweat. I was trying to remain anonymous for as long as I could and here I was having my details recorded in a book telling anyone who was interested exactly where I was staying.

"OK. One night will be £55. Breakfast will be from 7-10 and you will be required to check out no later than 11:30am tomorrow. I'm sorry but we are booked up tomorrow night and all weekend if you had planned to stay for a few nights."

Holy shit. 55 fucking quid a night. The money wasn't going to last long at that rate. I would have to find a job…and quick.

I gave her the money and she brought me up to the room. With a little wry smile, she commented; "Please do not bring any girls back. I want no fornication under my roof"

I almost laughed, but instantly turned red and muttered that I wouldn't.

"Good.", she smiled. "I'm sure a good-looking lad like yourself wouldn't have too many problems picking up girls around here…especially with that lovely accent of yours."

Was she hitting on me? I panicked once more. What if she was…what would I do?

I stood outside my room, frozen to the spot. Was she expecting me to invite her in? A few seconds passed and finally she turned and went back down the stairs.

I fumbled with the key to the room and eventually got the door open. I certainly didn't want to be going back down the stairs and asking the land lady to help me into the room, what kind of idea would that be giving her?

The room was very basic. A small bed, wardrobe, and a little television. It smelled faintly of paint. I dumped my bags on the floor and lay on top of the bed. It was hard and not very comfortable, but I couldn't care less. Tiredness overwhelmed me at that moment, and I fell asleep within seconds.

When I awoke it took me a few moments to realise where I was. For a brief second or two I blissfully forgot about my situation and thought I had awoken in my own bed. When I remembered where I was, I felt nauseous. It was now dark, and I could hear the hum of the city in the background. I looked at my watch. 7 p.m. I felt even more nauseous at the thought my parents would now be beginning to realise I was not coming home.

What would they be thinking?

Had they heard about Frankie?

It was very real now. I would have to stoke up the courage and phone them.

How the hell could I do that?

As We Sat Amongst the Sleeping Swans

I sat on the bed and thought for a minute or so. The sudden feeling of intense hunger took my mind off my troubles. I hadn't eaten all day and my body suddenly cried out for food. That feeling of waking from a sleep during the day hit me, the effects of low blood sugar. I put my coat on and headed out of the building, luckily avoiding the land lady as I went.

Like most places, there was a definitive change in atmosphere between the day and evening/night-time. There was a more relaxed, almost playful mood to the city. I met a group of girls who were all dressed up and mostly drunk, a group on a hen-party I presumed. I felt nervous and self-aware as I walked past them, but they didn't even notice me. Nobody in the city noticed me…I don't think I liked it. Anonymity, something I had always craved, like most things when achieved, didn't live up to expectations.

I walked for ten minutes or so before I came to a busy street with a few fast food outlets on it. My mouth began to water at the smells that wafted through the air and I could find myself becoming lightheaded and weak from hunger. Like a moth to a light, I was drawn into the first fast food joint I came across. Standing in the queue I had to lean up against the wall for fear I was going to faint.

Dread, stress, and hunger were not good combinations.

When I got to the counter, a young girl with greasy hair took my order. She looked like she bathed in the grease the food was cooked in, her complexion as greasy as her hair. I took a seat alongside the window and waited for my order to be processed. The city was awakening. Students prowled the streets in search of bars and parties, life was flowing, and people were enjoying themselves.

My mind raced back to home. The stress my parents would be suffering because of my disappearance dulled my appetite for a moment. I *had* to phone them...maybe tomorrow.

No, I would have to do it tonight. I couldn't leave them in torment overnight.

My number was called, and I went to the counter to collect. The girl with the greasy hair gave me the food and I returned to my window seat. I took a bite of the chicken burger and sat back in the seat with satisfaction. I had never tasted anything like it. I tore into it and ate it all in a few bites. I contemplated ordering another but decided to eat the chips before making that decision. They were equally as good, the salt and vinegar they were doused in accentuating the already delicious flavours. For those few minutes, I was lost in the pleasures of the food and all seemed right in the world.

When I had finished, reality hit like the most unpalatable dessert.

I left the restaurant with its delicious smells and warmth to head back to the B&B. The adventures awaiting in the city night could wait until tomorrow. My hunger satisfied; tiredness hit like a ton of bricks. Once out in the evening air, I seemed to feel the cold ten times more, and I longed for my warm bed. Sleep would offer sanctuary, my room a haven from the big bad world outside.

As We Sat Amongst the Sleeping Swans

Now, one of my weaknesses in life had always been a terrible sense of direction. Living in a small rural area like Lisnaderry, I had always gotten away with it, it didn't matter so much. But, when alone in a big city I had never really been in before, I was faced with a problem...a big fucking problem. I didn't know whether it was the tiredness I felt, or because I had severely underestimated my poor sense of direction, but once out on the street, I didn't know whether to turn left or right. I tried not to panic. Surely, I had to have had some form of card or flyer from the B&B I was staying in, surely to fuck. I stood in my tracks and checked all my pockets...nothing.

Shit!

I remembered it had taken me ten minutes or so to get from the B&B to the chippy. I wasn't that far away and I'm sure I could navigate my way back again, but it was crucial I set out in the right direction from the outset. I tried to gather my thoughts and not panic.

Think.

It was hard to think logically though. Knowing most of my money and all my clothes were in that room, brought a cold sweat to my body.

I scanned the street. Why the fuck had I not been paying attention to where I was?

I really was a dumbass sometimes.

At the bottom of the street to my right, I spotted a shop that sold guitars and musical instruments. My heart soared, and I headed in that direction as I remembered walking past it. My parents had always given off to me, especially my father, over the years about the way I would sleepwalk through life. At that moment, I could see their frustrations.

When I reached the shop at the bottom of the street, I was faced with another crossroad. I looked up both streets and this time didn't recognise any landmarks.

Oh fuck!

I was out of ideas. If I went in the wrong direction and walked for five or ten minutes, that meant I would be five or ten minutes further away from my destination. My heart began to accelerate, and I regretted eating so much, as the food was rumbling and gurgling in my stomach, seemingly determined to escape from my nerve wracked body.

I had an idea. Backtrack to O'Connell Street and take it from there. A wave of optimism washed over me, and I walked quickly in search of O'Connell Street, luckily enough finding a few street signs on the way. Five to ten minutes later I approached my destination but didn't recognise any part of it. Full scale panic began to resurface, and I began to run.

A headless chicken would have had more direction.

After a few minutes of light jogging, I had to stop and bend over to gasp for breath. I was in a quiet side street with not much life around. I knew I was lost and had no money, everything lost, all my possessions in that little room that I could never find again. I knew I'd have more chance of finding a needle in a haystack than finding that one tiny room in a city of a million rooms. Once I had gotten my breath back, I vomited all over the pavement. The food that had been so delicious to eat, now putrid and lying on the dirty pavement.

I wanted to cry but didn't have the energy for it.

Just then, an old man walking a dog approached me and asked me if I was OK. His interest in my wellbeing made me want to cry even more than before.

"Are you all right young fellah?", he asked, his features showing concern.

I wiped my mouth clean.

"Yep, I'm all right, thanks. Just had a dodgy chip in the chippie down the road."

"Are you sure? Do you have any friends or family close by who could come get you?", he asked.

"No. I'm OK. I'm just heading back to my B&B."

"As long as you're sure. I hope you feel better soon.", he replied as he went to walk back up the street.

"Sorry…sir."

The old man turned around.

Very self-consciously and wondering whether to pretend I was drunk to alleviate the embarrassment of my stupidity, I mumbled; "I can't seem to find my way back to my B&B. Could you help me?"

"Not a bother. What's the address you're staying at?"

As We Sat Amongst the Sleeping Swans

"Em, I don't actually know."

The penny dropped with the old man and he looked at me knowing I wasn't the full shilling.

"I've never been to Dublin before, so I was walking around trying to find a room for the night. When I eventually found an opening, I was so relieved that I forgot to take a note of where I was. I was hungry so decided to go for some food and now I'm...lost."

The old man's features changed from suspicion to one of humour. He laughed.

"Ach, God bless you son. I'm sure you're not the only one its happened to. Right, do you remember if there were a lot of B&B's on the street you were on?"

"Yes, yes there were a good few.", my confidence growing now because of the man's calmness and logical questioning.

"I've an idea it might be Gardiner Street. There's a lot of B&B's on that street. Take a walk along it and I'm sure your memory will be jogged if it's the one. If not, here is a list of other streets."

He took a pen from his breast pocket and wrote down a list of streets on the back of his fag packet.

"Try Gardiner Street first though", he said whilst handing the fag packet to me. "All the best...stay calm, don't panic."

He gave me some directions to Gardiner Street, and I thanked him and shook his hand.

As We Sat Amongst the Sleeping Swans

My dad always said that strangers would help a person far more than their own friends and neighbours, I could see his logic now.

I half jogged up the road, following the man's directions. I tried to heed his advice about staying calm, but it was easier said than done knowing I might have lost all the money I had in the world.

A few minutes later I found the street. The man's directions had been good. I walked up the street, but nothing in my memory stirred. Much like a city boy might visit the countryside and think everywhere looked the same, all trees and fields, I was the same in the city. All the buildings and streets looked identical; I couldn't differentiate anything. I walked for a few minutes and the panic rose in me further. I could imagine my father's disappointed expression if he was with me.

"Fuck sake boy will ye pay attention.", he would scold, his lingering look hitting me harder than his words.

I walked further up the street. Still nothing.

What was I going to do?

Was I going to have to sleep on the streets already?

I didn't think that would happen until a few weeks down the line, not the first fucking night!

Just as I contemplated facing the horrible thought of trying to find a park bench or an alleyway to spend the night, I heard a slightly familiar voice.

"Cold out tonight."

As We Sat Amongst the Sleeping Swans

I looked at the woman for a moment, my brain frantically working away in the background trying to work out who she was.

"Luckily for you, I have the heating on, so you have a nice warm room to head back to."

I almost hugged her! It was the land lady. She stood there like an angel, a beacon of hope. I laughed heartily.

"Yes, freezing out. Can't wait to get back to the room. By the way, where *is* the building? I'm sorry, but it's been a long day and I can't seem to remember the number.", I lied.

She didn't even bat an eyelid and directed me halfway up the street to a building with a yellow door. My heart soared, and the door seemed to have a golden hue, an aura...like the gates of heaven. All my worries and anxieties melted away, the thought of getting into my lovely warm bed overriding everything else.

The woman said goodbye and I jogged up to the building. Once inside, the warmth reminded me of home, and my joy and relief instantly turned to sadness and anxiety once more.

I ran up the stairs and opened the door to my room. I jumped onto the bed and lay on the mattress, never had anything felt so much like home.

I laughed.

I thought finding that room would be as difficult to find as a needle in a haystack, but somehow, I found it. Maybe someone was looking out for me? Lying on that bed, sinking into its softness, and feeling the warmth of the room, the hubbub of the city outside made me think how lucky I was. It had been cold outside, damn cold and would only get colder. I could only imagine how cold it would be lying on a park bench, not to mention the danger that came with it. The thought of that horrible predicament made the bed even softer. There I lay in my little cocoon, no-one in the world, apart from the land lady knew I was there. That bed and its comfort briefly lifting my spirit of the problems that weighed heavily upon it.

I turned off the light and stretched back on the bed. Tomorrow I would be rested, I would have a full day to get acquainted with the city and find work. That had to be a priority. I was willing to do anything as my money wouldn't last long in Dublin and its fabled expensiveness.

As sleep took hold of my exhausted body and mind, it only then dawned on me I had forgotten to phone home. Absolute fatigue wouldn't allow me to agonise on the reaction of my family at home.

As I lay there, peacefully slumbering on that soft warm bed, torment would prevent my poor family from doing the same that night.

I would worry about all that tomorrow I reasoned, as I fell into a deep sleep.

CHAPTER 4

In the weeks that followed my newly found friendship with Frankie, I piggybacked on his ascension through the popularity stakes in school and the school bus.

Although I had always been content with my mid-bus mediocrity, Frankie dragged me to the back seat, kicking and screaming. He was the newly crowned king of the bus. He sat at the centre of the back seat and I was his right-hand man...literally, sitting at his right-hand side. Having never craved the limelight or attention from others, I had to admit that having influence and popularity because of my association with Frankie was quite enjoyable.

I had never, nor had anyone else, classified myself as a funny guy. *I* thought I had quite a good sense of humour, but few ever got it. My trouble had always been I had no brain-mouth filter. Before I had fully computed a thought, I had broadcasted what was in my head before it had been filtered and understood. My mum had always complained that I had no tact, but my dad had always found it funny.

I was his polar opposite.

It used to infuriate me asking him a question. He would sit and literally look to the heavens in thought before answering. This was the case for every question...every fucking question.

"Dad...why is the sky and the sea both blue?"

As We Sat Amongst the Sleeping Swans

He would fold his arms, look to the heavens...maybe a little chin rub. Fair enough, the question required some thought.

"Dad, do ye want a cup of tea?"

Same considered approach!

I wasn't like that, however. I was more like my uncle Willie, my mother's brother. He was a complete lunatic whose lack of tact landed him with more broken noses and hidings than anyone I ever knew.

He wasn't nicknamed Wild Willie for nothing!

I didn't want to end up like him, wanting to be more like my dad, who was well liked and respected within the community.

Frankie seemed to think I was the funniest fucker ever. Every story I told he would laugh heartily. I think because *he* laughed so much at my stupid shit all the rest of the boys, who looked up to him, followed suit like the sheep they were. They never really found me funny before Frankie came on the scene, but now I was like Eddie Murphy sitting in the backseat.

To be sitting holding court in the backseat alongside Frankie, after all the years I spent in the audience of the big boys, would have had the same odds as Wimbledon winning the cup in '88!

I felt even the girls looked at me differently. I don't think they found me any more attractive than previously, but they'd certainly noticed my status boost. I got a few more smiles from the girls, whereas

As We Sat Amongst the Sleeping Swans

pre-Frankie I would have been lucky to have had a glance.

Frankie certainly had a way with the girls. He looked like an 80's version of David Bowie, with the spiky dirty blonde hair. Gaunt, lanky, and pale...he wasn't what could have been described as a heartthrob. He had a fashion sense that could only be described as confusing...but the girls loved him.

Why?

Because of his gift of the gab.

All the cool girls, the little cliques who sat near the back smoking and who everyone was terrified of, melted when he spoke. He had an aura, his sense of humour...even his laughter was infectious. When he laughed at my silly jokes and stories, I think people laughed simply because *he* was laughing.

Unlike most of the dominant boys that had went before him, he never belittled or made fun of any lesser kids. He joked with the nerds and weirdos, laughing with them...not at them.

When it came to teachers and those in authority, he was less generous in his kindness and understanding. The wit and humour he demonstrated so positively towards his fellow students, he sharpened into a vicious weapon against the authoritarians.

He had been expelled from the high school he attended in Ballymoy. Of course, he had been expelled for telling a teacher "to go fuck himself" one too many times. He didn't care. His mother didn't care either.

He came to the tech to study Politics, History and English, as he wanted to go to university and do a degree in Politics. He wanted to become a politician, an honest politician, and change the world.

Silly fucker.

He was a year older than me and the rest of the boys in our year, but years ahead when it came to life experience. He had grown up for the first few years of his life in England, then lived in Dublin until he was ten, before moving back to his father's homestead of Ballymoy. He had lived in rough areas in Manchester and Dublin and it had stood to him. He was as hard as nails and as wily as a fox.

One night when I was telling my parents over dinner about my new friend, I was delighted to hear my dad knew Frankie's father. Not only did he know him, he had been good friends with him when they were growing up.

"Frankie Harris, from Ballymoy?", dad questioned. "Does he have a real good-looking mother?", he whispered, as my mother had left the table to go and call the twins for their dinner. Embarrassed by my dad's intimate line of questioning and probably turning red too, I replied, "Yea, I suppose she's nice."

He smiled. "Boy, I don't know what she looks like now, but years ago..."

He sat back and smiled, lost briefly in his memories.

Growing even more embarrassed, I quickly directed the conversation away from his mother. "Yea, his dad was called Charlie. Did you know him at all?"

Again, my dad sat back, laughing this time. "Charlie Harris. Poor Charlie. Good fella he was too. We used to run around together. Serious man for the women. They loved him too. He moved to England years ago for work and ended up with a model...a nudey model into the bargain. , I never seen such a good lookin' woman."

He sat for another moment, satisfied in his thoughts. Uncomfortable, as I knew exactly what he was thinking about, I quickly interrupted; "What happened Frankie's dad? He's not around anymore?"

A sudden melancholy descended upon my father's features.

"Ach, poor Charlie. After he met your one and had the child, they stayed in Manchester for five or six years before he came back home. First to Dublin for a while, then back up to Ballymoy where Charlie was from. There was damn all for them but. Charlie, who was a great brickie, couldn't find work and went on the dole. The drink began to get the better of him and the rumours began that his woman was messin' around with one or two boys around the town. Drove poor Charlie mad. The states he used to get himself into...boy oh boy. Well, one night, around Christmas time, on a desperately cold hoor of a night, Charlie left the pub in Ballymoy, after drinking all day. He told the boys in the pub he was going to the lake to catch one of the giant pikes of renown the old people spoke of, told them he was goin' to bring it back the next day and hang it on the wall of the pub. They all laughed and told him to catch himself on. He only goes and does what he said...well, without actually catching the fish. He was a great fisher man in his day, but he was as drunk as a skunk that night and it must have been minus 3 or 4. Next morning he was found...face down in the water. Poor fella drowned in a few feet of water, must have lay there all night on his own. Ach...poor Charlie."

At that point my dad stopped speaking and sat looking out the window. It was the closest I had ever seen him coming close to becoming emotional. I didn't speak, letting him compose himself for a moment or so.

My mum came into the kitchen with the twins, and the subject was changed. It pleased me though that my dad and Frankie's father were friends. I knew my parents would approve of my friendship. It made a difference to a good sensible boy like me. I would have found it difficult to have a friendship with someone my parents didn't like.

As I said, I never gave my parents too much bother.

I never mentioned Frankie's father to him. Frankie never mentioned him either...when sober.

Over the next few months, our friendship was forged and strengthened further over our Saturday night drinking sessions. Those sessions would define our weeks. They gave us something to talk about on Monday and Tuesday and something to look forward to and plan for on Wednesday, Thursday, and Friday.

As We Sat Amongst the Sleeping Swans

Sometimes it would only be the two of us, those were probably the best nights. Other nights, there would be one or two boys from school invited. As Frankie was "the man" in school, it was an honour for others to be invited to our sessions. Girls would be met in the bars and nightclubs around the town, after the main event of drinking the carryout had taken place. Girls came easy for Frankie, but he would always put his friends before them. There had been many a night when I or one of the others in our group had drank too much. On all those occasions, Frankie left whatever girl he was with, to sit with us in the taxi and make sure we got home safe and sound.

I don't think I could have returned the favour to him if it had been the other way around.

He was good hearted that way. Good hearted in every way.

Money had never been a problem for either of us at that age, even though we spent most of our week in school. I had many odd jobs. My dad had many friends who were farmers, so the summer months would be spent helping men with hay, silage and cattle runs. The winter would be spent mucking out sheds and silos and feeding silage and hay to cattle and livestock. Many of the men were single, with no help from sons. Most of the other men had either very young children or sons who had moved away or worked all week.

Being a young fella between the ages of 13 and 18 in the country could be very profitable. Golden years for myself and many of the men who needed help.

As We Sat Amongst the Sleeping Swans

Most of the jobs I did would see me earning between 10 and 20 pounds...a lot of money for someone of my age. It bought a lot of sweets and toys between the ages of 13 and 15, and a lot of clothes and drink between 16 and 18.

Frankie worked part time in the evenings and weekends in the local supermarket in Ballymoy.

Every Saturday at around five p.m., I would rush home from whatever farm I had been working on during the day, eat dinner, shower, and sweet talk my mother to drive me to Frankie's house. Saturday night was my father's night out, so I would try to be away before he got home from work, usually at around 6.30. My father would normally give me warnings about not drinking and behaving myself, so I would try to avoid those lectures. My mother, bless her, would be more trusting and probably didn't think I would be getting up to any badness. My father knew rightly, he had probably been doing the same at my age too. I felt bad about the deception though, and the next day I would suffer. Having a hangover is one thing but pretending to be fine all day, whilst dying inside was no easy task.

Once I got into Frankie's house, any guilt I felt would easily dissipate. He would welcome me into his room where the music would be blaring. His room was very cool, very unlike mine. Posters of bands adorned the walls and candles lit up each corner of the room. Music from Bowie, Fleetwood Mac, The Smiths, The Pogues, The Dubliners, Johnny Cash...sometimes even Abba (his guilty pleasure) and many others would blare from his record player. He had a huge selection of vinyl records (that I later realised where his late fathers) that he cherished and looked after as if they were his own children. One night I spilt beer on one of the sleeves I was reading, and it was the closest I had ever seen him coming to hitting me. Luckily enough we got it cleaned up, but that was the obsession he had for those records.

The same ritual would occur every week when I entered his room. Almost hopping up and down with excitement, he would put both plastic bags behind his back and ask me to choose one of them. It didn't matter which one, as both bags usually contained the same contents, but it was our silly little ritual. The bags would always contain something different each week. We were young, still experimenting with alcohol and we liked to try everything. Some weeks there would be bottles of cider, others vodka, wine, port, sherry...there was one week when we even had a bottle of Advocaat!

"What's that shite?", I asked when Frankie produced the luminous yellow bottle from the bag.

"Advocaat. It's what the yanks call egg-nogg.", he answered. "Taste it, it's OK. It's also 17%. It'll get you nicely fucked."

I took a hit and winced.

"Yum, eggy.", I replied, both words laced with sarcasm.

He laughed and took a huge hit from his bottle.

"There'll be some stink of our farts in the morning after drinkin' this shite.", he said, and we both laughed and continued drinking from our bottles.

As We Sat Amongst the Sleeping Swans

After a while, it was actually OK...and it *did* get us nicely pissed.

We would drink some of our carry outs in Frankie's room, talking and listening to music until the alcohol began taking effect. Then we would venture out and head towards the lake on the outskirts of the town. It was only a ten-minute walk and that was when the fun would begin in earnest. Some nights there would be a crowd, other nights there would only be the two of us.

Those nights were usually the best.

When faced with an audience, drink in hand, Frankie was side splittingly funny. Stories, impressions, slagging, and jokes...he had it all in his repertoire.

The nights we spent alone; he was different. He would ask me about my family. When I spoke about them and told him about the seemingly tedious stuff we all got up to, he would listen contentedly. Smiling and listening to my every word, he would sometimes delve further, asking about my little brother and sisters, what we had for dinner during the week, where we had been on holidays...general life stuff. He would sit on his haunches or lie on the grass, gazing out at the lake. Like a child at bedtime, content...engrossed in what I was saying.

One night, after a full bottle of cheap wine and a freshly opened can of beer in my hand, I stoked up the courage to ask him about his father.

As We Sat Amongst the Sleeping Swans

He sat on his haunches, smoking, and gazed at me for a moment...contemplating the question. Then he smiled and looked out upon the lake.

"He's out there, Moz."

My dad had told me in the past that his father had been found in the lake, but this was the first time Frankie spoke about it.

We gazed out upon the lake. The stillness of the water allowed for a perfect reflection of the moon. For a moment, all was quiet, apart from the gentle lapping of the water against the bank. Neither of us spoke. The scene that spread out before us, heartbreakingly beautiful.

I gazed at Frankie for a moment and could see he was having the exact same feelings. That moment he spoke of his father, the scenery, the silence, and our inebriated state was enough to send shivers down my spine...again and again. We didn't need music, girls, friends...even any more drink, that moment was enough. Neither of us wanted it to end.

A minute or two later, after indulging in the beauty of scene we shared, I walked towards him and got down on my haunches to face him.

"I'm so sorry, Frankie. I'm...so sorry."

He hung his head. I hugged him. It was only then I could feel the deep rocking of his body and I knew he was crying.

We remained for a while like that. Not a word until his body became still once more.

As We Sat Amongst the Sleeping Swans

He got up and turned to walk towards the town.

"Fuck sake, Moz. All the girls will be taken if we don't hurry up and get up there."

We both laughed and ran towards the town and the life that lay within it.

He spoke no more of his father, that night. It was our mad night on the town, and I didn't want to bring the subject up again as I could see how upset he had been. There had been many occasions like that night, when the two of us were alone. We would talk briefly about his father but would always quickly move on when it got too much for him.

Saturday nights were not the only nights we spent together. Frankie would sometimes have dinner in our house after school, both my parents and siblings liking him. He was different in our house than he was on the bus. Always centre of attention, *the man*, whilst amongst his peers, he happily took a back seat when in our house. He enjoyed listening to all our stories and was reserved, almost shy in the presence of my parents.

Rarely would I go to his home, however. Saturday nights excepted, I spent limited amounts of time in his house. He lived with his mother, who was fine...a little ditzy but pleasant, and her boyfriend.

Her boyfriend, Geordie Quinn was a complete wanker. Ballymoy's version of Scarface for years, he had been in trouble with both the authorities and the IRA. Most people from around the area assumed he was an informer; such was the protection he seemed to command from the authorities. Sure, there had been periods when he spent time in prison, short periods of time, but the way he brashly prowled the streets in plain view of all, pushing drugs onto all and sundry in the community, was a little suspicious. On many occasions, threats had been made publicly about him in public houses from dangerous men around the area, but instead of the threats being carried out, those who had issued them would eventually be arrested. The guy was like fucking Teflon...a complete ballbag!

Needless to say, Frankie hated him.

I hated him too.

There were rare nights when he'd be in the house at the same time as me. Frankie would warn me of his presence.

"Cunty's here tonight. We'll drink a bit in my room and then fuck off quickly. I don't want us near that degenerate prick."

We would sneak past the living room where he lay watching television. On the way out, the alcohol consumption making us considerably less stealthy, he would sometimes call us in as we walked past.

"Where are ye's off to tonight boys?"

"Just into town.", Frankie would respond, coldly.

He would laugh. His fat guts showing below his tee-shirt that was too small for him, rippling like agitated waves.

"Away to fuckin' bum each other down the woods more like, ha ha ha."

"Whatever you say, Geordie. Have a good night.", Frankie would reply, stone faced.

Outside, he sometimes punched the nearest object closest to him. Wall, tree, bin.

"Relax, Frankie...it's OK. Don't worry about the fat greasy cunt.", I would advise, trying to calm him down.

"Moz", he would reply, "I'm used to that shit. But I can't bear him saying those things to you. Imagine what your parent's reaction to that would be? That piece of shit insulting a good fella like you. They'd kill him. I can't tolerate him sayin' that to you. My fuckin' doped up mother puts up with him, but my da certainly wouldn't have. Fuckin' cunt!"

I would put my arm around him and usually break into a song. Probably knowing what I was doing, he played along and sang with me. We would forget about the encounter and enjoy our night.

Not a lot of people knew, or would have expected it from Frankie, but he was very well versed in all things scriptural. Not belonging to any particular church like I was, he had an almost encyclopaedic knowledge of the Bible and its contents. I had never met such a deeply spiritual person. He spoke about Jesus with such affection, such deep love and faith, like he knew Him personally.

"How do you know so much about the Bible?", I asked one night whilst the two of us were drinking beside the lake, "I know fuck all...no-one I know does."

He smiled and took a swig from his bottle of cheap port.

"You know something, Moz, you've hit the nail on the head. Very few Catholics know scripture. From no age its drummed into children to pray to Mary. Asking some weirdo in a box to forgive your sins instead of asking Jesus. What the fuck is it with the Catholic church and these middlemen? Pray to Jesus. Pray to God. Ask them to forgive your sins and guide you, not a priest or the Virgin Mary. Fuckin' ridiculous, man. I bet you were confused growing up?"

"Well...yea, I suppose.", I answered, "It *is* a bit confusing...bit of a head fuck to be honest. I couldn't be arsed with it Frankie, loada shite. Sure, religion is for aul cunts who are gonna die soon and are afraid of what is on the other side."

Frankie took a swig on his drink, emptying it and throwing the bottle violently into the lake.

"See this is what fuckin' happens. They drum rituals and bullshit down children's throats, fuckin rosary beads and confession boxes. They drive people away from Jesus. Moz, its witchcraft. They practise pagan rituals. Easter, Christmas...even Halloween. These are pagan events, ceremonies, masquerading as Christian events. You see, my grandfather, my mother's father was a Presbyterian preacher. A good man, though still under Rome's orders and the rule of the dark lord, even unknown to himself..."

As We Sat Amongst the Sleeping Swans

He must have noticed my baffled expression as he stopped at that point to quickly explain; "The Sabbath day that must be kept Holy, Moz. All Christian churches celebrate on Sunday. Sunday is not the Sabbath, Saturday is. Another deception begun by Rome and both Protestants and Catholics are fooled into it. Anyway...fuck, I can't remember where I was, oh yea...my grandfather. He taught me scripture from a young age. No Hail Mary's, no rosary beads...no witchcraft, no Mass. He taught me the word of God...the Bible. I bet you have rarely even read the Bible, simply listening to some sexually frustrated lunatic preaching from an altar instead, the chapel decked in idols, gold, and other fine materials. Grandad taught me that God is always with us, Jesus walks with us. I have a personal relationship with Him, I feel blessed through life. I have no barriers in my way like Mary or a priest. God does not delegate to others...don't even get me started on praying to so called Saints. Open your heart Moz, invite Jesus in...all it takes is a word."

When he spoke like that, I got Goosebumps...I could feel Jesus there with us. He had a point, I never felt Jesus around me in a chapel. The Catholic mindset ingrained within me, always made me a little guilty and uncomfortable listening to Frankie's scathing criticism though.

I could only imagine my mother's reaction!

"So, what about your granda, Frankie? Is he still around?"

As We Sat Amongst the Sleeping Swans

He stood from his hunkered position and lit a cigarette. He took a deep draw and smiled briefly, contemplating his reply.

"My grandfather was a fuckin' great man. A true gentleman. No one...no one ever had a bad word to say about him. He was a preacher, but he practised what he preached, unlike most of the fuckers who are in it for the money, the car, and the parish house. No, he was humble, generous, gentle...a man I will never come close to being. My ma though...haha...my fuckin' ma, she gave him one hell of a hard time. Before she met my da, she became a glamour model. I mean proper glamour, posing buck naked in dirty magazines." He quickly glanced at me, "Don't you even think about lookin' up any magazine archives, Moz."

We both laughed.

"It would be hard on any father to hear about his little girl doing such despicable acts. You can imagine the gossiping from the self-righteous fuckers in his congregation...fuckin' hell. But he faced up to it all, brought it out in the open and talked about it. He certainly didn't agree with her choice of career, but he helped her quit. The poor guy sold his house, promised my ma he would give her half the money then, and the other half after he died, if she quit the modelling. She did. Then she met my father. Again, back in the day, late 70's England with the IRA at their work, the Irish wouldn't have been the most trusted of blokes."

He stopped and took another drag, a little smile resting on his lips.

"My grandfather, English and staunchly Presbyterian, welcomed the Irish, Catholic young man into his family. Both men forged a friendship that would last until my da's death. My da listened when my grandfather spoke. He was as amazed by my grandfather's teachings as I was. Growing up Catholic and confused, scared shitless of creepy priests, nuns, and Brothers, he was faced with a man of the opposite persuasion who spoke to him like a man. He taught him the Bible, spoke the fuckin' truth in a straightforward way, all without judgement or patronisation. My da loved him like his own father."

He stopped, shook his head ruefully and looked at me.

"I've been blessed with great male role models in my life, Moz. Just like you and your dad. Cherish and enjoy him. I had two great men to look up to...the two of them now gone, God bless them."

"What happened your grandfather?"

Frankie's features suddenly darkened, and I regretted asking.

"Ach, he was an awful man for fry-ups and fast food. Like Elvis, one of his heroes, he had an almost addiction to junk-food, if there is such a thing. The man never drank, never smoked a fag in his life. There wasn't a pick of fat on him either, but the fat from the bad food was obviously building on the inside of his body. A terrible worrier, he worried about my ma around the clock...probably warranted too, what with her whoring about and all. But the worrying and the fast food eventually caught up with him...his heart blew up in his chest one day and he dropped dead tending to his little garden out the front of his rented house."

He stopped and took another draw on his cigarette, before looking at me; "I was thirteen years old and sitting in our living room watching TV the night our phone rang. That fuckdog Quinn answered it. He didn't say much on the phone, said goodbye and hung up. My ma was in bed at the time, sleeping off one of her hangovers. He crossed the room, sat down on his seat, and with a little smirk on his face...I'll never forget that little fuckin' smirk, said "Got some news for you, boy. Your granda popped his clogs today, his heart blew up like a balloon. Now turn that shite over and go tell your ma."

Frankie stopped at that point, even in the darkness of the evening I could see tears forming in his eyes.

"You know something, Moz, it was at that moment, God forgive me, I vowed I would ruin that bastid someday."

He took another pull on his cigarette, his steely eyes locked on mine.

"And I will, Moz...I'll get the better of that cunt someday."

Realising what he was saying and seemingly snapping back to the present, he immediately changed the direction of our mood and conversation.

"C'mon Moz. I'm dying for one of these Cointreau and oranges you've been ravin' about all week. Let's go, man."

At that, we raced drunkenly and breathlessly to the bar to meet our friends and partake in the adventures the night would bring.

In the weeks and months that followed that night, I couldn't forget the rage I witnessed in Frankie's eyes when he vowed his revenge on Geordie Quinn.

It frightened me.

He never mentioned it again, but I was worried that something bad might happen, Frankie was not a man who minced his words or made insincere promises.

In the end, though, I shouldn't have worried about the fate of Geordie Quinn.

It would be poor Frankie who would meet an unfortunate circumstance in the end.

CHAPTER 5

It took me a little time to realise where I was after I awoke. I knew I had dreamt, many dreams, but couldn't remember any of them.

But I knew none were good.

The room was cold, and I could hear traffic and hustle and bustle outside. Awakening in my own room at home there would be silence…and the room would be cosily warm.

Once more, queasiness threatened to overwhelm me. "What the fuck am I doing?", I asked myself aloud.

I looked at my watch.

Shit.

The digital clock on top of the dresser read 11:11. I had to be out of there by 11:30. The sudden rush of activity the ensuing deadline brought offered a few minutes of rest to my agonised mind. I heard the vacuum cleaner out in the hall come closer to my door. I knew it was a cue from the cleaners for me to get the fuck out. When changed and my bags packed, I sat for a moment on the edge of the bed. Foreign women's voices could be heard outside my door, they sounded angry. I sat with my head in my hands and ruffled my hair, thinking frantically about what I was going to do next.

Then I thought about them.

As We Sat Amongst the Sleeping Swans

In the cold light of day, the thought of running away from my beloved family hit me hard in the guts. I rushed to my bag, pulled out the plastic bag my toiletries were in and vomited into it. I felt weak, weaker than I ever had been in my life. A cold sweat saturated my skin and I wanted to lie down. I wished I had booked the room for a few days, to lie there and sleep until those feelings passed.

The loud, angry, foreign voices outside the door began once more and I cursed and grabbed my bag on the way out. A large, middle aged, red-haired woman bustled past me into the room with what I took to be her daughter (red-haired, younger, and slightly slimmer) in tow, without registering my presence once. I descended the stairs and met the land lady at the bottom.

"You're too late for breakfast.", she scolded, not looking up at me as she mopped the hallway.

"I know.", I mumbled, "Wasn't really hungry."

Her features softened as she looked up at me; "Hungover, eh? What are ye like?", she laughed and went into the dining room for a moment. She came back out a few seconds later holding a banana, an apple, and a muffin.

"Here, take these and make sure you eat them. You don't look too good. Get some sugar into the system before you drop. You young fellas these days have no sense."

"Thanks", I mumbled in response. I was genuinely touched by her kindness and concern for my wellbeing.

As We Sat Amongst the Sleeping Swans

"Are you goin' back home to see yer mammy?", she asked.

My mum.

The thought of her almost made me break down in tears. Oh God, what must she be thinking?

I nodded. I couldn't speak, the risk I might begin to cry was too great. That would surely raise alarm bells with the land lady.

"Good boy. Now off you go. Don't forget to come back and see me again.", she called after me as I headed for the door. I looked back to wave at her and she gave me a broad wink.

At that I quickened my step out the door.

I stood outside on the street. The wind was up, and the morning was cold and very bitter. Standing there in the cold light of day I could have sworn I was in a dream…or nightmare. It didn't feel like I was really there, it was all very surreal. At that moment I had to put my hand out to rest upon a railing in front of one of the buildings, for fear I was going to fall. I was lightheaded and nauseous once more. Trying to act inconspicuously I fought with all my might not to throw up on the street.

"Fuckin' pull yourself together ye bollix", I muttered to myself through gritted teeth. There was no point in pining for my family. I couldn't go back home; I couldn't let them know where I was. I had to lie low in the city. I had to get a job, save some money, and get out of the country. Go to England, America…wherever the fuck, but I had to get out.

As We Sat Amongst the Sleeping Swans

The mental pep talk I gave myself did the trick and I walked with purpose up the street. No point in moping around, I had to sort myself out or it was all fucked.

First, I had to get accommodation for the night. I knew I couldn't stay in a B&B again after the prices I had paid the night before, so made it my mission to try and find a hostel. I knew it might be difficult though as it was Friday and the tourist and party element would be in town.

I headed down the street in search of accommodation and it wasn't long before I stumbled across a few hostels. They didn't look too bad and I loitered around for a bit outside, judging the people who were entering and leaving the buildings as a guide to what they were like inside. The people all looked the same, foreign looking and student-like. Nothing too threatening, no one looked rough or troublesome. A large group of dark-skinned young men carrying rucksacks left one of the hostels and I decided that was the one for me, knowing there would be a good chance of an empty bed.

I entered the building and two young men sat talking behind the counter. I waited for a moment or so, no response or acknowledgement from either of my presence. They gabbled away to each other relentlessly, thick Dublin brogues interlaced with bouts of manic laughter.

I coughed to register my presence.

One of them, a ferrety looking little fucker, looked up at me, clearly irritated.

As We Sat Amongst the Sleeping Swans

"Ye want somethin' mister?"

I was rendered almost speechless by his lack of customer service skills.

I glanced at his companion who was chubby and bald but didn't seem old enough to be so...like an overgrown baby. He too gave me the same irritated look.

"Are there any rooms goin?"

They both laughed.

"This fella must think he's at The Ritz, eh? A *room!*", the ferrety looking one said. "We don't do rooms, mister, this is an 'ostel. We have beds."

I should have told them to stick their beds and storm out, but just as I was about to, a very pretty blonde girl smiled at me as she walked out past us.

"See ya later Marianne", the baby looking one chirped on her way past.

Thinking I could have a chance to get talking to her that night, I reigned myself in.

"Could I get a bed for tonight...maybe a few nights?"

The ferrety looking one sighed and took out a large book from under the counter. Without looking up at me he asked how long I wanted a bed for.

"A week maybe?", I answered.

"A week...a week. Hmm, let me see. Can you pay up front? Cash?"

I jumped at the offer without asking for a price.

"Yep, no problem. How much do you need?"

"Well, its 15 punts a night, so 7 nights is...105"

I was brought up by my dad to always haggle.

"90 do ye?"

Both looked up at me in surprise.

"Well, if you want to stay for 6 nights, 90 would do us rightly. 7 nights is 105."

I could see those boys were not versed in the art of haggling, so pulled out the 105 punts from my wallet.

The baby looking one looked me up and down whilst the ferrety looking one counted the money.

"90 punts, eh?", he scoffed. "You northern boys, bunch of chancers, eh?", he said, without any indication of humour.

"Where you from, Belfast?"

His ear wasn't tuned to the northern accent at all. *He* sounded as Belfast as I did, and he was as Dublin as they came.

Trying to cover my tracks in case anyone came asking after me, I nodded my head in agreement.

"Yeah, Belfast."

The ferrety looking one gave me a key with a number 2 on it. He told me it would allow me to open room number 2 only. Curfew was 2am and we would have to vacate the building each day between 1pm and 4pm for cleaning. He asked me did I want a locker for my stuff, and I had to pay another 10 punts as a deposit.

I needed to get a job.

As soon as the money was handed over, they lost interest in me and I descended the stairs to room number 2. A wave of panic washed over me as I entered the room. The room was quite clean and tidy, a bit smelly, but not too bad. The daunting part were all the bunk beds. It seemed to be like a prison, and I began to panic thinking I could actually end up in one for real, if I didn't play my cards right.

There was no-one in the room, so I went and sat on the nearest bed. Some of the other beds had towels placed on them, so I took my towel out of my bag and placed it on the bed I sat on. Primitive shit, next thing we'd be pissing on our beds to mark our territory.

I felt like crying. I wasn't supposed to be part of this world. I was too sheltered, too normal. The idea of growing up to become a teacher, marrying a local girl and settling down in Lisnaderry beside my parents, an ideology I had always rebelled against so half-heartedly, now seemed like heaven on earth. My heart pined for that scenario now and I wished I could have turned back time and strove towards that life with all my might.

Just as I began to become lost in a deep yearning, a man walked into the room, wet and naked, all but for a towel wrapped around his waist. He nodded in acknowledgment to me on the way to his bed and sat for a while, drying his curly locks with the towel that sat on his bed. His breathing was very laboured, and I dreaded at once the thought of sharing a room with him that night. If he breathed so heavily simply drying himself, just how bad would his snoring be?

I stole a glance at him. Curly haired, big...very big, red faced with a belly like a pregnant woman. His belly was huge and wet, beads of water running down it and falling off the bridge like a tiny waterfall. Although his belly was ivory white, his face was red, almost purple. Twinned with his heavy breathing and grossly overweight body, the guy looked like a strong heart attack candidate.

He caught me looking at him and I quickly looked away, embarrassed.

"Ya on your own, buddy?", he asked with more than a hint of an American accent.

I nodded.

"Irish or European?", he asked.

"Irish"

"Good. You'll fit right in. There are two Irish guys staying here...two good guys, you'll like em. They'll be here for another night or so. How long you staying for?"

"A week"

"A week, good. Me too. I've been here for two, maybe stay for at least another week, maybe two. Not a bad place, good crowd."

"Where you from...America?"

He laughed. "Not quite, close though...Canada. Sorry, where are my manners.", he continued as he got up to cross the floor towards me. He put his hand out.

"Clive. Pleased to meet you."

"Canadian Clive", I said aloud unbeknownst to myself.

He laughed. "Yes, Canadian Clive."

"JP", I replied and cursed myself I hadn't thought of a fake name.

"JP? Lovely name...lovely name", he said, still holding my hand and giving me a long, uncomfortable lingering look.

Fuck!

I began to panic a little as he stood above me. What if he made a pass at me? He was a big man, a big *heavy* man. I glanced quickly around the room to see if I could grab anything to protect myself. Not seeing anything within my reach I decided I'd grab his balls if he made a move...grab them hard!

To my great relief he slackened his grip and moved back to his bed.

"What brings ya to Dublin, JP. Work, study...fun?", he asked, a little playful smile crossing his lips at the word fun.

The song YMCA suddenly came to mind. It couldn't possibly be that type of place, I thought, surely to fuck not. Then I remembered the pretty blonde who walked past the reception who smiled at me.

"Work", I replied. I certainly wasn't going to say fun. What kind of ideas would that give him?

"Good…good. I'm currently doing security at a big industrial estate just outside Dublin. Keeps the money coming in to keep me in delightful places like this…the lap of luxury.", he laughed.

Although I was sure he was gay and having never met one before, he seemed to be a good guy. I had always been wary of gays before, having the arrogant attitude most straight men had that all gay men would fancy me and try make a move. Canadian Clive seemed no more interested in me than I was in the B&B land lady.

"Doing much today?", he asked.

"No. Gonna try and get a job. Just arrived yesterday."

"Listen, JP, if you're stuck for work, I can give you my bosses number…they're always looking for people."

I almost cried. Strangers trying to help a desperate person was certainly a beautiful thing.

"Yeah, might take you up on that. Could you put a word in for me?"

He nodded.

"I'm goin to head out and see the city for a bit, Clive…do ye want to join me?", I asked, desperately hoping he would say yes.

"Maybe tomorrow. I have to go and meet a friend for coffee."

I nodded and got up to head out into the city. "Fancy goin' for a pint tonight?"

"Can't buddy...gotta work tonight."

"No problem"

Putting his jeans and tee shirt on, he probably noticed the disappointment etched on my face.

"I'm sure the Irish guys won't let you down tonight...crazy guys always up for beer."

I smiled and bid him farewell, looking forward to meeting the boys that night.

I walked past the two Jackeen's at the desk, neither of them stopping their relentless chatter to look at me.

Hungry, I went in search of food and found a greasy spoon in the middle of the city. As I sat perusing the dirty, laminated menu, a fat, bald man sat across from me reading a newspaper. The page that lay open had a photo of a young girl, probably around the same age as me. The headline "MISSING".

I read that headline over and over, the word echoing in my mind. I rushed out of the café onto the street. How long had I been gone? Over 24 hours surely, but how long since my family would have known I was gone? Probably 7 or 8pm the previous night, alarm bells probably wouldn't have been raised until 11 or 12. I heard somewhere in the past, probably on TV, that a person couldn't be deemed as missing until 24 hours had passed.

I couldn't be caught by the authorities and bundled back home...I couldn't.

I ran up the street looking for a phone box. I was sweating like a madman, even though the air was cold and fresh. I ran further, frantically looking for a phone, not finding anything and cursing in frustration. Finally, in the distance I spotted one. I sprinted towards it, mentally racing against my mother at home reaching for hers. When I reached it, there were two teenage girls on it, laughing and giggling down the line. They kept feeding coins into it and I knew they were there for the long term.

Fucking girls and phone calls. I don't think I ever spent more than five minutes on a call, probably only ever to my gran as I had to repeat every sentence five times to her, but girls could spend hours on the fucking thing!

Irritated, I knocked on the glass. They stopped giggling and glared at me. I pointed at my watch, stabbing an angry finger at it a few times. Both gave me the two fingers and returned to their call undaunted.

"Fuckin' wee hoors", I muttered under my breath.

Cursing my stupidity for pissing off teenage girls, knowing they would make the phone call last twice as long to piss *me* off, I stood and waited outside the box. Finally, after what seemed an eternity, they put the phone down and walked past me.

As We Sat Amongst the Sleeping Swans

"Wanker", both hissed. I didn't have the energy to argue back.

I put the coin into the slot and dialled our home number. My heart rattled in my chest and I thought I was going to throw up once more as the phone began ringing.

"Hello", the voice was my mothers. Anxious and riddled with sadness and fear it broke my heart. I had never heard her like that before...and it was all my doing.

"Mum"

"John-Paul! Oh, sweet mother of God! John-Paul, where are you son? Are you OK? Come home...*please* come home."

My poor mum. My heart cracking into a thousand pieces, I blurted the words out with all my strength.

"Mum. Don't worry. Everything is OK. I'm in Cork. I need a few days to myself. Don't alert the authorities, please don't. I will be home soon, everything is OK."

I caught a glimpse of my reflection in the glass and felt disgusted by the lies I told my own mother.

"Come home now, John-Paul. Please...please, please", my mother pleaded, and I knew she was crying.

"Be home soon, mum. Please don't worry. I'm OK."

I put the phone down and sobbed like a five-year-old. I never could upset my mother.

As We Sat Amongst the Sleeping Swans

Drying my eyes, I exited the phone box and went in search of work.

As We Sat Amongst the Sleeping Swans

CHAPTER 6

Growing up in Lisnaderry there hadn't been many role models to look up to. My father had always been my role model. I looked up to him and admired him...but he was my dad, I was biased. Then, when I was about nine years old and my father eventually persuaded me to go to the local football pitch on a Saturday morning for underage practice, I met the man who I truly looked up to.

I had no more interest in becoming a footballer than I had of becoming a ballet dancer. My dad played a little when he was younger and had a keen interest in making a footballer out of me. I was glad when Stephen came along and fulfilled my father's desire to have a footballer in the family. It took the pressure off me.

On that sunny spring morning at football practice, I met a real-life superhero.

The man was a giant, an actual giant. He must have been 6-4 and was built like a brick shit house. He even looked like superman, jet black hair and a chiselled jaw that looked like it could cut steel. Pat Joe O'Halloran was a Garda who worked and lived in Ballymoy but was prominent in the community of Lisnaderry due to his marriage to a woman from the area. He coached the underage football teams and girl's camogie teams in the area. He was heavily prominent within the local church and often participated in the mass, assisting the priest in the ritual of Holy Communion. He had been a major hurling star in his native county down south, years before relocating to the northern region as part of his Garda career. His presence in the community had even achieved the unthinkable...he brought hurling to the area of south Ulster and coached the team in Ballymoy.

Even friends of my father who were staunchly anti-police and Garda had showed a begrudging respect for him. Unlike other Gardai, he was a man of the people. A man of the church, a man of the community. On that first morning I met him, I tried my best for him...tried to emulate and be like him.

Over the years, my admiration and respect for him deepened. He coached and guided me to become a better player than I ever expected to become, fully average, but that was a great achievement for someone with my limited natural ability. Our teams never won any trophies but had come close at times. What we lacked in talent and numbers (we were a small rural area competing against teams from large towns and catchment areas) we made up for in courage and heart. Every player played for one man...Pat Joe O'Halloran.

I never forgot the day he came to our house.

He arrived unexpectedly one Sunday afternoon at the beginning of November. I was only twelve, and he had come to our house to personally tell me he was awarding me the "Most Improved Player" award at the upcoming club dinner dance. For me, that award was my life's biggest achievement. I knew I would never win a "Player of the Year" award, certainly didn't have the talent for it, but to win the most improved player was the pinnacle. Certainly, an award one could never win two years in a row, so I was going to enjoy it. I was so chuffed this hero of a man was in our house. I may have imagined it, but I think he had to stoop under the door at one point to prevent hitting his head. It was like the Pope had visited. My mother fussed, and my father was as speechless as I was. To take the time out of his day to personally deliver the message that a twelve-year-old boy was to be awarded something as trivial as an underage club, most improved player award, showed the character and humility of the man. Although I hadn't much interest in football, that day I thought I could achieve anything on the field. It was the most motivated I had ever felt or indeed would ever feel. He stayed in our house and accepted a cup of tea and a biscuit from my mother. Encouraged, my mother even got the family camera dusted off, so I could get a photo with him in our home. As I grew up, my childhood fascination with him didn't fade, surprisingly, as most things did.

At mass every Sunday Pat-Joe would assist the priest administering the communion. When I was younger, I remember looking up at him thinking he was like God himself, such was the admiration I had for him. He had a distinctive walk, more a swagger, like John Wayne, that he used walking up through the aisle. Every Sunday he wore a fitted suit that accentuated his shoulders and made him look like a cartoon hero character. During the week in school I would try and imitate his swagger, like many of the boys in my class. When I grew a little older it became evident to me the admiring glances he would get from the females of the congregation, as he swaggered up to the altar. When queuing, I always made sure to verge to the side of the altar where Pat Joe would be handing the communion out, much to my mum's annoyance.

"I don't agree with this whole layman trend.", she would complain after every service. "Make sure you childer always receive communion from the priest...not from whatever local celebrity or big fella's assisting him, ye hear?"

We always agreed that we would, but every Sunday I "accidently" veered to Pat Joes side of the altar. Every week he would offer me the small wafer of communion and wink at me in acknowledgement. I would walk back down the aisle feeling like I was ten feet tall...even when I was sixteen or seventeen!

To my surprise (and slight disappointment), Frankie didn't share my admiration of him.

We were in Ballymoy one evening, heading towards the lake for our carryout. As we stood at the pedestrian crossing, laughing, and joking as usual, Frankie's features darkened.

"Young Morrissey", the unmistakable, deep voiced southern accent boomed.

I looked towards the Garda car where Pat Joe sat with the window down.

"Pat Joe!", I exclaimed, embarrassingly like a teenage fangirl.

"Ye behaving yourself?", he joked.

"Not one bit"

"Good lad!", he laughed and drove away.

"*Pat Joe*", Frankie mocked as we crossed the street.

Trying not to get annoyed I laughed. "Sorry...but he's a bit of a legend, you have to admit that?"

"Legend?", Frankie almost spat the word, "What's legendary about him? Big meathead cop who drives around roughing up drunks. Made his name by whacking a tiny ball around a grass park...fuckin' degenerate that's what he is."

"Now, now, Frankie...don't get jealous.", I joked.

"Ha, jealous. Look at you. Did your fanny get wet when he looked at you? Fuck sake Moz, I expected better from you. *Ooh, Pat Joe*"

Inside I was fuming. I must have turned red from his insults, but I didn't react. I was old enough to know how I reacted when angered, especially in public. I cared too much for Frankie to have a bust up with him in the street.

When we got to the lake, after a half bottle of gin was drank by both of us, I decided to break the silence.

"Not cool earlier, Frankie."

"What wasn't cool?", he asked but I knew he was playing for time to think of a response.

"Saying I was basically hot for O'Halloran. What kind of shit talk is that? I did *not* fuckin' appreciate that...you prick."

Frankie pulled deeply on his cigarette, never losing eye-contact with me. Then he turned away and kicked a stone into the lake.

"Sorry Moz. Didn't mean to upset ye man."

"Well...you did. O'Halloran was good to me growing up. I have always admired the man, Garda or no Garda."

There was an awkward silence for a minute or so.

"How was he good to you? I didn't know any of this."

"He taught me how to play football and coached me."

Frankie looked at me, dumbfounded.

"You jokin' or what?"

I began to get irritated; he wasn't giving up on this topic.

"Why would I be fuckin' jokin? What's funny about that?"

"You admire some big meathead bully because he taught you how to feel up other boys on a pitch, whilst running around after a leather inflatable object, trying to put it between two sticks more times than the other bunch of lads? Fuck sake Moz...it doesn't take much to earn your admiration."

My blood began to boil, and I could see Frankie's face was crimson with anger too. What was he so angry about, *he* was the one insulting *me?*

"The fuck is wrong with you?", I asked.

As We Sat Amongst the Sleeping Swans

Frankie walked back and forth across the shore, staring into the lake before shaking his head and answering me; "Sorry Moz. Just really hate that big cunt O'Halloran. I'm surprised you like him, to be honest...really surprised."

He looked at me with a mixture of surprise and disappointment. I felt embarrassed, but defiant.

"He's not my usual type of role model, I admit...but the guy has to be admired. Look what he's achieved in his life, look what he does in return. He coaches kids and tries to put them on the straight and narrow and teach them a skill. He does work for the church...all in his own time. He..."

I was cut off mid gush by a loud cackle of laughter.

"Are you seriously tryin' to wind me up Moz, seriously...referencing his church activities?"

I took a swig of my gin to dampen my temper...it didn't work.

"Ye know somethin' Frankie, you are the quickest to pass judgement. What do you do with *your* time? Fuck all, that's what, apart from slaggin' everyone in front of ye."

Frankie sat stone faced looking at the ground and I began to feel guilty for saying what I said.

"That what you think of me Moz?", he asked in a very small voice without looking up.

I took a swig of my drink to give myself some thinking time. I had huge admiration for Pat Joe, but also for Frankie and didn't want to insult him. But he was so fucking sceptical.

"Sorry Frankie. I didn't mean to annoy you man, but slagging off big Pat Joe...the man's a legend. I mean, come on, what has he ever done to you? Do ye even know him?"

Frankie's features suddenly became very animated.

"Know him? Oh, I know the cunt all right."

"*Cunt*? Fuck sake Frankie is there any need to call him that?"

"You know me Moz. I call a cunt a cunt. And he is a *proper* cunt"

I sat and shook my head. Then I did the unthinkable.

"Frankie, you know somethin', you're out of order. Calling a man like that who means so much to me and my childhood *that*, is unforgiveable. Shit...you might as well have called my dad a cunt. Fuck this, I'm headin' home...I'm not puttin' up with your shit anymore."

I took a final swig of my drink and flung the bottle into the lake.

"Ach, Moz...come on man, let's not fall out over that prick, let's not let him ruin the night."

I walked off towards the town. "No, you're the prick Frankie", I shouted over my shoulder.

He remained sat where he was, and I got the first available taxi home.

As We Sat Amongst the Sleeping Swans

It was Monday before I seen Frankie again. We waited at the bus stop together in silence. When the bus came, we headed straight for the back seat and he took up his role as king and court jester seamlessly. He even got a few reluctant laughs from me and coerced me into the slagging and craic he generated. By the time we got off the bus, our friendship had been mended.

"Any fags on ye, Moz?", he asked as we headed towards the smoking area. I nodded and got two out of my packet. The smoker's area was another arena for Frankie, even students who didn't smoke, flocked to the area for the craic. That morning was quiet, just us and a couple of weirdo hippy looking dudes, who walked around with their heads down all day and communicated to each other through the medium of grunts.

Frankie took a large drag and exhaled for longer than usual. I could tell he was nervous through all the bravado. "Listen Moz, sorry about the other night."

"It's OK- don't worry about it." I said, without truly meaning it.

"But we have to agree to disagree on that prick O'Halloran.", Frankie replied, a coldness in his tone I had never heard before.

We stood smoking for another minute or so in silence until the two hippies sloped off to whatever class they had to get to.

"The fuck's your problem? *Prick*? Is there any need to call him *that*?" I spat, annoyed with myself I was getting angry.

"Every fuckin' need!", Frankie shouted, before reigning himself in, looking around to see if anyone overheard, before hissing, "*Every* need. He's a prick of the highest degree...and a *bad* prick at that."

I stubbed my cigarette out against the wall and shook my head. "Whatever, Frankie. Fair enough. I like the man, you don't...as you say, lets agree to disagree."

I walked towards my class.

"Moz...you *shouldn't* like him you know.", Frankie shouted after me.

"Ok, Frankie, whatever you say.", I sarcastically replied over my shoulder.

"He's fuckin scum, I tell ye man...fuckin scum."

I walked back towards him.

"What is it? Has he done something on ye? I know you don't like him, but you're worrying me now. What happened to stoke up so much intense hate for the guy?"

"He's scum Moz. He put my da's head away back in the day. The bastard was shaggin' my ma behind his back...nice guy eh? I blame that piece of shit for my da's eventual death."

My legs felt like jelly. Pat Joe was a stalwart of the community. He was a happily married man with three children of his own, two of which were younger than me and Frankie. I couldn't comprehend what Frankie was saying. I sat on the wall. When I looked up at him, he was visibly shaking. I took another cigarette out of my packet and gave it to him to calm him down. He lit it and dragged deeply. He was as white as a sheet, I'm sure I was too.

"Fuck. Really?", I asked, half hoping Frankie would say he was exaggerating. He simply nodded, and I fully believed him.

I sat for a moment with my head in my hands. My mind bombarded with an avalanche of thoughts, memories, and images.

Not Pat Joe, surely not.

Hurling hero, football coach, Garda, the communion at the chapel and all his community work. Surely, he couldn't have cheated on his own wife with another woman, herself married with a child.

"I'm sorry, Frankie. I can't believe it.", I quickly glanced at him, "Well, obviously, I do believe it...just a figure of speech."

Frankie nodded; "I know what ye mean."

He finished smoking his cigarette and walked off towards his class. I had never seen him so deflated. All through that day I couldn't help thinking about it. I remember my dad telling me about the men that were "at" Frankie's mother back in the day, but I would never have imagined, never in a million years, that Pat Joe would be one of them. Poor Frankie. Geordie Quinn was a scumbag, and everyone knew it, Frankie's hatred for him vindicated by everyone who knew him. But, to watch Pat Joe strut around like a god, loved and admired by all walks of the community from 10-year-old boys, to middle aged men in admiration of his sporting achievements, to little old ladies who admired his work in the church, must have been killing him inside.

I couldn't believe I had misjudged a snake so badly.

That evening on the bus, Frankie was back to his usual self and the craic was good once more. When we got off, his mother was sitting in the car waiting to pick us up.

"I'm gonna walk home, Frankie. I'll see ye tomorrow.", I said, as I didn't really want to be in the same car as his mother after the revelations of that morning. Hurt and disappointment etched themselves suddenly on Frankie's face.

"Ma, go on ahead home. JP and I want to walk to his house, get a bit of fresh air. JP's mum will drop me home after a while.", he said whilst nodding his head at me, encouraging me to agree.

"Yeah…no probs", I replied.

Without saying anything, his mother drove off. We walked in silence for a few minutes, enjoying the quietness of the country evening after the hustle and bustle of the bus.

"Moz, don't judge my mother alongside O'Halloran. It's not fair, she's different."

As We Sat Amongst the Sleeping Swans

I was a little taken aback by his request. Were they not as bad as each other? It took two to tango did it not, and I knew my own mother would ever do something as selfish, thoughtless, and irresponsible...never in a million years. As if reading my mind, he continued; "My ma's not like yours, she's'...different."

"Damn right she's not.", I blurted out very childishly and felt instantly embarrassed.

"My ma's always been a bit of a girl. This is hard for me to say, pretty fuckin' embarrassing to be honest, but that's just the way she is and always has been. It's like she has some sort of screw loose. I love her to bits, don't get me wrong, and she is a loving, caring mother with a big heart. But when it comes to any man who pays her attention, she's desperate. I don't know what's wrong with her. She put my da's head away and my grandad's too"

I didn't want to say what I was thinking, but once more Frankie seemed to pick up what was on my mind.

"Yes, I do blame O'Halloran fully. Usually I would say it takes two to tango, but my mother is...I wouldn't say easy, like a lot of fuckers think, but vulnerable, very vulnerable. O'Halloran the bastard took advantage."

I was beginning to understand. I remember watching a documentary on television about women who were nymphomaniacs, maybe Frankie's mother was one of them? Once more, Frankie put an end to my presumptions.

As We Sat Amongst the Sleeping Swans

"I don't think it's a sexual thing. By the way, this is as cringey as fuck for me, more an attention issue. My mother can be very childish and innocent in a way, craving adoration and interest from anyone, but especially men. Because of her past in the glamour business, she seems to need constant validation on her beauty, and I know she is petrified of losing her looks with age. Snakes like Geordie Quinn and O'Halloran pick up on those vibes and take advantage."

I was beginning to understand. She *didn't* seem a bad sort. We walked towards my house in silence and I asked him in for dinner. He accepted, and we had a nice evening, although I couldn't help thinking about how poor Frankie's home life differed, living with a deeply flawed mother who he adored despite everything, and a snake like Geordie Quinn.

Worst of all was the snake who masqueraded as an angel within the community.

After dinner and a few cups of tea, my mother and I drove him home to Ballymoy. I sat in the front and Frankie sat quietly in the back. Just as we approached the turn to Frankie's estate, we met O'Halloran, stooped over a car, laughing, and joking, probably reminiscing about his glory years to some sucker in the car. My mother waved at him and he waved back at us, that winning, wholesome grin beaming at us like the streetlights illuminating the street...bright and equally as artificial. I stared stony faced ahead, looking at him from the corner of my eye. I could see his reaction change from cheerful to one of deep concern, as he noted my reaction, obviously spotting Frankie sitting in the backseat.

The penny had dropped for him at that point.

I couldn't help but to peek in the wing mirror at him on the way past. He wore an expression like I had never seen before...anger. A shiver ran down my spine.

There began a war with O'Halloran that would kickstart a chain of events that would have devastating effects on us all.

CHAPTER 7

I walked aimlessly around Dublin streets for half an hour or so, my mum's cries over the phone piercing my almost broken soul. I had to hold the tears back. If I began crying in the middle of the street in broad daylight, I'd surely be lifted by the men in white coats. I tried to hold it together for a while and wandered into the first pub I could find. I was never one for drinking during the day, usually only on Saturday nights, but I couldn't think of anywhere else I could hide out for a while.

The pub was smoky, the usual barfly's present. Old men smoking strong cigarettes and pipes, drinking strong drink. The music was good (mostly traditional Irish) on the jukebox, and the fire was blazing with a good heap of peat sat in reserve, ready to be turfed on when needed. The barmaid made her way up to where I sat at the bar. I could see her mentally weigh me up and I began to panic a little that she might ask for ID to confirm my age. She didn't, thankfully.

"What can I get you?", she asked, her Dublin accent subtler, posher.

I instantly fell in love.

She was perhaps mid-thirties, blonde with a body to die for. Big green eyes gazed at me expectantly and I found myself lost in them. I must have gazed into them for a second or so longer than I should have, as she repeated, "What can I get for you?"

Feeling myself going red and without any prior thought, I replied, "Whiskey…neat".

She turned and walked towards the optics and I couldn't help but gaze after her. I became lost in thought once more about what kind of man could get a woman like that. I knew I certainly couldn't, and she was out of Frankie's league too. Then a wave of nausea hit me as O'Halloran's big head popped into my mind. *He* could get a woman like that; she'd be putty in the bastard's hands. The thought of how she would react to O'Halloran if he was sitting next to me, dampened my desire for her almost totally.

She walked back with the pathetic measure of drink in the glass and I gave her a fiver and didn't receive much change in return. I took a sip and grimaced. What the fuck did I order whiskey for? I must have thought I was John Wayne or Clint Eastwood when I walked in…what a dick!

I looked up from my glass and the barmaid was looking back at me, laughing.

"That whiskey not agreeing with you? Want another?"

I began to laugh too. "No, it's fine…its good. I love a good scotch."

She laughed again. "It's not scotch, its Jameson."

I could feel myself turning red.

"Yeah, I meant Jameson, sorry. Its good stuff, good vintage."

She laughed even more. "OK, mister whiskey connoisseur. What do they call you then?"

Her beauty was so striking that I blurted my name out without even thinking of making up a false one. She told me her name was Hilda.

I downed the rest of the whiskey and tried to keep it down as best I could. Hilda noticed my attempts and asked if I wanted another. I shook my head and concentrated on keeping the vile liquid in my stomach. Fucking whiskey, horrible, I had never drunk the stuff before, even on one of my nights with Frankie.

"Beer this time, maybe?", Hilda asked, trying not to laugh.

I agreed, and she poured me a cold pint. I sipped it, vowing to make it last a while. The bar was comfortable, warm, and offered solitude from the harsh outside world. I remembered going into bars at home with my dad and looking at all the old-timers, feeling pity for them drinking their whiskeys and pints. Now I was beginning to think those aul boys had the right idea.

The beer was going down well, too well, and I ordered another. I cringed as I gave Hilda another fiver knowing that my funds were running down like sand in a timer. The beer and whiskey were beginning to give me a little buzz and I began to feel good, more confident. Hilda began to come over for a chat more often and she began to tell me of her family. She had two children and was married to an accountant who worked in the city. One of her

As We Sat Amongst the Sleeping Swans

children was a teenager in secondary school and I began to like her much more, less in a sexual way and more in a human way. She told me her father owned the pub and she managed it. I couldn't believe how such a beautiful woman could be so down to earth and I admired her even more for that. We talked for twenty minutes or so before she asked if I wanted another. I looked at my glass to see it was almost empty and agreed. She brought me another and after a sip of the fresh, cold beer I knew I was beginning to get a little drunk. Hilda went over and mingled for a while with the aul Dubliners at the bar. Their wit was vicious, and the craic was getting better with every pint and whiskey consumed. I sat for a while on my own, glad that Hilda was conversing with the other men at the bar. As much as I enjoyed her company, it was good to sit and contemplate for a while, the booze slowly chipping away at my mountainous anxiety. The music was nice, traditional Irish, soothing my inner turmoil. Just as one song ended, I took a sip of my beer and looked around to see a group of youngsters sitting in a booth. They were all similarly aged to me, probably students. They sat chatting, laughing, and having a good time. I sat for a while, transfixed by them, smiling along with them. It was nice to see, people happy and at ease, enjoying their lives and friendships. It reminded me of how Frankie and I used to be, along with the other boys we used to hang around with. One of them got up to put a coin in the jukebox and the music eventually drifted out across the bar. I sat, dumbstruck for a minute or so, listening. The music struck a chord with me. I don't know if it was because of the booze or the atmosphere in the pub, but the melody almost brought tears to my eyes, such was the beauty of the piece. Hilda came back over to have a chat.

"Hilda, do you know the name of that song? I've never heard it before."

"Oh", she replied, her eyes drifting to the left, searching her memory, "Ah, yes…it's "The Lonesome Boatman" by…"

"The Furey's", a gruff Dublin accent interrupted over a cloud of smoke.

"Yes, The Furey's, you're right Jacko. Good tune, but I prefer something with lyrics in it."

I threw another fiver on the counter and asked Hilda for some change for the jukebox. She gave me a handful of coins and I walked to the machine, found the song, and put it on. I sat at the bar and listened. The sound of the water lapping at the shore and the birdcalls at the beginning, transported my mind to the lake where Frankie and I spent our best…and worst times. It was uncanny. Then the sound of the whistle and time began to stand still. The music was haunting, no other description I could think of was more apt. I looked around the smoky room and my mind wandered to Wednesday night at the lake.

The music an antidote to the tragedy that occurred.

It seemed to be a piece that was made for a smoky bar in the middle of Dublin, on a Friday afternoon. When the song ended, I sat for a while, the melody

As We Sat Amongst the Sleeping Swans

replaying over and over in my mind. I went over to the jukebox, careful not to put the song on again first, so not to annoy the other customers with overkill. I put on a few good ones including "The Man Who Sold the World" by Bowie, a song that always reminded me of Frankie.

I went back to the bar, sat, and ordered another pint and let the music work its magic. Ten minutes or so later, The Lonesome Boatman came over the airwaves once more and I was transfixed. This was my third ever hearing, and the imagery produced in my mind had an intoxicating effect. As I sat hunched over my pint, I caught Hilda looking at me with a look of concern in her eyes. She walked towards me; "Are you...*crying*, John-Paul? What's wrong?"

Oh fuck! I felt my face and to my surprise found a river of tears running down it.

I wiped my cheek.

"*Crying?* No, I just yawned a few seconds ago and my eyes must have watered."

"You sure?", she asked, her eyes searching mine.

Her concern for me made me want to break down. I imagined her taking me in the back, hugging me and looking after me in a motherly way. I stayed strong however and laughed it off.

"That song Hilda, "The Lonesome Boatman", I've never heard anything like it...maybe it did make me a little emotional.", I laughed. If she didn't believe my bravado about not crying, I would try and fool her into thinking the *song* made me emotional, not all the shit in my head the song stirred up. She smiled and walked back to tend the others at the bar. I felt annoyed with myself for letting my emotions get the better of me, I had to toughen up or I would arouse suspicion.

I sat for another while, soaking up the atmosphere in the authentic old Dublin pub. More people came in as the day grew later and I began to enter conversation with some of the aul boys at the bar. All were very funny and knowledgeable on all things sport, music, and history. I drank a few more beers and began to lose count of what I had consumed. Most worryingly I was beginning to care less and less about what I was spending. I knew the evening was growing late when I began to find it difficult to get served at the bar and the music began to get louder. The bar began to get smokier and livelier and I looked at the clock on the wall to see it was approaching 7pm. I sat with my head in my hands. I had wasted a day, a day that I was supposed to be searching for a job and getting my shit together. There I was, pissing my grandfather's money up against the wall. I dreaded to think of what he would make of me.

As I sat, head in hands, lost in the bosom of self-pity, I felt a hand on my shoulder.

"You all right mate?"

I looked up. The accent was Australian and the man standing in front of me was long haired and bearded.

"I'm OK...too much of this stuff.", I said pointing to my pint glass.

"Too much piss.", he laughed, "Mind if I join you?"

"Be my guest."

He sat down on the recently vacated seat beside me, calling Hilda over with a confidence and assuredness that I could only dream of having. To my annoyance, she seemed to like it and her eyes lit up when taking his order.

"What do you want...pint?", he asked me.

"No thanks. I'm OK man. I've had enough."

"Have a pint with me you tosser. An Irishman turning down a drink? Don't let the side down mate?"

"OK", I reluctantly agreed.

Hilda served us up two pints and we clinked glasses and introduced ourselves.

"John-Paul."

"G'day John-Paul, I'm Kurt.", he said and offered me a very strong handshake.

"What are ye doing in Ireland?", I asked.

"Doing a tour of Europe. Me and a few mates. We started in Scandinavia, then Britain, then headed to Belfast moved down to Dublin, Galway next, then Cork. After that we're heading to France and then making our way down through continental Europe."

"Sounds good. How long are you doin' it for?"

"Bout three months or so."

"Ah man, I'd love to do something like that.", I said, thinking aloud.

He took a sip of his pint and looked at me. "Why don't you come with us?"

Once more, my lack of brain-mouth filter kicked in. "You're not trying to bum me are ye? I'm not a fuckin' rent boy in case you're wonderin'?"

He laughed heartily. "Bum you? I wouldn't even kiss you mate. Get over yourself man. If I was looking to bum guys in Dublin, there would be plenty of places to find willing victims around the city, not some smoky old man joint like this."

I waved my hand in submission. "Ok, ok. You can never be too careful these days."

"Yea, I know. No, the reason I asked is because I got two guys to tag along with me in the last few weeks, one guy in Sweden and the other in Belfast. Great guys. I'm like the fucking pied piper, man."

We both laughed and drank some of our beer. He began to tell me about himself. He was twenty-six and had broken up with his long-term girlfriend the year before. He had travelled all around Asia and was now doing Europe. He made his living simply by turning up on building sites in the morning and volunteering to perform a day's labour for a set fee. Most of the time he was told to get lost, but other days he struck lucky and sometimes was even asked back for a second or third day. In more rural areas he had visited in Asia and Northern Europe he had

As We Sat Amongst the Sleeping Swans

showed up in farmers' fields offering the same labour, with approximately the same percentages of success. He was an interesting guy and took my mind off the anxiety my spirit was overrun with. I told him very little about my situation, lying that I was visiting friends in university.

"Hey Kurt, do you think you could get me a job on one of those sites?", I asked.

"You're more than welcome to tag along in the morning, as long as you're at my place by six."

He asked Hilda for a pen and wrote down the name of his hostel, also in Gardiner Street. He told me to call at 8pm the next night to go out on the town if I didn't wake up in time for "site trawling" as he termed it. Very earnestly I told him I would definitely meet him at 6am the next morning, to which he responded only with a wry smile.

I bought him a pint and had one myself. He told me he was going to have to go back to his digs soon as he had an early start, reminding me I had one too. He went to the toilet and I sat back in my barstool, lit a cigarette, and basked in the notion everything was going to be all right. One day in Dublin and I had met two friends, a potential girlfriend (the blonde at the hostel) and got myself sorted with a job or two…all from the comfort of a barstool.

I was some boy.

Why bother with education and trying hard, when one could sit up in a Dublin bar, drinking beer, smoking fags and using ones God given charm to get everything one wanted whilst having a great fucking time? The music played on and Hilda smiled reassuringly at me from time to time, and I felt like the king of Dublin itself.

Anything seemed possible in this magical city.

Kurt came back from the toilet, gulped down the last of his beer and asked if I was walking back with him. Gratefully I agreed, as I was sure I would get lost on my own. We walked out into the cold night air and stereotypically, I became twice as drunk when the fresh air hit me. The night around us was lively, even livelier than the night before.

"Kurt lets go to a disco or something. Try and pull some girls…ye up for it?"

Kurt laughed. "There's no chance of you getting into any club's mate, the state you're in. No, let's go get some chips and I'll take you out tomorrow night after we earn our money, show you around the city and hopefully pick up some chicks then."

He was right. A sudden hunger come upon me when he mentioned chips. I hadn't eaten all day.

"OK. Good idea.", I conceded, and we walked to the nearest chippie. We got some food and I headed back towards the hostel with Kurt, satisfied, confident, and looking forward to the next day and the adventures that lay ahead.

As we stood outside my hostel, Kurt reminded me to be outside his at 6am the following morning and if I couldn't make it then to meet him at 8pm the next night. I assured him I'd be there at six, no problem. It was 11pm, I'd get at least six hours sleep, no issue. He laughed once more and shouted over his shoulder as he walked off; "We'll see."

"We fuckin' *will* see. Six it is.", I shouted after him.

I stumbled into the hostel and into my room. The room was dark, and a few sleeping bodies lay in the various bunk beds. I found my bed and began to take my clothes off, tripping over my jeans and falling onto the floor in the process. I began to laugh and a few irritated "shush" sentiments resonated around the room. I got into the bed, which was relatively comfortable and lay back, relaxed. What a difference a day could make. Last night I was lost in the streets of Dublin like a fucking street urchin, afraid and lonely. Now I lay in a comfortable bed, contacts and friends made, a job to go to in the morning and plans for the future. I lay back satisfied with my progress until sleep took me for the night.

I woke from a fitful sleep, my head pounding and my throat as dry as sandpaper. What the hell was I doing sitting in a bar all day, pissing the little money I had up against the wall? I knew I would be fit for nothing all day; I would spend the day hungover and depressed…another crucial day wasted.

Then I remembered Kurt and the job. I reached for my watch that lay strewn on the floor and checked the time.

11am

I lay back in bed and cursed myself. I overslept by over five hours. What kind of an asshole was I? How could I expect to ever make anything of myself by behaving like that?

Did I get up and rough it out, trying to make amends of a bad situation?

No.

I lay back in the bed feeling sorry for myself and tried to make the horrific hangover disappear. Then I was awoken by the cleaners who told me I had to get out until 4pm. I quickly dressed and left the hostel, walking out into the bitterly cold Dublin afternoon. I checked my watch, 1.03p.m. My head pounded, and I felt sick. I walked quickly, trying to find somewhere I could sit down. Once more, I had to stop and lean up against a wall for fear I was going to faint. Once steadied, I walked for ten or fifteen minutes until I found a café. I entered and sat at the window seat. The place was empty and a young girl with a foreign accent came over to take my order. I ordered a tea, my stomach not ready for food yet. She brought me a small teapot and a cup. I gave her a fiver and again didn't receive much change. How was I going to stick these prices I wondered? Every fucking thing seemed to cost the guts of a fiver and my fiver supply was running out...fast.

I sat at the window and watched Dublin pass by. I felt it was literally passing me by too. Yesterday I wasted a day in a pub, spending money I didn't have, thinking in my drunken stupor that I had it made, that everything was going to be OK.

Today not too many things seemed to be OK...far fucking from it.

As We Sat Amongst the Sleeping Swans

As I sat drinking my overpriced tea, I spotted a young man very shabbily dressed arranging his bits and pieces at the entrance of an alleyway. At first, I presumed he was a busker until he began to get his sleeping bag out. He began to organise himself and I found myself mesmerised by him. A sudden horror rose in me at the prospect that I could end up like him very soon. How many more nights could I afford to stay in the hostel, how many more days could I feed myself in Dublin at those prices? Was I being reasonably pessimistic or was it a result of the hangover? Once again, I cursed myself for wasting a day getting drunk, and my head pounded even more because of it.

When I returned from my doom filled thoughts, I took a closer look at the young man sat on the pavement across the road. A sudden cold sweat came over my body as he returned my gaze. I rubbed my eyes to make sure they weren't deceiving me, but when I looked back over, I realised it was *him.*

It wasn't possible...surely it wasn't him.

Impossible.

But it *was* him.

Frankie.

I got up from my seat, my eyes never leaving those of Frankie's across the road. What was he doing? Why was he begging on the streets of Dublin? My mind was overwhelmed, my senses and emotions at breaking point.

As We Sat Amongst the Sleeping Swans

Outside, I waited patiently for the traffic to subside, my mouth as dry as the desert and my heart pounding so hard I feared it would burst through my chest.

What would I say to him?

I found an opening in the traffic and ran across the road, my eyes locked on his. As I got closer, I realised it wasn't him. He was a little older, thinner, his face more weather-beaten.

I didn't know whether to feel relieved or disappointed.

The young man continued to stare at me, probably thinking there was something wrong with me as I had followed him across the street, glaring at him the whole time.

"Sorry.", I said, "Thought you were someone I know."

"No bother.", he replied in a strong Dublin accent. "Could ye spare any change mister?"

Put on the spot and still feeling embarrassed, I put my hand in my pocket, rummaged around, and produced a few coins and a fiver. His eyes lit up at the paper money, and I handed it to him.

"Thanks mister."

I had probably made his day but took no satisfaction from it. I walked away, cursing myself at letting another fiver slip through my fingers.

CHAPTER 8

In the months that followed Frankie's revelations, I kept my distance from O'Halloran. Because of his immense size, it was easy to see him coming so I avoided him skilfully in and around the town. To be face to face with him would be difficult as I was never one to mask my feelings and I certainly didn't want to get on the wrong side of a man like him.

One evening in late spring of the following year, I came home from school to find my mother flustered, busily preparing herself for work.

"John-Paul, a girl has phoned in sick tonight and I have to go in early to cover. Typically, your father will be late home too, so you are going to have to finish preparing dinner, then leave Stephen over to the pitch for training."

"No bother, mum. Will I take your car?"

"Yes", she replied, "Rita is picking me up in 5 minutes, so run the twins over to the pitch. Claire can do her homework in the car whilst you wait."

"Ah fuck sake ma, I have to wait for him? Can I not just leave him there and come home for an hour?"

She stopped what she was doing and glared at me. "Watch your language mister! Seriously, John-Paul, I hope you don't talk like that in school. Why don't you take a run around the pitch when you're waiting on Stephen? No harm to young Harris, but since you met him you've lost all interest in sport. You used to be such a good wee footballer, what with your awards and all. You should try and get back into it. I mean, look at you…you're as white as a ghost, a bit of sport would bring a bit of colour to those cheeks."

After issuing orders and insulting me like only a mother could, she kissed me on the cheek and rushed out through the door to the awaiting Rita.

I cursed under my breath and rounded up the twins. There was no way I was waiting around for an hour, so as I approached the pitch, I had an idea.

"Listen, Stephen, I'm gonna leave you here and go to a friend's house to study for a bit. Be back in an hour."

Without responding he got out of the car and made his way to the pitch, transforming from grumpy little brother to cock of the walk among his peers in a few footsteps.

"OK Claire, we are going to Frankie's for an hour. You can do your homework there. Do you want to get into the front seat?", I asked my little sister.

She shook her head without saying anything. I didn't take offence. I wouldn't want to be seen with me either.

I laughed and headed to Ballymoy.

I pulled up outside Frankie's house and prayed Quinn wasn't in. He wasn't likely to be, as there was surely a vacant bar seat somewhere in town needing occupying. I told Claire to wait in the car, just to be on the safe side as I went to check. I knocked the door and Frankie's mother answered.

"Hi love.", she greeted me, unusually friendlier and more upbeat than normal.

"Is Frankie about?"

"Moz...what's up man?", Frankie greeted me as he walked down the stairs behind his mother. I explained I had an hour to kill and it would be good to sit and have a bit of craic to pass the time.

"That your wee sister in the car?", Frankie asked.

"Yes"

"Well, don't just stand there, go get the little darling.", his mother interrupted.

"Well, OK...I suppose...", I muttered half-heartedly.

Frankie laughed. "Don't worry Moz, he's not here...probably not be back for a good few hours. Bring her in."

Relieved there was no chance Claire would be in the same vicinity as Quinn, I went to get her.

Frankie's mother took her by the hand and led her into the kitchen.

"Go you boys up to the room, little princess and I will go into the kitchen and have some girly chats...I might even have some sweets somewhere."

Claire smiled, beguiled by the woman's charm, beauty and promise of sweets. When I got to Frankie's room, I asked; "Is she OK? She's a bit more friendly and upbeat today. What's up?"

"Ach, she gets like that from time to time. One day she won't speak to you, the next she's all over ye. Women, all the same…fuckin' crazy."

"Don't I know it.", I lied to strike a rapport. My mother was one of the most level-headed people I knew, and Claire was even more grounded and sound than Stephen and I were.

"So, what do I owe the pleasure?"

"My mum was called in to work early and I had to leave Stephen over to the football. Didn't fancy the idea of watchin' O'Halloran poncing about like he's He-Man, so I thought I'd call round and shoot the shit for an hour or so."

Frankie leaned over and fist pumped me; "You're starting to see my point of view Moz."

We sat and listened to music for a while and planned the weekend that lay ahead. The craic was so good that when I finally went out to look at the clock on the landing, a cold shiver ran down my spine.

7.30.

The training finished at 7.

Shit!

I rushed down the stairs and grabbed Claire, apologising to Frankie and his mother that I had to rush off to pick up Stephen. The pitch was about a fifteen-minute drive and I drove like a maniac to make it in ten. When I got to the pitch, O'Halloran was standing in goal and Stephen was taking shots.

The two were laughing and joking, to the stranger they could have been father and son.

I stood on the edge of the pitch and called Stephen's name. I prayed inwardly that Stephen would run over and O'Halloran would go about his business on the pitch, picking up cones and bibs or whatever he did. To my great annoyance, both strolled over to where I stood, fist passing the ball to each other and chatting.

"Sorry I'm late.", I uttered sheepishly.

"It's OK, sure we had a ball, didn't we Stephen? I'll be watching this boy playing in Croke Park someday I'm sure. You keep at it, mind Stephen, not like this brother of yours."

"Yes, stick at it Stephen.", I agreed non-committedly.

"I've been telling Stephen to always stick with his team-mates in life. Team-mates have been through all sorts of hardships together and they'll have a common bond all through their lives. They're your brothers. Take my aul teammates from back in my playing days. We had a couple of glories, glories that I still take great pleasure in looking back upon. Playing in front of 70-80000 people in Croke Park and winning...beyond words. But those weren't the moments that forged the bonds between my teammates and me. It was the dark nights in January when we were being flogged in training, men being sick and still pushing on because they didn't want to let the rest down. Getting stuffed in matches and getting booed off the pitch by the fans, then getting a bollocking by the manager in the changing rooms, those were the moments that made brothers out of us more than the glories. Stephen will realise this growing up, but the key is endurance. Dedication, commitment, and sacrifice make champions. Isn't that right Stephen."

"Yes, Pat Joe."

"Now run you on Stephen and get into the car. I want to have a word with your brother."

Stephen ran to the car and my stomach began to churn.

"You know what I'm talking about, don't you? You've neglected your brothers on the pitch recently. Good lads who have focus and motivation in their lives. You're more than welcome back on the team, you know. We've a half decent minor team this year, there's a spot for you in the half-back line if you're willing to make training a few nights a week."

"Aye, I'll have a think about it, sure.", I lied.

He gazed at me for slightly longer than is deemed acceptable, searching my eyes for truth; "Make sure you do. It's a big few years for you young fellas what with exams and all. Healthy body, healthy mind. It would be a shame to see someone like you not reaching your full potential. A lot of you fellas are like sons to me...I've known and coached ye's since you were wee tots."

Again, he gazed into my eyes with full sincerity, those big blue eyes. A man like that, a man of his standing with all his achievements in life speaking to me with such feeling...it made the hair on the back of my neck stand on edge. All Frankie said about him at that point began to fade into insignificance and I began to idolise him once more.

"Thanks Pat Joe. I'll have a think about it and try and get down next week."

He threw his head back and laughed.

"You think too much, young Morrissey. Instead of saying you'll *think* about it and you'll *try*, say you *will*. *Do* it, don't *say* it...*do* it. OK?"

"I will.", I said, and meant it.

"Good lad. Now get that boy home.", he said as he patted me on the shoulders with those shovel sized hands.

I headed towards the car motivated and confident. Maybe I *should* hang around more with the boys on the football team, cool it off with Frankie for a while. Maybe Pat Joe was right. I was drinking at the weekend and killing brain cells I couldn't afford to kill if I was to pass the exams and get to university.

But the boys on the football team were so dull in comparison to Frankie. I didn't really like football either. I liked music and having a laugh with him. To subject myself to O'Halloran's stewardship would also feel like a betrayal to my friend, after the revelations he'd made known to me about him.

But he was so damn charismatic...as was Frankie.

I drove the twin's home and not a word was spoken about my poor punctuality by anyone.

The next morning as we stood waiting for the bus, I told Frankie about my encounter with O'Halloran. I told him about his request for me to go back and play football. We both had a good laugh.

"That meathead! All he thinks about is football. He must be over *all* the underage teams in the parish. He must really hate his wife, eh? I mean he must spend every night at the pitch instead of being at home. Ah well, suppose running after wee boys on the pitch is better than running after other men's wives, eh?", he said, his words laced with a deep bitterness.

I laughed nervously and tried to change the subject. "Good craic in your house last night though. Claire really liked your ma."

Frankie didn't respond, merely shaking his head and looking at the ground reflecting on his previous comment.

"You're not gonna go, sure you're not?", he asked looking at me through squinted eyes.

"What do you think?", I answered with a nervous laugh.

"Good man. The cheek of that big bastid. He fuckin' knows we're buddies. What's he up to?"

"Let's not talk about him Frankie. Don't get yourself annoyed over him."

As We Sat Amongst the Sleeping Swans

He snapped out of his trancelike state and became more like his old self as the bus approached. We spoke no more about it for the rest of the day.

A week passed since I spoke to O'Halloran and I began to forget all about our conversation. Hearing the boys on the bus talking excitedly about their upcoming football season stirred nothing in me, no excitement or passions were raised. My passions were music and craic. Next stop was university where I would undoubtably get my fill of both.

Then, one evening that week, that all changed.

I was sitting at the table eating dinner when Stephen bolted out of his chair and ran to the door. "Dad, dad...its Pat Joe. He's outside, he's coming *in*."

Unlike the last time he came to our house to notify me of my award, my excitement had dulled considerably. In fact, my stomach turned at the prospect of speaking with him. Stephen greeted him at the door.

"That layabout brother of yours here, Stephen?", he boomed.

"He's in there.", Stephen replied, a hint of disappointment in his voice that Pat Joe wasn't there to visit him. O'Halloran play fought with him on the way into the kitchen.

"Get your gear Morrissey. Your coming with me. You broke your promise last week and I'm going to make you pay for that tonight boy. I'll make a man out of him yet Ed, maybe make him a bit more like this boy.", he joked with my father whilst taking Stephen in a play headlock.

"Good luck with that.", my dad joked in reply and I cringed at their jokes at my expense.

"Run up and get your gear, there's a good lad. Don't keep the man waiting.", my mum instructed, and I went upstairs very reluctantly to get my stuff. When I came down, O'Halloran was holding court once more, all my family eating out of the palm of his hand. I felt nauseous at the thought of sharing a car with him on the way to the pitch and dreaded what Frankie would say if he found out. But, what could I do? There was no way I could turn him down after he so brazenly called at our house. My parents would probably kick me out of the house before they would refuse the hero of the country what he wanted.

He knew that too.

He bid his farewell and my family, much to my great embarrassment, waved us goodbye from our doorstep.

If only they knew.

He drove slowly to the pitch, in silence for a minute or so before he spoke. There was no talk about football and all its glories this time. His motivational pep talk hadn't worked on me, my absence from training last week affirming that, so he began to change tact to a more direct style to pick my brains.

"I've seen you around the town with that Harris boy, haven't I?"

As We Sat Amongst the Sleeping Swans

"Frankie? Yea. I knock around with him a bit. He's one of about five boys I would hang around with from time to time.", I lied.

Still driving very slowly and never taking his eyes off the road, he continued; "Listen, I'm gonna be straight with you. You're a good lad, I've known you for a long time. You're from a good family and you have a bright future ahead of you, believe me, the world is at your feet if you want it. But these are important times and you need to pick your friends very carefully."

My blood ran cold and a clammy sweat suddenly covered my body. I felt extremely uncomfortable about this prick's anticipated attack on my best friend, especially when I'd known what *he'd* done.

"I *always* pick my friends carefully, Pat Joe.", I responded, trying not to get angry.

"Do you? Well what about that Harris lad? Do you think he's a good choice of friend?"

I paused for a moment before answering. The cheek of this big bastard.

"Yes. Frankie's one hundred percent. Do *you* not think so?"

O'Halloran laughed without humour, rolled down the window and spat before rolling it up again.

"He's a hundred percent…that's a good 'un."

We arrived at the pitch and he turned the engine off. We sat in silence for a moment or so before he turned to me and spoke.

"John-Paul, as I said you're a good lad and I think a lot of you. I'm going to speak to you off the record here, OK. Before I do, you must promise not to tell anyone about this information I'm going to divulge. Do I have your word?"

"Of course.", I answered without consideration as I was so eager to hear what he was going to say.

"OK, now this information is very classified and if word got out that I told a civilian about this, especially a minor, I could lose my job. This is the length I am going to protect you John-Paul, and it's because I think so much of you and your family."

I nodded without speaking, my mouth dry and my tongue like sandpaper.

"We have been monitoring Harris for a while now. We have very good reason to believe he is in dealing drugs around Ballymoy. We have a good case against him currently, and in the next few months we plan to prosecute him for his crimes. If he is found guilty beyond reasonable doubt in the courts, he *will* go to jail. He has been caught in the past when he was a minor, but this time he will not get off so lightly...mark my words"

He paused to let his words take effect before continuing; "Now, I ask you the question, John-Paul, is this the type of friend you should be associating with? A *friend* who will eventually drag you down and lead you to wreck and ruin. I cannot stand by and let that happen to you, and I hope you will heed my words and stay clear of him."

I sat in stunned silence for about a minute.

As We Sat Amongst the Sleeping Swans

Frankie dealing drugs! A drug dealer?

I had grown up believing drug dealers were the scum of the earth. Could I have misjudged someone so wrong? Could I have gotten it so wrong that I let someone like that completely poison me against a man I idolised growing up?

Shock eventually turned to anger. Aware as anyone the sheer size of O'Halloran and the damage he could do to me if I angered him, I spat the words out viciously, words powered by hatred and an intense sense of justice for my friend; "You're a rotten liar! A stinking rotten liar."

I was shaking. I was ready for action, I would take the big fucker on if he wanted to, I didn't care what he could or would do to me. His reaction was not what I expected though. He didn't meet my anger with his, instead he shook his head and looked out the window sombrely.

"John-Paul…John-Paul. I may be a lot of things, but I'm not a liar."

"No…no? Well what about Frankie's…"

"Mother?", he answered before I could get the words out, stopping me in my tracks.

"Yes.", I hissed, the anger subsiding in me, making room for curiosity and surprise.

"I can't believe he's still pursuing this.", he replied, now sounding very defeated. "The trouble that boy has caused."

"What do you mean? What trouble has he caused?"

"What *trouble* has he caused? You mean he's never told you? He came to my family home one evening, obviously off his head on something, ranting and raving at my wife and children...in my own home. Throwing accusations around about me having extra marital affairs with his *mother.*"

"That's not like Frankie...not like him at all. I've never known him to take drugs either, never in all my time has he done them or talked about them.", I responded defiantly.

"Well, he was obviously getting high on his own supply that night for whatever reason. OK, I can understand he was upset, but to blame *me,* about stuff like *that.*", he stopped at that and gripped hard on the steering wheel, so hard I could hear the leather squeaking.

"You know Frankie's mother. Let's be honest John-Paul, man to man...she's a bit of a girl, always has been. It was well known there were a few boys from around the country up to no good with her, her present live in lover one of them. I can tell you that I certainly wasn't one of them. I've been married 25 years and have never even looked at another woman, never mind doing something like *that.*"

Once more he paused and waved at some of the boys arriving at the pitch.

"Let me ask you something. What was your initial reaction when he told you about what I apparently did?"

As We Sat Amongst the Sleeping Swans

I paused before answering, as I knew he knew what it would be. I decided to be honest and tell him, "Well, I didn't believe him at first."

He became more animated and turned to look into my eyes.

"You *see*. You didn't believe him; your gut wouldn't allow it. Now, in the force, one of the first things we were told is to believe your gut. Guess what- in over 90% of our gut reactions, we are correct. Your gut, your subconscious smelt a rat and alarm bells rang. You didn't believe him. You didn't believe him because you have known me since you were a child and you knew it wasn't in me to do something like that. You believed in my character over what he was telling you. Do you think my wife would still be with me if she believed him, or had one inkling of doubt? Of course not. She is a bright woman who can account for every one of my mornings, evenings, and nights, who's known me since I was a very young man. Now, John-Paul, please use a bit of logic and think critically about this situation."

"But why would he accuse you of something like that? It doesn't make sense. *None* of this makes any sense."

O'Halloran let out a belt of laughter.

"Why would he accuse me? Well it might have something to do with the fact I was the one who caught him dealing around the town. Took a bit of a dislike to me, did young Harris. Did he ever tell you why he ended up at your school? Why he left his last school in Ballymoy?"

"Yes. He had an altercation with a teacher. Told him where to go.", I responded, my confidence in Frankie diminishing by the second.

O'Halloran let out another belt of laughter.

"Does he ever tell you the truth I wonder? He *didn't* have an altercation with a teacher as he puts it. The school expelled him. Why? Because he had been caught dealing drugs…that's why."

I sat, deflated. I felt sick and defeated. What could I say to defend him?

O'Halloran sat in silence too, letting his words marinate for a while.

"You see John-Paul, this is why I don't want you associating with that boy. He's a liar and a cheat. You have much more to do with him and you'll soon be out dealing or even *taking* drugs. I don't want that to happen to you. You've too much going for you, think of that lovely family of yours…if you ended up on drugs or in jail it would kill them."

I looked up at him; "Is this the truth Pat Joe?"

He put a hand on my shoulder. "One hundred percent truth. Ask him. Look into his eyes. His lips may lie, but his eyes wont."

He took the keys out of the ignition and pinched my kneecap. "Come on then. Let's release some of that anger out on the pitch. Are you OK?", he asked, concern writ across his features.

"As OK as I can be after losing my best friend."

"As I said before John-Paul. You have 15-20 best friends up on that pitch. Get out and reignite that friendship with those brothers of yours."

I went out on to the pitch with my usual half-hearted approach, despite O'Halloran's motivational words. I resolved to save my aggression not for the boys on the pitch, but for my so-called best friend who would feel the full brunt of it the next day.

CHAPTER 9

Once more I found myself wandering Dublin streets like a lost soul, after my encounter with the young man outside the café. I blamed the hangover for tricking my mind into thinking the young man was Frankie. Either that or admit I was beginning to *lose* my mind.

I walked quickly around the city to try and clear my head.

It didn't work.

The city was different that day. It was a Saturday and the place was hiving. Young people walked around in gangs of three and four. Young people enjoying their weekend and the break it gave them from their studies or work. Full of life and enthusiasm, shopping for clothes and arranging their nights out. I tried to feed off their energy and life, but the hangover had made me queasy and drained my appetite for everything.

I walked past a café with a sign stuck to the inside of the window.

HELP WANTED-ENQUIRE WITHIN

Without thinking I walked into it. It was busy, and an extremely flustered looking lady stood taking orders from a table of four. I waited until she had finished before following her to the counter.

"Excuse me", I said.

As We Sat Amongst the Sleeping Swans

"One minute, love.", she replied whilst she communicated the order to the kitchen staff.

A few moments later she came over to me. "Sorry love, table for one?", she asked, smiling whilst wiping an arm over a glistened brow.

"Em, no I'm not actually here to eat, I came with regards your sign outside."

"Oh.", she replied, a little surprised and probably a little relieved she didn't have to serve me, "That position is actually filled love, sorry."

My heart sank, and I turned to head back out the door.

"Sorry, love...wait a minute.", she called after me.

"The girl who is taking the job is starting tomorrow, she couldn't work today. I could do with some help now to be honest. Have you any experience in this line of business?"

"Yes. I worked in a pub at home.", I lied, instantly feeling guilty. It was a white lie, but I felt bad lying to this woman as she reminded me of my mum in looks and mannerisms.

"OK, good. Would you mind helping now? I'll pay twenty punts for four hours labour and you'll get a share of the tips too. How does that sound?"

"Sounds good.", I replied trying to restrain my excitement.

Her face lit up with glee and she rushed into the kitchen, coming back out with a pinafore for me to put on. She gave me some very quick and basic instructions, and told me to get out and take orders, armed with my pencil and notepad. After five minutes, when the excitement wore off, I became as flustered as the woman. Although flustered and under pressure I began to enjoy the work as it took my mind off my troubles and more importantly at that very time, my hangover.

The work was intense, not as physically demanding as the jobs I had done on the farms around home, but *mentally* intense. There was a lot to remember, people always looking attention, with a lot of back and forth to the chefs, who were stereotypically very shouty. The lady who granted my temporary employment, Kay, was the manager. Although she kept me on my toes, she was also kind and patient. Kay's daughter, Kayla, a young girl of no more than fourteen years old, completed the team. Kayla was every bit as good as her mother, constantly surveying what was in front of her, staying on top of every order, one step ahead of the customers. Between them they worked like clockwork and I couldn't help but feel I was putting a huge spanner in their precision work, despite Kay's kind words and encouragement.

Most of the customers were friendly and understanding. There were a few times when I messed up an order and Kay or Kayla swooped into my rescue, explaining to the customers it was my first day. A little joke (not at my expense) and the customers laughed the issue off and went about their conversations without any further issues. There was only one customer who proved difficult in the four hours of my shift.

As We Sat Amongst the Sleeping Swans

Two elderly ladies sat in the middle of the café. One of the ladies was Irish and had the aura of a retired nun about her, very conservative and upright in her mannerisms. She seemed pleasant enough. The second lady was American, speaking with a drawl that I guessed to be Texan, or somewhere where the cowboys lived. The old American woman kept calling me over.

"Hey sonny, those people over there.", she pointed to a group of four young people sat a few tables away from her, "Can you have a word with them? Tell them to turn the volume down a little?"

"OK", I replied, embarrassed at being put in such an awkward position. Walking towards the group of young people, knowing the old ladies' eyes were on me, I bent down and quietly asked if they needed anything else. They all very politely said they were fine, and I walked towards the kitchen to pick up another order. I couldn't see the old ladies reasoning. The group of young people were all very mannerly, not loud, or obtrusive in any way. After I had completed the next order, the old lady clicked her fingers at me, "Hey...hey, sonny. What'd ya say to them, what'd ya *say?*"

I bit hard on my tongue.

"I just asked them to tone it down a little.", I lied and went to walk off.

"Is that what they call toned down, is it? Just listen to *that!*"

I couldn't hear anything except the normal murmur of a public domain.

"Sorry Miss, but this is a public café and I can't demand people keep quiet, unless they are disturbing the peace for other customers."

"What? *What?* How are they *not* disturbing the peace? I mean the din from their big mouths is incredible…*incredible*", she was almost screeching now, so much that other diners began to look over.

"Marjorie, please…not in here", the other old lady pleaded with her.

"Bunch of loud mouths", she spat, "Bunch of loud mouths! You have a word sonny, or you can kiss goodbye to any tip, I'll tell you that for nothing."

My blood boiled, and I felt very embarrassed. I'm sure my face was visibly burning. I wanted to tell her where to go, but I only had an hour or so left, and I badly needed the promised £20.

"I'm sorry madam, but if you feel that strongly about this, I will have to get the manager."

"Go get him then…go get him", she screeched.

I went over to Kay and told her what was happening. She sighed and went over to speak with the old lady. I got on with my business and went back and forth to the kitchen to pick up orders. I checked on the table the old lady was complaining about, all oblivious to the fact they were the subject of an ever-increasing rant. As I walked past her table all I could hear was the "loud mouth's" sentiment being repeated over and over. Her rant became shriller in volume and most of the diners began to notice now.

"You tell them sweetie; you tell them to shut it...frickin' LOUDMOUTHS"

"I'm sorry madam, I cannot see or hear how these people are causing any disturbance to the peace. If *you* continue this behaviour, I'm going to have to ask you to leave."

"Ask *me* to leave? Oh, I will make it easy for you sweetie. Come on Beatrice, let's get out of here. I do not care for the company...*or* the staff, very much."

Kay stood aside to let the ladies get to their feet. The crazy American one glared at Kay, and then at the table of four young people she complained of.

"Bunch of LOUDMOUTHS'!", she screeched once more, this time the sound absolutely blood curdling.

The four young people sat for a moment confused, until they all began laughing. The lady stood where she was and shook with rage, I think I even saw her stomp her feet in bad temper. She turned on her heel and the two of them headed out the door, slamming it on the way out.

A few minutes after the old ladies had left the café, Kay came up to me and said, "Those old witches didn't pay. Can you believe that?"

I scratched my head in bemusement. "How the hell? Did they run up much of a bill?"

Kay laughed, a laugh that seemed to have won narrowly against a sob and handed me their bill.

"Fuck me.", I blurted out and instantly turned red, feeling ashamed of myself swearing in front of a lady like Kay. She didn't say anything but headed back to the customers. Between the old ladies they had four cups of tea, two hamburgers and chips, two side salads, two soft drinks, two apple tarts with ice cream and two espresso coffees.

When the shift ended, I helped Kay and Kayla tidy up. Just as I went to get my coat, Kay approached me and handed me the £20. It was the hardest £20 I had ever earned.

"I'm sorry John-Paul. There would normally be a few extra punts thrown in on top of that, but unfortunately we have had to put all the tips we received into the till, to cover those old witches bill."

"Kay, its fine. I only expected to get the £20 as agreed and I'm very glad of it…thanks for giving me a chance today. I feel bad for you and Kayla though. You have been working hard all day and didn't get any tips. You know, you should call the cops on those two, they shouldn't get away with that."

Kay flashed a defeated smile.

"There's nothing the gardai could do. Firstly, how would they track them down, and more importantly, technically I kicked them out and it should have been up to me to obtain payment first."

The penny dropped. The old American lady had been making a huge fuss over nothing and had become more troublesome because of her unfair accusations.

"You don't think…", before I could finish, Kay finished my sentence; "We've been conned?

As We Sat Amongst the Sleeping Swans

Absolutely. I've seen it before, rarely, but I've been conned before. Those old witches knew exactly what they were doing."

I stood for a moment, mouth open in astonishment, replaying in my mind how the old lady had cranked up her verbal assault on the young people and had become more troublesome and difficult to deal with.

Kay shrugged her shoulders. "Listen, it happens. Thanks for your help John-Paul. You worked hard today, and I appreciate it. Have a nice night and call back in to see us again."

I took that as my cue to leave and bid them farewell. At that I walked into the fresh early spring evening towards my hostel. I felt as if I had salvaged the day somehow. Earlier that day I had felt as low as possible after waking up so late, passing up the chance to work and earn some money, now I felt proud I had gone into the city and earned my keep for the day.

I arrived at the hostel. The place felt different. There was more life about, it didn't feel as depressing as it had done. When I entered the room, Canadian Clive lay on his bed reading, and two other young men sat on top of opposite bunk beds.

"Ah, JP. Was wondering where you were. I was telling the guys here about you. Ger, Liam, this is JP. JP, meet Ger and Liam."

"Ger, Liam.", I muttered, surprising myself how shy I had become, attributing it to my seemingly permanent hangover.

"Good man JP. Where are you from?", asked Liam, a big friendly faced fellow with a red face and a pair of glasses.

"Ach, just up north. Yourselves?"

"I'm from Tipperary and Ger here is from Kerry."

Both seemed to be friendly from first impressions. Liam seemed bookish. He was on a long weekend in Dublin after an interview in one of the universities the day before. He was trying to get into vet school. Ger was a builder who was spending a week in the capital on a big building job, rather than travelling back and forth to Kerry. He was a body builder in his spare time, huge muscled who spent most of his time eating and drinking protein shakes.

"Munster men, eh?", I replied and instantly turned red at my inane response. There was silence for a moment or two before Canadian Clive spoke.

"Are you guy's heading out tonight?"

"No", answered Ger, "Not me. Early start in the morning. Yourselves?"

"Might do, if I can get anyone to come with me?", Liam replied, looking expectantly my way.

"Well, I can't Liam". Canadian Clive said. "I've been working all day and I'm shot…maybe tomorrow."

Ger laughed loudly.

As We Sat Amongst the Sleeping Swans

"This cunt Clive. You've been saying that every night. You must have a stack of money built up and you're afraid to spend it. I didn't know Canadian men were such tight bastards."

"I didn't know the reputation Kerry men had for being stupid until I met you…and you confirmed everything.", Canadian Clive quipped and Ger laughed good naturedly.

I knew I would get on with them. They seemed up for a laugh and no one took themselves too seriously. I had my doubts about Ger at first because he looked like a hard bastard, but he was sound and very down to earth. He had a mullet hairstyle which unnerved me a little, and he seemed to preen it a lot, which I took as confirmation he didn't grow it for irony.

"What about you, JP?", asked Liam, "Are ye heading anywhere tonight?"

At that I remembered Kurt from the night before and his offer to meet me outside his hostel at 8pm. "I'm supposed to be meeting a boy for pints at 8pm tonight. You're more than welcome to join us."

Liam's face lit up and he jumped out of his bed and grabbed a bottle of vodka from his bag and some deodorant. He sprayed some deodorant under his armpits and offered some to me. I did the same and gave it back to him. He took a slug of the vodka and handed it to Ger who also took a hit. Canadian Clive declined the offer and passed the bottle to me. I took a sip and winced, to the great amusement of the others.

"Fuck sake, JP. Take a bigger slug than that. I thought you nordies could drink.", Ger laughed. I took another drink and could feel the vodka blaze a trail the whole way down to my stomach, before sitting there like a lake of lava.

Ger took a huge slug of the vodka when it was his turn; "It'll help me sleep, this stuff. Another dose and I'll be out like a baby. Here JP, redeem yourself this time.", he said, handing the bottle to me. To avoid their slagging, I took a bigger slug, but still they laughed.

"My God, JP. You nordies drink as well as you play football.", Ger quipped, before continuing; "Where are you from anyway? Where's that accent…Armagh…Monaghan…maybe Tyrone? It doesn't matter, there's a grand total of zero All-Irelands between them all, eh?", he laughed.

I took another drink and winced, but the foul spirit had finally given me a little Dutch courage; "No, not from any of those counties.", I lied, "I'm a Down man. Think we have five All-Irelands. Not as many as you boys have, but just trying to think how many times you've beaten us in championship football…oh that's right…none."

Liam laughed loudly, and Canadian Clive joined in too when he realised I had got one over Ger; "Good man JP. You got him there, haha. Now you're learning how to talk to these guys."

My dad had always admired Down football teams through the years and I remembered him jumping around the house in glee once after Down had beaten

Kerry, reciting that very fact. I wouldn't have known it otherwise and was glad I retained that information and used it to my benefit to win that argument. My dad had always loved to see Kerry getting a beating as he was sick seeing them winning all the time. I'm sure he would have approved and admired my white lie, to get the better of a Kerry man in an argument.

Ger took it well. He sat shaking his head, laughing; "Well, that's me told. You got me JP...ye nordie hoor.", he said, with a friendly wink.

I was glad to be with them. The craic was good, and they took my mind off the trauma that lay within it. We drank the bottle of vodka between us and I began to feel good again, the lava in my stomach now pumping fire through my veins. My confidence was growing with each sip and I began to tell them the tale of the crazy American lady. They all laughed, and it felt good to have people to share those moments with again.

"JP, if you're still interested in a little security work let me know and I will get you an interview. My boss is a pretty good guy and we're always looking people...would beat taking shit from Yankee geriatrics...it would probably pay better too.", said Canadian Clive.

I told him I was interested, and he promised he would ask the next day. Again, at that moment I felt I could take on the world, that mornings depression a dot on the horizon, those feelings of sorrow and loss surely never to return.

As We Sat Amongst the Sleeping Swans

Liam reminded me of the time, and we asked Ger and Canadian Clive once more if they would reconsider. Both men lay in bed comfortable and warm, satisfied with the prospect of a night tucked up safely in bed, instead of a mad night in the cold city.

We bid them farewell and headed towards Kurt's hostel. I saw his silhouette in the distance, as he stood, lit cigarette in hand. When he spotted me, he began to laugh.

"Where were you this morning, ya cunt?"

"Liam, this is my friend, Kurt. Kurt, this is Liam", I replied, ignoring his question.

"Pleased to meet ya Liam. Now, where were you this morning ya pussy? Thought you Irish guys could drink all night and work all day? Letting the side down, mate.", he continued, laughing.

I shrugged it off and admitted defeat. "Sorry. Slept in…forgot to bring my alarm clock with me."

"Ha, alarm clock. Forgot your balls you mean."

"I forgot how abrasive you Aussie cunts can be.", I replied, trying not to snap and make it sound too much like he was getting to me. He took it in the manner I hoped and laughed, punching me on the arm as he walked past me, leading us into the Dublin night.

The streets were packed, various accents and languages providing a soundtrack to the evening. We entered a bar in the O'Connell Street area of the city and Liam ordered three pints. The bar was relatively quiet, and we found a booth in the corner. We sat and quickly drank the pints. Liam and Kurt were setting a swift pace I worried I couldn't keep up with. Forcing huge volumes of beer down had never been my strong point and I knew the sooner we moved onto shorts, the more I would be able to keep up. I was halfway down my pint when Kurt disappeared and returned a few moments later, plonking three fresh pints down in front of us. Liam was ready for his and took a huge draught, producing a mighty burp, sitting back in his chair very satisfied. It didn't take long for the three of us to form a bond, considering we had barely just met. Subject matters of sport, music and women were always good barometers of another's personality. The craic was so good that I barely noticed both sitting swilling very empty looking glasses.

I had barely begun my second.

"Shit, you boys are thirsty. Same again or you fancy moving onto the half'uns?"

Both looked at me with astonishment.

"Bit early for that JP.", said Kurt.

"Not at all. I'm getting a vodka and coke. Beer's for pussies.", I lied as I didn't really fancy going on the shorts either, but knew I had no chance of keeping up with them drinking beer.

I brought the drinks back and concentrated on finishing the second pint. When I had done so, both Liam and Kurt were finishing their third and I had to down the vodka and coke in two gulps. I sat for a few moments trying not to vomit, until Kurt jumped up and decided it was time to leave for another bar. Liam and I gladly followed as neither of us were familiar with the city and Kurt seemed to know where the best places were. We went to another few bars and had a drink or two in each of them. The prices were hurting my ever-diminishing funds badly. The £20 I had worked so hard for, now a distant memory. At around 11pm, Kurt asked us if we wanted to go to a disco to pick up girls. Liam, like an over eager puppy nodded and smiled, too drunk to even speak. I was aware getting into a disco would cost us at least a fiver or a tenner, money I couldn't justify spending. Kurt laughed and reminded me if I had have got up and went to work with him that morning, my wallet would be bulging with money, just like his.

He was becoming a little annoying.

"Your beginning to get on my tits, Kurt.", I sniped.

He laughed.

He told us not to worry about paying into a disco as he knew of a disco-bar a few streets over. Admission was free of charge.

Luckily for us, when we arrived there were no bouncers at the door. I doubted Liam, or I, would have been allowed in, the state we were in. Kurt, as usual strolled to the bar, long hair flowing in his wake like he owned the place. I noticed there were a lot of pretty girls in the bar and annoyingly I noticed a lot of them looking at him, as he paraded himself like a peacock. After he bought a round, he wasted no time in harvesting the admiring glances his rugged looks and confident stance had produced. He reminded me a little of Frankie in the way he went about picking up girls, but his confidence, unlike Frankie's, crossed the line into cockiness the drunker he became. Frankie would have ingratiated himself into a group of girls and welcomed his friends in, setting *us* up with jokes and sacrificing the punchlines to make us look good. Kurt was more selfish, and from time to time even made jokes at our expense to boost his own agenda.

"Your man Kurt is a bit of a gom, isn't he?", Liam said, as the two of us retreated to a table of our own. I didn't know what a "gom" was, but I agreed, knowing from his tone what he meant. Liam and I became embroiled in our own drunken conversation and the night was becoming more enjoyable, as we could let our guard down when Kurt was preoccupied. He was funny in a self-deprecating, geeky kind of way, and it was nice to spend time with someone of my age. He was desperate to move to Dublin and live it up for a few years as a student, away from the small town in Tipperary where he grew up, with its small-town opinions and prejudices. I could relate to him but when he began to speak of his family and his love for them, how much he'd miss them when he fulfilled his dream, I almost broke down and told him my own story. Pulling myself together and avoiding embarrassing myself in a crowded bar, I stood up and began dancing. Liam sat, bemused, drinking his beer. Then he began to laugh, obviously at how ridiculous my dancing was (I hadn't meant it as a joke at the time). Standing up to join me, he began to dance in a bizarre over the top way too. When we ran out of gas, I went to the bar and ordered another round for us. I tried to get Kurt's attention which was difficult as he was talking to a group of girls, and when I finally accomplished eye contact and pointed to the beer pump, he dismissed me, waving me away. Although I raged internally at his lack of respect towards me, I felt relieved I didn't have to buy another drink. The thought of how I was going to carry on my exile with the ever-diminishing funds visited my mind fleetingly, before the alcohol diluted it accordingly.

As I struggled through the crowded bar with our drinks, I noticed Liam speaking to a pretty blonde girl. I handed him the drink and stood to one side, not wanting to impede on his conversation. A moment later, Liam tapped me on the shoulder. He stood grinning at me.

"JP, this is Nina. Nina…JP".

"Hello, Nina.", I said and shook her hand.

She smiled at me and shrugged her shoulders in a cutesy, shy way. She was very pretty, very cute. Small with large blue eyes and elven features. I felt a little jealous that Liam had nabbed such an attractive girl but felt glad for him too. Liam excused himself to go to the loo. As he walked past me he whispered in my ear; "Talk to the girl, JP. She came over to ask me to introduce you both. Good luck!".

Flattered and a little shy even through my drunken haze, I asked Nina where she was from.

"Finland. You? Here in Ireland?"

"Yes, up north.", I replied and took a sip of my drink buying myself time to say something witty and clever.

Nothing came.

She laughed and asked me how old I was.

"Twenty-three", I lied.

Again, she laughed. "Aww, only a baby."

I cursed myself, wishing I had said twenty-five, but I may not have gotten away with it. My lack of tact once more kicked in and before I could filter my thoughts I blurted; "A baby at twenty-three? What age are you then? You only look about eighteen, the same age as...my little sister."

Once more she laughed. I was either doing really well with her, all the giggles I was earning, or she was amusing herself at my idiocy. I didn't really care as it was nice to have female company either way.

"I'm twenty-eight. Thank you for the compliment, but it's been a long time since I was eighteen."

"There's obviously good water in Finland then.", I remarked, and she laughed once more.

"You're cute.", she said, looking at me with those big blue doe eyes.

"So are you."

"Do you want to kiss me?"

This was too easy I thought, and a million thoughts raced through my brain, the most prominent one being that I should move to Finland. My thought process had obviously hesitated my motions and Nina pulled me towards her, and we kissed for a while.

When I came up for air, I took a sip of my drink and noticed Liam standing beside me, grinning. He finished his drink, nudged me and said, "Here, I'm gonna head back. You've got your hands full, fair play to ye. I'm wrecked. I'll see ye later. Good luck!"

I half-heartedly asked him to stay but knew he didn't want to play gooseberry every much as I would have, Nina seemingly on her own with no other friends for him to chance his luck with.

I spent the rest of the night in the bar speaking with Nina and it turned out we had a similar interest in a lot of the music we liked, although most of her musical tastes were more heavy-metal than mine. She was in Dublin for the weekend with her friend to watch some obscure death-metal band play a concert. She was staying in a B&B not far from the bar and she asked if I would walk her back. I agreed, and we left soon after.

Outside, the air hit me, and I became twice as drunk as I had been once more. It was more of a grogginess than an energetic drunk and I just wanted food and sleep, the torrid week I endured truly catching up on me. It was Nina who suggested we get something to eat and I heartily agreed. We walked down the crowded streets hand in hand and found a busy pizza shop. We ordered a large pizza and some chips, I paid of course, in my attempt at chivalry. We sat in the busy shop and got stuck into the food, the alcohol and the cold Dublin night giving both of us a ferocious appetite. Once finished we walked towards Nina's B&B and I felt much better, fortified by the food. We kissed outside her front door and with a mischievous little smile she asked if I wanted to come in. I agreed and began to panic a little as I didn't know what she would expect from me. I was eighteen and a virgin. She was twenty-eight, foreign and most likely experienced.

A mismatch of epic proportions but I gladly accepted the role of plucky underdog.

She took my hand and led me into the B&B, trying to stifle her giggles and putting her finger over her lips ordering us both to be quiet. Once we ascended the stairs, she took me aside, saying she shared the room with her travelling companion. My eyebrows raised involuntarily as my mind had immediately raced to the conclusion her travelling companion was a hot, blonde Finn with the same desire for me as Nina had.

I had hit the jackpot.

I was definitely moving to Finland!

Once inside the room, Nina flicked the bedside lamp switch, illuminating the room dimly. She threw her arms around me and we kissed, this time a little more passionately. Just then, I noticed a movement in the bed across from us. A loud yawn and then up stood a little bald man, wearing only a pair of Y-fronts.

I stepped away from Nina and looked at the man who walked towards the toilet. He and Nina began speaking in what I presumed was Finnish, and he took what seemed to be the longest and loudest piss in history.

"Who the fuck is that guy?", I whispered to Nina.

"Pessi. He's my brother."

Finally, after he finished his urination, after many stop-start episodes, I quipped; "Pessi? Your parents named him well." and wished someone else was in the room who understood and appreciated my wit, Nina staring blankly at me.

Pessi came back into the room and quickly got changed into his clothes, stumbling around the room , half asleep trying to put his boots on. When dressed and ready, he stood in front of us, slightly groggy and awkward.

"JP, this is Pessi...my brother. Pessi, this is JP...my new lover.", Nina spoke and they both laughed heartedly. We shook hands and they continued speaking in Finnish.

"OK, Pessi...bye bye.", Nina gestured towards him, shoving him towards the door. Just then, Pessi turned and winked broadly at me.

When he left, Nina came towards me and pushed me onto the bed before beginning to undress.

"That was the friend you mentioned?", I asked.

"Umm-hmm."

"Could you not have told me your friend was your *brother?*"

She was continuing her striptease, but all my desire had been extinguished.

"Friend, brother...what's the difference. He's my best friend. We do everything together. What's your problem?"

"Do you not think it's all a bit weird? I mean, where's he off to now?"

She stopped gyrating in front of me and began to glare at me.

"We had an agreement. He's going to sleep in the television room downstairs. I would have done the same if he had brought a girl back."

"This is all a bit weird.", I said.

Her glare intensified, and she began to cover her bare torso with a previously discarded top.

"What's *weird*?"

"What's *weird*? The fact you and your brother are so open about either of you getting off with some random person is more than a little strange. And what the fuck was that wink he gave me about...one of the creepiest things ever. I don't know if this openness is a Finnish thing, and I apologise if it is, but it's all a bit strange to me...sorry."

"Get out. Get out of my room. There is nothing weird going on here, the only weird thing here is you...little *virgin*."

She began to laugh and put her top back on. She looked into my eyes.

"You *are* a virgin...aren't you?"

I got up from the bed and walked to the door, Nina's cackles raining down upon me like poisoned darts.

"I expected better from an Irishman. Of all the men I could have had tonight, I get a little boy like you."

I slumped out of the room and descended the stairs. Just as I was about to open the front door, Pessi appeared behind me.

"You finished? That was quick.", he said, shrugging his shoulders and heading back up the stairs to his bed once more.

I opened the door and walked back out into the cold Dublin night, once more alone. My drunken stupor had evaporated, and an intense tiredness grew over me. I headed back towards the hostel, passing a phone box on my way. I couldn't bring myself to call my mother.

I needed her too much. Needed all of them too much.

As I walked back to my hostel, I vowed that tomorrow would be different...better. Then realising the next day was Sunday I realised nothing much would happen again.

My money...and time, were running out far too quickly.

As We Sat Amongst the Sleeping Swans

CHAPTER 10

The next morning, I stood waiting for the school bus. Frankie must have been running late as there was no sign of him. My heart pounded, and my mouth was dry. I didn't know how I would react when face to face with him. I felt relieved when he didn't show up. I was most volatile in the morning; it was best not to be in contact with him until later during the day.

I got on the bus and sat on one of the empty seats at the front. A few of the boys at the back shouted down to me, asking why I wasn't coming up. I lied that I wasn't feeling well, and they asked no further questions, continuing their smoking and chatter. I sat and looked out the window, O'Halloran's words ringing in my ears.

Just as I was beginning to enjoy the bus journey, I saw the old beaten up Nissan overtake the bus and knew Frankie would be getting on at the next stop. My heart pounded, and I began to sweat. The bus seemed to grow smaller and I suddenly wanted an escape route.

The bus stopped and I considered lying down on the seat to hide from him as he got on. My pride wouldn't allow it though and I sat, upright and proud to face him as he got on. Weirdly as the confrontation grew nearer, the anxiety and fire I had experienced a few moments before was replaced with a coldness.

Ice insulated my veins...I was ready for the cunt.

As We Sat Amongst the Sleeping Swans

A few kids boarded the bus and walked past me, a few surprised expressions that one of the "boys" from the backseat was sitting amongst them, probably worrying what I was up to, before Frankie came into view. I initially thought he wasn't going to notice me as he walked with his head down, putting the receipt back into his wallet as he went. Then he lifted his head just before he walked past me and did a double take.

"Moz...what are ye doing? Why...?", he asked, before his face fell, obviously reading my features knowing something was up.

"Keep walking dickhead.", I said, almost shocking myself at how cold and hard it sounded. He stood in shock for a moment before he traipsed up the bus. The bus was quiet that day, the ringmaster of the backseat having a rare off day. He didn't speak to me that day, or the rest of that week. In the mornings that followed, he sat in his mother's car and I stood at the bus stop. That evening his mother was waiting for him and he jumped into the car, speeding off home. It went on like that for over a week until one day we got off the bus when his mother wasn't there. I stalled for a while behind him, bending down to tie my shoelace two or three times to put some distance between us. Suddenly, he turned on his heel and walked with purpose towards me. He wore an expression I had rarely seen, one of anger and menace.

It scared me.

I was game for most confrontations and never backed down from a fight before, but I knew I was no match for him if it came to blows. He was too tough...too quick and strong. I decided to fight fire with fire and walked towards him regardless of the consequences.

"So, I take it O'Halloran's had a chat with you then?", he asked.

I nodded; "He has."

"And I suppose he told you some *truths,* did he?"

"He sure did."

"Like what?"

"Like *what?* Well, the fact that you're a drug dealer, a stalker and a fuckin compulsive liar."

I looked into his eyes and as O'Halloran predicted, they didn't lie.

He stood for a second, before turning to gaze into a field at nothing in particular.

"That bastard.", he muttered to himself. He turned to look at me and I swear I could see tears standing in his eyes. He turned around again quickly to gaze back into the field.

"He's right. Well, he's telling two truths out of three. I have been done for dealing...drugs, and I did visit his house once. I'm not proud of it, but he pushed me over the edge, and I couldn't just let the bastard get away with it. His wife or children weren't home though-I made sure of it. But let me tell you something, I'm no fuckin' liar."

I laughed.

"Not a liar Frankie? All you ever do is tell lies. You're a *compulsive* liar."

I tried to remain calm. I didn't want to get into a fight with him. I just wanted to tell him what I thought of him and get him the hell out of my life. O'Halloran was right, he *was* bad news.

He looked at me without saying anything and shook his head.

"Thought you were different Moz. Thought you might have understood. You're just like the rest of the pricks around this country. Idolising some piece of shit like O'Halloran and taking his word as gospel. Good enough. Go back to living your little life in this little community…fuckin' numpty."

I laughed.

"Numpty? Rather be a numpty than a drug dealing low life."

Once I said the words, I regretted them.

This time it was his turn to laugh, bitterly.

"Low life? You'll learn in time Moz that I'm not the low life. I hope you learn that sooner rather than later."

We stood staring at each other in silence for a few moments. I didn't know what to say to him. I didn't know whether to feel sorry for him or not. He admitted everything O'Halloran said, yet remained adamant O'Halloran was the one in the wrong. Behind his shoulder I saw his mother's car come into view. I shook my head in defeat.

As We Sat Amongst the Sleeping Swans

"OK, Frankie. Whatever you say. Look there's your mother."

Without saying anything he stepped into the car and sped off, his mother not even looking at me. I wondered then what drugs *she* had been taking that day.

The next day I remained sat at the front of the bus and for the next few months after that. Frankie and I didn't speak again for the rest of that school year and I went back to my safe life and safer future.

When the summer holidays came and went, and we returned in September, there was no sign of him. A few weeks went past, and we all knew then he had dropped out. The bus was a lot quieter without him. I was glad to be shot of him though and concentrated instead on trying to get into university.

A few weeks later, on a slow Friday afternoon, I had gone to see my careers teacher after school to chat about university options. We spent half an hour talking, him trying to convince me what a great teacher I would make, me telling him how much I detested the idea. After the frustrating and time-wasting conversation for both of us, I walked into town to get the late bus home. Feeling pent up and frustrated, I went into the corner shop at the top of the town to buy some cigarettes, even though I had promised myself for the tenth time that week I was going to quit. Elsie, the owner and town gossip was engrossed in her usual chat with another old hen from around the town, slandering as per usual some other unfortunate soul to much; "God forgive me, but I shouldn't be saying this." and "Is that wrong of me to say, me being not one to judge and all."

The pair of them every bit as poisonous, yet pious as the other. The term wolves in sheep's clothing never seeming as apt.

I must have stood waiting for five minutes without as much as an acknowledgement from either of them, when I heard the bus rumble up the street behind the shop. I coughed attempting to get noticed but still nothing, then in panic I interrupted their conversation; "Elsie…you wouldn't give us a ten pack of B&H there, would you? I need to run here and catch the bus."

The two of them stood and stared at me in astonishment. How dare I interrupt their conversation.

"You shouldn't be smoking, young fella…it's bad for you.", Elsie said, turning to pick the packet from the shelf and gladly accepting my money.

Once I received my change I turned and bolted out the door, hearing their tut-tuts at my perceived lack of manners by not sticking around to indulge them in small talk. I was the quickest runner in my year at school and knew I would need to really put on the after-burners to reach the bus, the last of the queue now ascending the steps about three hundred metres up the street. I put my head down and sprinted with all my might. The indicators on the bus flashed to turn out onto the road, luckily the road was quite busy so it couldn't pull out at that moment. I pumped my legs and arms like pistons. I must have been about one hundred metres away, my speed decreasing like all good sprinters, stamina not being a strong point. Just then, a kindly bastard flashed the lights to let the bus out when I was closing in. The bus pulled out, flashed its hazard lights in acknowledgment and sped up the road.

I cursed and bent over, gasping for breath, ruing at that moment I smoked so much, my lungs on fire. After a minute or so, I began the long walk home, not for the first time. Just as I was coming to the edge of town, I walked past one of the many pubs it was known for. Dunbay was a drinker's paradise, this one, Connolly's, one of the more notorious. It was the one pub my dad always said the townies of Dunbay were truly territorial over. He reckoned if someone from the country areas or an outsider of the town walked in, the music would stop and there would be big trouble in store for the stranger, just like the Western movies. My dad had a prominent dislike, often verging onto hatred, for the townies of Dunbay.

It was a little bizarre as my mother herself was a Dunbay native. Such was the small town/country mentality of where I lived.

True to form, I heard a racket inside the pub. There was a fight going on and it seemed to be heading towards the door. I stalled and waited outside, intrigued to see what was going to spill out onto the street. Two men busted out through the door and onto the pavement. One larger man had the smaller one in a headlock.

"Enough...OK", the larger one was shouting.

"Lemme go ya bastard. I'll kill him…fuckin' kill all of yez."

"Enough", the larger one repeated and threw the smaller man to the ground. As he walked back into the pub, he called back over his shoulder, "And your barred too."

"Stick it up your ass.", the man on the ground shouted after him.

I would usually play the good Samaritan and offer to help someone up off the ground, but on this occasion, I turned a blind eye and walked on ahead. The man was drunk and obviously aggressive. After walking about ten yards up the street, I heard the man calling after me; "John-Paul. Is that you?"

I turned to look at the man who was now getting to his feet.

"Willie. What the hell?"

It was my uncle Willie, my mother's brother…Wild Willie.

Willie was standing, dusting himself off.

"What was that all about?", I asked.

He laughed; "Some prick beat me at pool. You know me…I never could lose."

I shook my head and laughed too.

"What are you doing? No bus today?"

"Missed it. I was on detention.", I lied to impress him.

"Detention. Ah, the memories. Don't let your mother know…she'll say you'll end up like me."

She'd say exactly that. The two of them didn't see eye to eye.

Willie was a lot younger than my mother, probably only around thirty or so. He was a small, powerfully built man who did a little painting and decorating around the town when sober enough to do so. He lived alone in a council house in one of the estates in Dunbay. A bachelor who lived a true bachelor lifestyle.

"You're not walking home, are you?", he asked.

"Ach sure it's only a few mile out the road. I'm sure I'll get a lift."

"Bollocks to that. Come back to my place for a can or two. I'll run you out the road later."

I agreed and we walked the short distance back to his house.

Once in the house, Willie went to the fridge and came back with two cans of beer. We opened them and toasted each other's health and drank deeply. We sat in the living room and he put on some music. I always liked him, he was a cool uncle and offered an edgy alternative to the rest of my strait-laced family.

"How's your da?", he asked. I nodded and said he was doing well.

"He's a good man.", he said. Then with a wry smile, continued; "Don't know how he ended up with *her* though."

If anyone else had said that I'd have went for them, but I could accept it from him and laughed, saying nothing in reply.

I pulled two cigarettes out of the packet and gave one to him, lighting his then mine. He inhaled deeply.

"Any girls?".

I laughed; "Girls? No interest."

He had a slight look of horror on his face.

"Sorry. Me and my big mouth. Any boys then?"

I laughed again; "Fuck off you. Boys! Cheeky prick."

It was his turn to laugh and I knew he had been winding me up.

"No. Too busy for girls. Big exams coming up next year, pressure's on."

"Ach, exams? I take it you're doing them to please your mother. Do what you want John-Paul. Fuckin' waste of time doing exams and goin' to university. Most of the boys around the town go to Belfast for a piss-up for three years and end up back here on the dole. Get a job…earn a few pound."

I didn't reply. He was probably right, but I knew I wouldn't return when I went. We sat and drank a few cans and talked. He mostly talked about what was

As We Sat Amongst the Sleeping Swans

going on around the town and about all the women in his life. I rolled my eyes at that and continued listening to his bullshit. I remember one night a few years back, when one of my dads' friends, Gerry Wilson, came to visit. During small talk Willies name was mentioned.

"Was talkin' to your brother in law, Ed. Wild Willie. He was telling me about all these women he's at these days. Some boy that.", he laughed.

"Some boy surely.", my dad said, rolling his eyes. "I've heard about these women. Pam and her five sisters." Both men laughed but I didn't get the joke back then.

I was going to joke with him about Pam but reasoned against it. Poor Willie had enough people taking the piss out of him without his teenage nephew doing it too. After a while the drink began to get the better of me. I got up to go to the toilet and stumbled, almost falling. Willie laughed and got up to put his coat on.

"You need to eat something kid. I'm gonna head to the Chinese here. Be back in a few minutes. The phones over there. Ring your mother and tell her you're OK…she'll be worrying. We'll get you a taxi after we get this feed."

I went to the toilet then phoned home. Stephen answered and I lied I was in Frankie's and would be home soon. He grunted something in reply and hung up. At least I could say I rang if my mum started on me when I got home. A few minutes later Willie came back with the takeaway. We sat at the table and ate,

As We Sat Amongst the Sleeping Swans

Willie opening another couple of beers for us. When finished we retired to the sofas and watched television for a while. I rang a taxi and the girl said it wouldn't be for an hour at least, as the town was so busy, it being a Friday night. I sighed and told her I could wait, slumping back onto the sofa.

We talked for another while, Willie telling me funny stories about his past, growing up around the area. He asked about my friends and I told him about Frankie, eventually telling him about our falling out.

"Why did you fall out? Seemed to be a good kid this Frankie.", he asked.

"Well, I found out he was telling a lot of lies, in-fact he was a compulsive liar. He...was up to no good and I had to find out from a Guard about what he was up to.", I replied being careful not to mention anything about the drugs. I heard stories around town that Willie was connected to certain organisations, if not directly then very indirectly through various close friends who were certainly involved. Willie was not a man who would take too kindly to such a story of drug-dealing in the local area. Repulsed by what Frankie had done, I certainly wasn't going to broadcast his crimes and put him in any risk of danger.

"Up to no good? What kind of no good?", Willie asked, his eyes narrowing into little slits. A cold shiver ran down my spine and my heart thumped. If I let my mouth run like it usually did, a family trait both Willie and I shared, then Frankie was in trouble...big trouble.

"Well, Frankie had a lot of family issues. His dad died a few years back and his mother...well, she's been a bit of a girl. One of the men Frankie believed was having an affair with her...when his dad was still alive, was a Guard. After his dad died, he went a bit crazy. Vowed to get his revenge on the Guard and ended up harassing him at his home...pretty bad shit.", I summarised, glad I held it together without revealing the dealing issue.

"This Frankie kid...what's his surname?"

"Harris."

He's not a son of Charlie Harris, is he?"

"Yep. Did ye know him?"

"Everyone knew him. Your father was friendly enough with him too. I knew *of* him, didn't have any dealings with him, but from all accounts he was a good decent fellah. Bit too fond of the drink, but sure who isn't? His missus, holy shit! Never seen a woman like her, used to be a model, modelled in dirty mags and that."

I nodded in agreement. She still had it.

"Yeah, well pretty girls make graves as the saying goes. She's caused quite the trouble with her looks for a lot of people."

A troubled look dawned upon Willie's features for a moment before he spoke. "Hold on a minute, who is she shacked up with now? It's not that wee cunt Quinn...Geordie Quinn, is it?"

My heart quickened. I didn't want Willie to make the association between a known drug pusher and Frankie.

"Yeah, it is", I mumbled before continuing, "Where's this taxi?", attempting to change the subject.

"That Quinn's a bad bastard, John-Paul. He's dangerous. By the way, who's this Guard that was supposed to be involved with Harris' old lady?"

"Ach, there was no Guard at all, Willie. Frankie's head was that messed up that he accused the Guard for some reason."

"Why would he do that?", Willie questioned, and my heart raced once more.

"Just took a spite against him, that's all. The Guard's this pillar of society that everyone loves...the type of fucker Frankie naturally hates and rebels against."

Willie sat back in his chair, his mind wandering. I felt nervous and wanted the topic of conversation to change quickly.

"Now I remember. Jeez, that's a good few years back. I wouldn't have been much older than you are now, but I remember. I used to knock about with a few boys from Ballymoy, went to discos and that with them. I remember there were a few hushed rumours that the big fucker who used to play the hurling was knocking off Harris' woman. He'd been spotted with her in his car a few times and apparently Charlie caught the two of them in the act. Fuck that's a few years back now."

My blood suddenly ran cold.

"Are you serious?"

"Yes. Shit, I forgot all about that. Nothing ever came of those rumours though. You might as well have blamed a priest of doing the dirty deed back ten-fifteen years ago as a hurling hero Guard. No-one would ever have believed that."

I sat back, head swirling. How could I have bought O'Halloran's lies over Frankie's truth? I felt sick to the stomach.

"Are you sure?", I asked.

"Well, there was some hefty rumours around the pubs at the time. Charlie seemed to confirm them too with his rantings and ravings about finding his wife and the Guard in action. Poor bastard."

He sat silent for a moment before a wry smile broke across his features. "Good lookin' women, John-Paul…very dangerous. Stick to the fat girls and those lacking in any beauty…no problems and very grateful too…if you know what I mean."

He laughed and stood up to clear the dirty dishes from the table. I sat, numb. I hated myself for jumping to conclusions so easily, what kind of a friend was I? Everyone had let Frankie down and now I had too. Was that one of the reasons why he didn't return to school this year? And O'Halloran. What a dirty lying bastard. All that bullshit he had told me in the car that day. So convincing, lies flowing like slurry from his mouth.

"John-Paul…John-Paul", Willie spoke, awakening me from my trance.

"Taxi's here."

I got up and headed towards the door. Willie followed me out.

"I enjoyed this, kid. Come back again soon. You and your friends are welcome to come around anytime for a few beers, safer than being out in the town. Tell your da I was asking about him…and your ma too…aul bat", he said with a wry grin.

We shook hands and I went home. My Dutch courage fortified by the cans I had in Willies house; I rang Frankie's number once home.

"Ello.", the gruff English voice answered once more, a voice I never thought I'd hear on the phone again. I asked if Frankie was there and she shouted up to him. Such visual beauty certainly hadn't been paired with its audible counterpart.

"Yea-who's this?", Frankie asked over the line, his tone confrontational. God only knows who or what he had been expecting.

"Frankie, it's me…Moz."

A long silence.

"Yea…what d'ya want?"

"Just wanted to say I'm sorry.", my voice quivering a little before I coughed to clear my throat.

As We Sat Amongst the Sleeping Swans

"Why?"

"Can we meet…tomorrow?"

Another long pause.

"Alright then."

CHAPTER 11

After waking I looked at my watch.

10:05 am.

I stretched, surprised how well I felt. No sign of a hangover or the weariness that lumbered me the day before.

"You get up for a little while each day?", the distinctive accent of Canadian Clive drifted across the room.

I laughed; "Morning Clive."

"Morning JP. Liam's in the shower. He told me about your antics last night. You're quite the dark horse."

I laughed again and stretched out in the bed. Just then, Liam entered the room, wrapped in a towel.

"Oh…he's awake. Casanova himself. Any joy last night with your one?", he asked.

I yawned and stretched once more. "What do *you* think?"

"Lucky bastard. She was a nice wee yoke too. Fair play, boy. You nordies and that accent!"

I laughed.

"Might as well use it down here. It sure doesn't work up north."

Liam busied himself folding and packing his clothes and possessions.

"Are ye heading home today Liam?", I asked, hoping he wasn't so we could spend a little more time together.

"Yeah, back down to Tipp. Hopefully back up in September if I can pass these fuckin' exams."

My heart pined for home at that moment. I should have been getting ready for exams in the summer. I should have been relishing the pressure and deadlines final year in school brought. Readying myself for the excitement of leaving home in September, with my parents blessing, for three or four years of fun times in University. I had been on the right track, but one night in my life had destroyed all that. I felt sick at the thought.

Liam halted his work and stood looking down at me; "Are you OK JP?", he asked, reading the melancholy that had obviously clouded my features.

"Yeah...of course. Just thinking about your one last night. Wait til you hear this.", I replied trying to distract from any unwanted attention or questions. I told them the story about Pessi, exaggerating and eliminating certain parts of the story in equal measure. They both had a good laugh and my sad thoughts left me momentarily.

In a few minutes Liam was changed and ready to go.

"Lads, it's been a pleasure. I need to rush off. There's a train leaving on the hour and I'll have to sprint all the way."

He took out a pen and piece of paper from his bag and ripped it in two before writing on both pages; "Here lads, this is my number. Give me a call during the week and we'll arrange to meet up again."

Both Clive and I took his number and I lied I'd phone. He shook us both by the hand and rushed out the door. I knew I would miss him, but by now I was becoming hardened to loss. I lay back in my bed and fell asleep.

When I woke again it was 12.30pm. I called out to see if Canadian Clive was there, but there was no answer. Ironically after feeling so good when I had initially awakened, I now felt like shit. My head pounded and I felt as weak as water. I wanted to sleep all day but remembered that I would have to get out by 1pm to allow the cleaners in. I sat up and tried to compose myself. I tepidly walked across the cold floor and pulled my jeans and jumper on, before sitting back down on the bed to tie my shoelaces. I left the room and headed back out into the cold Dublin afternoon.

It *felt* like a Sunday. There weren't many people around and the traffic was much lighter than the first few days. The afternoon was grey and cold, lifeless, and uninspiring. I knew it would be a difficult day. I remembered my Walkman in the rucksack and stopped to sit down at a bus stop to load Urban Hymns by the Verve into it. As I walked along with *"Bittersweet Symphony"* blaring into my ears, I imagined myself as Richard Ashcroft in the video for the song, walking along bumping into everyone not giving a shit. There was no one around to bump into until I met a large bald man and I put my head down and avoided his gaze at all costs.

Some fucking Richard Ashcroft I was.

I almost laughed at how pathetic I was but didn't have the energy for it. The music perked me up and put a spring in my step until *"The Drugs Don't Work"* came on, one of my favourite songs, and I had to skip forward to the next track as I knew the lyrics would surely make me cry. Crying and walking the streets of Dublin in broad daylight would surely attract unwanted attention.

To stroll without abandon or constraint through a large European city like Dublin for a young man should have been like a dream. But, when money was slipping through one's fingers like sand, and the city seemed to discriminate against anyone who roamed it alone, without a partner or a friend, it was far from dreamlike. I spotted a pharmacy in the distance and walked towards it. Canadian Clive had told me to get passport photos if I wanted to get a job on the security hut where he worked, as I'd need them for my identification card. He had arranged an interview for me on Monday and said I'd have a good chance of landing the job as he'd put a good word in for me. He told me at my age I would get about 5-5.50 an hour and I could do twelve hour shifts three or four times a week if I wanted, as they were always looking for men.

As We Sat Amongst the Sleeping Swans

With money like that rolling in I could buy a ticket to Australia or America in no time.

I went to the counter of the pharmacy to get change and then sat in the booth to get my photo taken. After a few minutes of waiting, the machine finally produced the small slip of paper with my photos on it from a slot near my feet. I picked it up and sat for a few moments in complete shock looking at the horrific images. Most people complain about terrible passport photos and share some embarrassment about their appearance in them, but this...this was different. I looked like how I felt...haunted. My eyes conveyed a terror that horrified me. I thought I had a better poker face than that. What were people thinking of me if I was walking around like a terrified zombie? My skin was as white as a sheet and dark circles framed my eyes. My mouth was crooked, and my hair was wild. I looked like I had escaped from a mental hospital. I sat for a few moments further and tried not to cry. My appearance upset me that much and I wondered how my mother would react. The thought of her pushed me over the edge and I began to sob, fat tear droplets splashing over the horrific image on the paper I held in my hand. I cursed myself and tried to get it together, before drying my face and exiting the booth without attracting attention from anyone in the shop.

Once out in the cold afternoon air, I walked aimlessly as I had done the day before. I had another few hours to kill before I could go back to the hostel at 4pm. I cursed the two little pricks who worked in the hostel and their stupid fucking rules and thought

As We Sat Amongst the Sleeping Swans

of what I could do to put the time in without spending too much, or *any* money. I walked into a few music and book shops, browsing for a while until some annoying sales prick would inevitably come over, pressurising me into buying something. As a last resort when I traipsed into a café to get a piece of toast and a cup of tea to get out of the cold, even the waitresses began to clean the floor around me after I had been there after a certain time. To deter their circling, I ordered another tea and sat over it for half an hour, until they very untactfully began their passive intimidation techniques to shoo me out of the shop.

This fucking city! If one didn't have money or was reluctant to spend it, the city of "A Hundred Thousand Welcomes", quickly turned into the city of "A Hundred Thousand Fuck You's!"

I slipped out of the café and made my way slowly back to the hostel. It was almost 4pm and I waited outside for a few minutes before entering. The two Jackeens stood watching me as I went past. I nodded my head at them in acknowledgement, but they ignored my sentiments. On cue, after I had walked past them towards the bedroom, I heard them howl with laughter and knew it was most likely a joke made at my expense. Again, I was the only person in the communal room, the others who stayed there obviously living their lives to the full and enjoying the experiences the city weekend could offer. I lay on my bed and stole another glance at my passport photo. I didn't know whether to laugh or cry, quickly putting it back into my wallet and vowing not to look at it again. I closed my eyes and exhaustion took hold of my wearied body once more.

When I awoke, the room light was on and a few bodies were present, lying on beds. I looked up and saw both Canadian Clive and Ger lying sleeping and checked my watch to see what time it was. 10:03pm. I cursed myself knowing I would struggle to sleep later after sleeping for six hours already. I wanted to be fresh for my interview tomorrow but knew I would wake up wrecked and looking like shit. According to Canadian Clive I was almost guaranteed a job, but I still wanted to make a good impression to my new employer. I had wanted to chat with Canadian Clive before the interview, but he was sleeping like an overgrown baby and I didn't have the heart to unsettle him. He had written on a piece of paper the name of his boss and the address of the building I was to go to. He didn't specify a time, just telling me to be there any time before 12pm. I walked up to the communal television area with a little spring in my step. In 24 hours, I would be employed with a plan to move out of the dive I called my temporary home.

There were five people sitting watching a film. Two men, one a young Chinese guy who didn't speak English and a fat man from Birmingham whom I wished didn't speak English, as he never shut the fuck up throughout the film. Three girls lay almost on top of each other on the sofa, one being the pretty blonde I spotted on my first day, and things began to look up. The film had just started a few minutes and it didn't take me long to get the gist of what it was about, a very violent and disturbing film about a Maori family in New Zealand. During ad breaks the

As We Sat Amongst the Sleeping Swans

three girls engaged in conversation with me as I sat on the floor in front of them. They were backpackers from Scotland staying in Dublin for a week or so, the next day being their last in the hostel. The pretty blonde was called Marianne and she was around the same age as me, the other two older, in their mid-twenties. They were all very friendly and as the film progressed, they began to break away on their own, leaving Marianne and me to talk more privately. It was beginning to turn into a very enjoyable night, bar the fat loudmouth giving a running commentary of the film. When the film ended, the two girls got up and said goodnight, leaving myself and Marianne in the room along with the mute Chinese man and the loud fat man. We talked for a few minutes more before she yawned and said she was going to bed. I walked her out to the foyer, spotting the two Jackeens sitting in a backroom smoking and watching television, their eyes almost popping out of their heads in astonishment as I was engaged in conversation with the blonde beauty...and making her laugh. I smugly smiled and buoyed by their jealousy, my confidence high, asked if she wanted to go for lunch the next day after my interview. To my gleeful surprise she agreed and said she would meet me at the foyer at 1pm, just when she was checking out. She retired to her room and I skipped to mine, hoping Canadian Clive or Ger were awake so I could gloat. Unsurprisingly they weren't and I lay on the bed for an hour or so wondering how I'd landed myself a job and a girlfriend with no hassle or much effort at all. Life was beginning to look good again and I fell into a deep satisfying sleep.

As We Sat Amongst the Sleeping Swans

I awoke the next morning and knew it was early, due to the hive of activity around me and the smell of deodorant in the room. Usually when I awoke, the room would have been empty, everyone out and getting on with their lives. This time I was joining them, my enthusiasm from the night before surviving the test of my sleeping nightmares. I looked up and Canadian Clive entered the room, waddling in like an oversized baby wearing nothing but a white towel around his waist. I was glad to see him.

"The man himself! Clive...how ya doin? Every time I see you, you're sleeping, good to see you're awake for once."

He laughed and sat down on the bed to finish drying himself whilst putting on some fresh clothes.

"What are you doing up so early? Party all night, sleep all day is more your style is it not?", he asked.

"Have to get ready for this interview you've arranged, don't I?"

"Interview?", he repeated, looking up to the ceiling as if a large confusion cloud had drifted by.

I laughed. "The interview *you* landed for me...remember?"

"Oh yes. I got you an interview with Davo, didn't I? Well, good luck. Give it your best shot and don't be too nervous. Davo doesn't like nervous people as he can't exactly put a bag of nerves in a security hut at night."

"Fair enough, I understand that but I thought you might have been sitting in on the interview too, being second in command and all?", I asked hoping he would confirm, as it would be good to have a biased and friendly person in my corner.

He stood up and put his trousers on; "Afraid you're on your own JP. It's my day off today and I'm going to visit friends."

My heart sank. I hoped he was not only going to be on the interview panel, but he would be able to come with me to the site as I hadn't a clue where I was going. Reading my thoughts, pulling his jumper down over his generous belly he came over and patted me on the back; "You'll be fine. You'll need to catch a few buses, so I'd set off sharpish."

I sat, now slightly deflated, my confidence beginning to haemorrhage. I showered and put on the most respectable clothing I had in my possession. A pair of black jeans, black boots, and a blue denim shirt. Probably not the most suitable interview attire but it was all I had. I stood in front of Canadian Clive as he lay on his bed reading a magazine.

"How do I look man?"

He did a double take when looking at me; "Do you not have a suit or a shirt and tie?"

"No", I replied sheepishly and realised that today wasn't going to be the walk in the park I thought it was going to be.

Canadian Clive stood and delved into his suitcase, producing a navy coloured sports jacket; "Here, try this on."

I put the jacket on and felt immediately like a child trying its fathers' clothes on.

I laughed and he stood back in assessment; "Bit big on you, but it's an improvement. It will have to do."

"Bit big? It's a fuckin' tent. I can't go for an interview looking like this."

He looked at me, hurt writ across his face; "Well if you don't want it, give it back to me then."

Realising I had hurt his feelings as he was only trying to help, I walked to the mirror and straightened myself up. I looked ridiculous but nodded my head in agreement; "Not bad I suppose...thanks Clive."

A little smile crossed his lips. I liked Canadian Clive. He was like a big harmless child. Very easily insulted, but any insults laden upon him could be very easily retracted by a kind word.

"Good. You'd better get off then. Good luck and let me know how you get on.", he said after looking at his watch.

"OK-I'm off.", I replied before turning towards him, "Clive...thanks again. I really appreciate this."

Again, the childish smile as he reacted positively to my complimentary comment. He gave me a thumbs up and I left to embark on my journey.

Three buses and a twenty-minute walk later, I had arrived. He had told me the industrial estate was just outside Dublin, but it had felt as if I had travelled to another country altogether. The whole journey from start to finish had taken almost two hours and had cost a substantial amount of money. The term "speculate to accumulate" came to my mind and I suddenly felt better, and knew the money spent would be an investment in the long term.

The building was bleak and depressing looking. Large, grey, and imposing it looked like a prison. I walked to the entrance and an old lady behind the counter asked me who my appointment was with. I told her I was there to see Davo. She sighed heavily and lifted the phone. She mumbled something down the line, put the phone down and then mumbled something in my direction.

"Sorry?", I asked.

"What ya sorry for?", she scowled.

"I didn't hear what you said...sorry"

Again, she sighed and shook her head; "I said he will be down in a few minutes."

I took a seat without saying anything in reply. What was it with these fucking sourpusses and their extreme attitude problems in customer facing roles? I tried not to let it phase me and concentrated on making a good first impression. I must have been waiting there for at least twenty minutes when suddenly a very flustered and irritable looking little bald man came down the stairs and spoke to the receptionist. She gestured my way and he turned to look at me. I stood and extended my hand to him.

As We Sat Amongst the Sleeping Swans

"You must be Davo? I'm John-Paul. Pleased to meet you."

He accepted my handshake, mine firm, his limp as a wet lettuce. He turned back to the receptionist; "Davo, eh?"

They both laughed.

"My name is David, Sean-Paul. Not Davo.", he said, condescension dripping from every word. I wanted to correct the little prick as he got my name wrong also, but let it go…I needed the job badly.

"Follow me", he continued, and I walked behind him like a naughty schoolboy behind the headmaster. He directed me into a little office that was very messy and stinky.

"So, what is it you want to see me about?", he asked. He had a squint and the term "one eye was looking at me and the other was looking for me", came to mind and I almost laughed aloud.

"Well, I came about the job. Clive said he spoke to you…put a good word in for me."

He sat back and guffawed with laughter.

"So, how do you know Clive?", he asked.

"Well…I live with him."

"You *live* with him?", he asked, one eyebrow raised in surprise.

"Yes."

"Clive stays in hostels in Dublin. Do *you* live in a hostel?"

"Yes. I'm staying there for a while."

"OK. Do you have your paperwork with you?"

"Eh...paperwork?". I was beginning to feel very stupid and stitched up now.

He gave an irritated sigh and continued, "Your papers. Your qualifications to show I can employ you as a security person. You do have them...don't you?", a little smile creeping across his lips.

"No. I've got GCSE's.", my response pathetic.

"GCSE's, ha!", he got up from his chair and opened the door, gesturing for me to leave.

"Are there any jobs going around here I could do? I'm a good worker."

"No. Please leave now.", he replied coldly as if I were an unwanted dog on the street.

"But Clive told me I was as good as hired. I mean, come on man. Give me a fuckin' chance. I'm desperate."

He guffawed with laughter once more; "Sonny, Clive is a fool. A likeable, harmless fool...but a fool. If you want to be taken seriously, stop hanging around in hostels with people like Clive. You will earn a certain reputation for yourself."

My uncle Willies genes kicked in.

"I'd rather associate myself with someone like Clive rather than a little fuckin' weasel like you. Look at you on your power trip. Enjoy it while it lasts you cross-eyed mother fucker.", I ranted at him as I stormed out the door.

As I walked past the surly receptionist on the way out, she glared at me like I had just farted under her nose.

"The fuck you looking at?", I hissed at her and walked out the door of the building. I stood outside for a minute or so, my head swimming and my blood boiling. I felt like rushing back in and taking the wee bollocks by the throat. What was I going to do now? I had relied on getting that job and now I was back to square one whilst haemorrhaging money by the day. I steadied myself and walked back towards the bus-stop.

When I had caught the three buses back to Dublin, it was well past half-two. I remembered about the date I had arranged with Marianne and realised I was an hour and a half late. She would had to have been very keen to still be hanging around waiting on me, but my ego made me walk past the hostel anyway to see if she was.

She wasn't.

I went to bed the night before, high on the prospect of a steady job and a beautiful girlfriend, the cold light of day delivering neither. I went to an off-licence, bought two litres of cider, found a park, and drank the whole bottle.

The cider was like an old friend making everything better. Once finished, I needed more. So, I went to the nearest pub and spent the next twelve hours or so repeating the process until I woke up once more in my bed.

CHAPTER 12

I borrowed my mum's car the next day and drove to Frankie's house. When I arrived, Frankie must have been watching for me, as he walked out his front door as soon as I got there. He got in and we sat in silence for about a minute.

"Listen Frankie...I'm sorry. O'Halloran...he..."

"He got inside your head. I know. I know what he's like."

We sat there for another minute or so, before Frankie broke the tension with a joke.

"Let's get the fuck out of here before you get done for kerb-crawling, ye creepy prick."

I laughed and put the car in gear. We drove around for a while before we got hungry and went to Dunbay for some chips. We sat in the car and ate them, then I drove him back to his house. We didn't talk much about anything, but it was good to spend a few hours together to release any awkwardness or tension that remained between us. He had met a girl in the meantime, and he was going to meet her that night. The feeling I had was not one of jealousy, more annoyance that I had let O'Halloran put our friendship on hold for so long. Frankie had moved on and found himself a girlfriend. He was the type who was meant to be in a relationship with a girl. Girls loved him and I could see how he would be good to them; it was in his nature. I was more immature and knew I would struggle to find a girlfriend anyway. I didn't want one either. I was more than happy to spend my weekends getting drunk and talking shite and having a laugh with Frankie. My father had always joked, a joke with a jag at my mother's expense, that the beginning of the end of his youthful good times was when he and his friends met girls and settled down. When he went to get out of the car, he shook my hand.

"I enjoyed this Moz. Good to be back friends with ye again. Fuckin' missed ye man. Let's arrange a night out next Saturday…I'll give Dawn the slip for the night."

I drove home satisfied I had my best friend back again, feeling cooler and more popular for it, his coolness and popularity contagious.

The week dragged in at school and I bragged to all the boys on the bus that I was heading out on the piss with Frankie. I even began sitting at the back of the bus again. When Saturday arrived, Frankie rang and arranged for us to meet by the lake at 8pm. He was supplying the booze and I agreed to supply the fags. I bought two twenty packs and arrived early at the lake at about 7:40. I opened one of the packs and was on my second smoke when Frankie appeared shortly after 8.

"Moz…I got the good shit for us tonight", he said, beaming from ear to ear. "Good aul Buckfast. Made by monks …but it is *the* shit"

We cracked the bottles open, clinked them in salute to each other and took a hit. Sickly sweet and quite thick with a distinct aftertaste, I took a deep breath and looked at Frankie's delighted expression.

"Whoa! Certainly is unique. Not bad though.", I commented and took another swig. The more I drank the more I liked it.

"Wait until your halfway down. This shit does strange things to you. It's like drinking a bottle of wine and about five coffees at the same time. The buzz is like nothing else…but the shits you get the next day are horrific. I thought I was giving birth the next day after drinking Buckfast for the first time. But, hey, worry about that tomorrow."

We clinked our bottles once more.

"To tomorrows mega dump.", I toasted and we both laughed and drank. For the next hour or so we drank and talked. It was just like the old times. The Buckfast made everything flow better. I had found my drink. I buzzed with confidence and energy. The label denied that the tonic classification held health giving or medicinal properties, but that must have been a humility exercise by the monks who made it. By the time I had finished I was ready to take on anything. I put my arm around Frankie.

"I'm sorry for doubtin' ye man. I never should have listened to that scumbag O'Halloran. Please forgive me, aul friend?", I said, the Buckfast enabling somehow my heart to speak. To my surprise, Frankie shrugged his shoulder away from me, swigged down the last of his drink and flung the bottle into the lake.

"Are you OK?", I asked.

He shook his head and laughed without humour.

"Not really Moz...not really."

"Why. What's wrong? I said I'm sorry, didn't I? We are friends again...aren't we?"

He sat on the ground for a moment and lit a cigarette, inhaling deeply before replying; "Yes. We're 100% Moz. I love ye man. But I'd be lying if I said I wasn't very disappointed by your doubting of me...and very worried."

My Buckfast buzz bubble had been very quickly punctured and deflated by Frankie's brutally honest words. I sat beside him and lit a cigarette too.

"Ye don't need to worry, Frankie. I'll not let you down again.", I assured him sincerely.

Again, Frankie laughed.

"You're not getting' it, Moz. I don't mean I'm worried about you letting me down again. You see, I get it how you would believe what O'Halloran said about me. And you did...every single fuckin' lie that was uttered from the cunts mouth."

He sat and took another drag of his cigarette, as did I to steady my nerves.

"I hold no grudge, Moz...otherwise you'd know about it.", he continued whilst catching my eye, his steely and intense.

"No, what worries me is how O'Halloran could convince my best friend to think the worst of me. Believe me, he *won't* care if you now know the truth. He has won his little battle. He knows now that if he can turn you against me, he can turn anyone. This shit worries me and has worried me for the last few months."

I scratched my head reflexively; "What is O'Halloran's game then? I don't understand. I mean, he had…relationships with your mum, but that was then, everybody's moved on. Why would he tell me about doing you for dealing? That shit is dangerous, especially around these parts. Is there something I'm not getting here Frankie?"

He pulled on his cigarette deeply and flicked it high until it fizzed out in the lake like a defeated firefly. He stood and patted himself down. "There is history with O'Halloran and me. I reacted in the past emotionally and rashly. He will be dealt with again, but as for you Moz, the less you know the better…for the time being anyway."

His words were intense and uncharacteristic of him. I had a sense of foreboding and didn't probe any further. Getting involved in their feud in the past had led to trouble that I didn't want any further part of in the future.

"Let's go Moz. That Buckfast has given me a serious thirst for some pints."

I knew Frankie didn't want to speak any more of the situation, so I played along and laughed and joked into the night in search of beer and girls.

A few weeks passed and I didn't hear much from Frankie. Much to my annoyance and great sadness I knew that our relationship had been irreplaceably damaged by O'Halloran's accusations. The times I had spent with him weren't the same as they had been before. His trust in me had been broken and I knew I would have to work hard to regain it, if indeed I ever could. Although he had found a nice girl in Dawn, he didn't seem as happy as he should. He had found a job in a meat packing factory and was working long hours, making good money, in an attempt to move out from under Quinn's roof. Steady job and steady girlfriend, I would have loved to have either, but it didn't seem to be cutting it for him. Every time I saw him, he appeared sadder, more down in the dumps. Alarm bells began ringing for me one Wednesday night, a few weeks after our night out drinking Buckfast. My mum was at work and my dad had went to the pub with his friends. I sat in my room studying for exams that were fast approaching. The phone rang and Stephen answered. He called up the stairs and when I asked who it was, he shrugged his shoulders and replied; "Dunno...didn't say, but he sounds very pished."

"What the fuck?", I asked irritably and presumed it was Willie. I took the phone. "Hello."

"Moz...what are ye at?"

It was Frankie, and Stephen was correct, he did seem very drunk. It wasn't like him. I never knew him to drink during the week and if he did it would have been a few beers, nothing major.

But he was steaming drunk.

"What's happenin' Frankie?"

"Not much Moz. How's that lovely family of yours...all OK?"

"Yea, not bad. What's up man? You've had a few drinks ye cunt? Why didn't you call me earlier...I would have joined ye?"

There was a long silence on the other end.

"Just had a few after work. Nothing major...couple of pints or something."

"Couple of pints...your fuckin' steamin' man.", I blurted, again my lack of tact getting the better of me.

Again, silence on the other end for another moment or two, before he replied, "Steamin'? Are you judging me like?"

Taken aback at his confrontational line of questioning, it was my turn to pause before answering; "No...not at all. Sorry, maybe it's a bad line, that's all."

"Yea...must be. Anyhow, I must go. Got shit to do and that. Tell all I was asking about them, OK?"

"OK", I replied, and he hung up.

The conversation worried me. It was like talking to a different person on the phone. At our age, getting drunk was fun, something that was done with friends at the weekend. Listening to Frankie slurring his words and denying he had drunk a lot on a random Wednesday night seemed too grown up and problematic for me. Drinking was for the craic, not to drown one's sorrows...surely to fuck we hadn't reached that stage yet.

The week passed and I didn't hear any further from him. Disappointingly he didn't call me at the weekend either and I presumed he had made plans with Dawn. I didn't want to put him in an awkward position, so I left him alone and stayed in, watching Match of the Day with Stephen on the Saturday night. Just as I was brushing my teeth and preparing for bed, I heard my dad downstairs, home from the pub. I decided to go down and spend half an hour or so with him. I liked it when he had a few pints in him. He was more relaxed and funnier. Unlike most people I knew, he was more affable after a few drinks, never nasty nor violent.

"Well, dad. Any craic tonight?"

Before replying he went to the fridge and lifted a can of beer, before looking up at me. "Want one?"

Surprised by his offer, I hesitated before answering, "Aye...well if you don't mind?"

He lifted another can of beer. "I don't mind. Its Saturday night, you've been studying hard all week. Let your hair down, have a drink with your father."

I happily opened the can and we both lifted our beers in the air. "Slainte", we both saluted simultaneously.

I drank deeply and we sat for a moment or so in silence.

"I like this, John-Paul. I never got to have a drink with my father. Enjoy this…you'll remember in years to come when I'm not around."

We took another few drinks from our cans and he got up to get us another couple. My father could drink more pints than anyone else in the local pub but never seemed too affected either that night or the next morning. I gulped down a few mouthfuls to try and keep the pace. He noticed and laughed.

"Don't worry about keeping up with me. You'll be on your ass in twenty minutes. I'm a seasoned gulpin…just enjoy the beer."

I nodded my head in agreement; "You *are* a gulpin of the highest degree"

We both laughed.

"I want to talk to you John-Paul, man to man about something."

I straightened up in my chair, tension gripping my body. "What the hell have I done now?", I wondered.

Reading my thoughts my father raised both his hands.

"Relax. Nothing you've done wrong. There was talk in the pub tonight about a few things going on in both Ballymoy and Dunbay. A lot of the boys are worried about their youngsters in the area."

I took another swig of my beer.

"How's that beer? Good?", he asked.

"Its good stuff."

"You know, I don't mind you having a drink. You're of age so there's nothing I can do about it anyway. You're a good sensible fella and I know you'll do no harm. As long as you don't go overboard drinking, which I know you wouldn't, and use it in a sociable way, you'll be OK. Boys will be boys, and I know what I was like at your age and you're a better fella than I was."

"Don't know about that.", I laughed and took another swig.

"You are. You listen to your mother and me and you work and study hard. You have a plan and direction in your life. I didn't."

It pleased me when my dad praised me like that, but at the same time it confirmed the bore I was. Sometimes I yearned for a disappointed look from my parents or a stern talking to about how I was going "off the rails" or something. I wished to be a rebel and to hell with the consequences but didn't have the balls when it came down to it.

"So, what was the talk in the pub tonight?", I asked, a little anxiety creeping in.

He gave a concerned look, not at me but at the issue in general before continuing; "A few of the boys were saying that there's a lot of drugs creeping into the area. Ballymoy is supposed be gettin' very bad altogether and Dunbay is catching up with it."

My heart began to race, and I took a swig of my drink to try and steady my nerves. I had to act as surprised as he would expect. If he thought I knew about this already, there would be further difficult questions I would have to answer, and undoubtably Frankie's name would be mentioned.

"What?", I asked, hoping I didn't sound too overly flabbergasted. He took my incredulous reaction as genuine and continued; "It's not good. Obviously, around the border here, there's a lot of boys who take great exception to scum bags dealing drugs to the youngsters of the area."

I was beginning to sweat now and fought the urge to wipe my forehead. I couldn't rouse any suspicion in my dad. If he found out about Frankie and his past convictions, or the fact that I *knew* about it...I couldn't even let my mind go there. If my parents knew that I was best friends with a convicted drug dealer they would probably go to such drastic measures of leaving the area...or ship *me* off somewhere. I wasn't a good liar and knew I wouldn't get away with denying what I knew about him. I nodded my head in agreement.

"Yea...not good. Well, you don't need to worry about me. I wouldn't know what to do with a drug. None of the boys I know would touch them either, too afraid of the boys around the town, who as you say, would take great umbrage to that kind of activity in the area."

My words hung in the air for a while and he sat contemplating the situation, before I continued in an attempt to change the subject; "Did ye see Match of the Day in the pub tonight...those United pricks winning again, sickening." As expected, he perked up at that. He was a huge Manchester United fan, I followed Liverpool a little and there was always a bit of slagging between us when it came to the fortunes of the two clubs. He got up and walked to the fridge to get some more cans, singing "Glory, glory Man United" as he went.

We drank the beers and made some more small talk before I got up and yawned. "Gonna hit the sack here dad, those beers have done me in"

He laughed, "Lightweight. I enjoyed this son."

"Me too", I replied and went up to bed. Although the beers had made me sleepy, I lay awake in bed for an hour or so. I felt sick to the stomach about what was happening. People had suspected Quinn of dealing in the past, but there hadn't been enough drugs in the area to confirm he was up to anything dodgy. He was known as a scumbag around the area, but if it was confirmed he was indeed dealing, he would surely drag Frankie down with him and only God knows what would happen to them...but it wouldn't be good.

The next day I rang Frankie. His mother answered and said he was in bed. It was after lunchtime. I left a message with her and he called back later that evening at 8.30pm.

"What's up Moz?", he sounded tired.

"Not much Frankie. Just thought I'd give you a call and see how things are."

"Not bad. Was out last night with Dawn and a few others...bit rough today."

There was a long silence. I felt a pang of jealousy Dawn had stolen away my best friend from me, enjoying the good nights I should have been having.

"Listen, Frankie. I spoke to my dad last night. He said the boys in the pub were giving off about drug dealing in the area. It's not good, man."

This time the silence lasted longer than the last time.

"And why do you feel the need to share this with me?", he asked very irritably.

"I dunno. Just thought I'd tell you the craic like.", I answered feeling very pathetic at that moment.

"Well, next time keep that shit to yourself, Moz. I'm not interested in what's goin' on around this shithole country, sooner I'm fuckin' out of it the better."

"What do you mean by that? Are you not happy…do ye wanna talk about it?"

"No. Listen, I have to go here."

"Have I done somethin' wrong Frankie. You sound very pissed off?"

"No Moz, I'm just very hungover. Need to go, give ye a shout during the week."

He hung up and I sat for a while thinking things over. He wasn't himself. A change had happened in him since we had our fallout. I hoped to God my doubting of him hadn't caused the change…but deep down I really suspected it had.

As We Sat Amongst the Sleeping Swans

The following Wednesday I came home from school, had dinner, and went to my room to study. I was putting the finishing touches to an essay that had to be completed for the next morning, feeling very sleepy after another intense day, when Claire shouted up the stairs to me. "John-Paul...phone."

I looked at the digital clock on my dressing table, 21:33. "Who the fuck...", I wondered, before realising it would be Frankie. I braced myself and descended the stairs. The phone sat off the hook, on top of the little oak unit. I picked it up.

"Hello. John-Paul speaking"

"Oh, hello John-Paul speaking, it's your friend Frankie speaking.", he laughed, again his words slurred, and I knew he was drunk again.

"You OK Frankie?"

A long pause.

"Not really Moz."

"What's wrong man?"

"It's that cunt Quinn. Things are getting' bad Moz. I don't know how long I can take this. The shit I have to take from that bastid. And what can I do...my stupid fuckin' ma loves him. What can I do to him? It would kill her if I hurt him. I need to get out. I need to leave this shithole town before somethin' really bad happens."

It was the first time he had opened up and been completely honest with me in a long while. I knew if I asked him when he was sober, he would snap at me and tell me to back off, so I seized the opportunity.

"Frankie, has any of this got to do with what I was saying the other day, about drugs in the area?"

He hesitated before answering; "Yes."

A silence hung in the air once more. I could hear his breathing increasing over the line.

"What is it Frankie, tell me. We can help you?"

He laughed once more, this time with a hint of bitterness. "What are you gonna do...tell your great mate O'Halloran?"

"No...fuck ye, no. I'm hardly gonna tell O'Halloran. My family can help, *I* can help."

"You keep to hell away from O'Halloran...underfuckinstood?", he demanded.

"Of course. What do you think of me?"

"I'm fuckin' serious. He can sweet talk you, he's done it before. You think you're this man of the world, but you're only a sheltered kid when all's said and done, very easily influenced by the big local hero, like every other cunt in this shithole country.", his voice was becoming raised.

I bit my tongue.

My temper was easily raised, and I could feel it becoming triggered. I couldn't let it get the better of me when my friend needed someone to be there for him.

"OK, OK. I'm not gonna fuckin' go runnin' to O'Halloran...we've established that. What's goin' on with Quinn? Tell me."

"He's getting worse with the shit he's up to. He's getting bolder and taking more risks...getting a lot bigger, if you know what I mean."

I nodded my head.

"I know what you mean. But you have nothing to worry about. It can't do you any harm what he's up to. Save your money up man and get the hell out. Nothing will happen to your mum, if anything it could be a blessing in disguise. If the boys in the area catch Quinn up to his antics, let's just say he will be out of the picture for quite a while and you and your mum can live your lives in peace.", I said very confidently.

To my surprise, Frankie laughed.

"Oh Moz, Moz, Moz. How I would love to live in your idealistic safe little world...just for one day."

Again, my temper began to rise in me.

"What do ye mean by that?", this time irritation evident in my tone, and I cursed myself inwardly.

"Do you think Quinn is stupid? Do you think a scumbag like that is so naïve to be blatantly doing what he's doing without havin' a fall guy already in place? Jeez, Moz...stop being so fuckin' naïve."

My blood ran cold. To my shame, in that moment, I thought about myself and the consequences my involvement with Frankie would bring to my family and me. As I had thought earlier, my family would move away from the area, so proud they were. They were never subjected to ridicule, never had to deal with it before in their lives. They would never forgive me.

"Are ye still there, Moz? Don't worry, you will never get dragged into this. People see me as a scumbag, mostly by association with Quinn and because I come from a broken home. A mongrel with no place to call home with an easy, whore mother, and a piece of shit stepfather. There will be too much mud to fling in our direction, people won't even give you a second thought. That's why we should distance ourselves from each other. People's memories are short. The less we are seen together the better."

The phone seemed hot and heavy against my ear and when I put my hand to my cheeks, I could feel tears on them. Some friend I was. I had betrayed him in my head already and his response seemed to confirm he knew. I didn't know what to say.

"It'll be OK Moz. Don't you worry. Study hard, pass those exams and get into university. You are clever, man. Don't worry about this shit."

I sat further without saying anything.

"Moz, I have to go. See you soon.", he continued and hung up.

I went back up to my room and lay on the bed. I cried myself to sleep at the cowardly betrayer I had become.

As We Sat Amongst the Sleeping Swans

Just before the Christmas holidays, a few months later, one of my friends on the bus, a lad I used to play football with, Declan Phillips invited me to his 18th birthday party in Dunbay the following Friday night. Declan was a good guy and very popular in the school, thanks to his prowess on the football field and his easy-going and likeable personality. I was honoured he invited me and looked forward to the night out, as it had been a long time since I had one. All work and no play were making me a very dull boy.

The craic was good on the bus, the day of the party. Declan got a few pranks played on him on the way home and everyone was upbeat for the night that lay ahead. I rushed home, got changed and sweet-talked my mum into driving me to Dunbay. I met the group in "The Dunbay Inn", a pub that was frequented by a younger crowd due to its leniency in serving minors. There was about a dozen of us and we sat drinking, getting drunk and listening to the Jukebox. The talk quickly turned to football and O'Halloran's name was bandied about in God-like terms. Maturity seemingly settling in, I got up and excused myself to go out to the shop at the top of the street to buy cigarettes.

"Buy them from the machine over there, JP. Freezin' out there.", Ryan Byrne said as I got up to leave.

"No way Ryan. Rip off in here. I'll head up to Elsie's...get them for half the price."

He nodded in agreement and I made my way out into the cold night air. The town was lively and festive. Christmas parties were in full swing and there were people everywhere in high spirits. I leaned against the wall outside the pub and watched the merriment of the town. The old adage of feeling alone in a crowd came to mind as I felt no part of the party that was occurring inside the pub or the local feel-good factor around the town. Listening to the boys in their worship of O'Halloran and local small-time sport confirmed to me I wanted something bigger, something better. I didn't think I was better or bigger than anyone…but I thought bigger. I didn't want my life to be wasted in a small town where small town false idols loomed large. I braced myself to the cold and made my way up to Elsie's. When I got there, as per usual, Elsie was deep in conversation with another aul biddy from the town. I cursed to myself knowing that neither would pass me the time of day until they had finished their gossip, both like dogs with a bone. I perused some of the magazines, none very exciting, all about fishing, farming, and mainly geriatric pursuits. Just then the bell above the door rang, neither woman turning to look who it was. It could have been an armed robber for all they cared, but they were not going to stop their chat.

"Moz! What's up man?". It was Frankie.

"Frankie! What the hell! What are ye at?"

"Ach, just out for a bit of a party. Its Dawns Christmas work do tonight, so I came into town with her. This is Tony, Dawns cousin. Tony, this is JP."

Tony and I both shook hands. "Call me Nosey."

"OK", I replied a little bemused.

As We Sat Amongst the Sleeping Swans

"Wait to ye see this." Frankie said before I could ask Tony why he wanted to be referred to as Nosey. Frankie strode up to the counter, confidence oozing from his stance. The two old ladies stopped their conversation and stared at him.

"Sorry to interrupt ladies, but I couldn't help but notice your impressive range of magazines and literature you have in stock. A broad range of interests and hobbies all catered for."

Elsie smiled at Frankie and at one stage I thought I saw her playing with her hair.

Playing with her fucking hair!

I was invisible to her, then Frankie walks in and she's putty in his hands. I wished I could bottle what he had.

"Thank you, son. We've got a good supplier and a good customer base who buy these magazines. As you say, there are a lot of hobbies and interests catered for. That's a very nice thing you said and I'm glad the younger generation notice these things."

"Certainly. It's hard not to notice. The reason I commented is because I'm trying to get into Architecture school, so I have a great interest in buildings and literature associated with the whole subject in general. Also, my brother is a keen fan of cars and wants to become a mechanic. I was wondering, would there be a way I could set up a subscription to these magazines on a monthly basis? You obviously have a good supplier, so I don't think it would be a problem for an entrepreneur like yourself."

There was a brief pause, before Elsie replied. "Let me get a pen and paper, son."

"Excellent...excellent stuff. I'm so excited. I've been trying to source these magazines for a long time. I'm *very* excited"

Elsie disappeared into a back room for a moment before returning, beaming from ear to ear with a pen and notepad.

"Let me write this down for you, young man. Tell me what you want me to order."

"OK-first for myself, could you order *Mayfair* and *Penthouse*. Two fantastic architectural magazines that will help me get an edge on my classmates. Do you want me to spell that for you?"

"No-I've got it. *Mayfair* and *Penthouse*...no problem", replied Elsie, finishing off her notes.

I was standing beside Nosey who let out a huge snort, trying not to burst out laughing. He excused himself and waved it off as a sneeze.

"For my brother, the car fan. Could I order three magazines? Is that a bit much?"

"No, no. I'll put an order in for you in the morning...not a problem."

"Brilliant. So, my brother's order will be *Escort* and *Fiesta*. He's a Ford maniac. The third magazine is called *Razzle*...its some sort of terminology these petrol heads use, don't ask me."

It was my turn to laugh. Elsie and her friend glared at me and I had to leave before I got worse. I stepped outside and laughed until I almost threw up. The image of Elsie's face when she opened her package to be greeted with a handful of porn magazines was too much. Tears were streaming down my face when the door opened and Nosey came out to join me. He rushed out and paced ten yards or so up the street before I could hear his howls of laughter above the night wind. I walked towards him.

"You missed it JP. The crazy fucker ended up getting her to order *Reader's Wives* too."

I burst out laughing again.

"What...how the fuck did he explain that one?"

"He told her his mother used to get it when she lived in England. Convinced her without even trying that it was a magazine for posh little ladies in England...like a WI subscription."

I was out of breath. My body felt like it had just run a race, I was exhausted after laughing so hard.

"Ah, that's too much. Fuckin' hell, only that prick could get away with that. *Readers Wives*...fuck me."

Frankie came out at that moment and we all fell around laughing once more.

"Ah fuck, my fags.", I said when I got my breath back. "That was the reason I went into the shop. How the hell am I supposed to go back in and face aul Elsie after that?"

"Don't worry about fags Moz. Nosey's uncle was on holidays last week and he brought back a couple of hundred for him."

As We Sat Amongst the Sleeping Swans

"I'll buy a packet or two from you Nosey if that's OK? I can't face that aul bag in there after that."

Nosey got a packet out of his jacket pocket and gave it to me; "Get me a pint down the pub here and we'll call it evens."

"Cheers", I replied and opened the packet giving one to both and lighting all three one after the other. I took a drag and then laughed again; "You're a bad hoor Frankie. Can't believe you got away with that one. Poor Elsie."

Frankie's features suddenly changed. He was no longer smiling.

"Fuck Elsie. That aul bag was very vocal around the town years ago about my ma's past career. Everyone in the area soon knew about it. She's not afraid to spread a bit of shit, so when she gets a big box of porn delivered to her door, it'll be a bit of comeuppance for her."

My heart sank. The Frankie that I knew and loved had briefly resurfaced in brilliant style when he had brazenly charmed and fooled Elsie in equal measure for our entertainment. But, instead of using his unique talent and humour for the fun of others, there had been a sinister and vindictive edge to his actions. It wasn't that he was either sinister or vindictive by nature, merely a reflexive response to the many that had been vindictive to him and his family in the past. He shouldn't have been that way, but he had been *made* that way by circumstances in his life that had been no fault of his own.

It was sad.

As We Sat Amongst the Sleeping Swans

"Let's get some pints and get out of this fuckin' cold.", Frankie said, the smile returning effortlessly.

We walked briskly back to "The Dunbay Inn". When we got there and the rest of the boy's spotted Frankie, a roar went up from their corner, so loud that everyone in the pub stopped to see what was going on. Frankie walked in, shaking hands and high fiving people like he was Elvis himself. I felt like my old self, happy to bask in his shadow but having my social status and credibility boosted a hundred times merely being in his company. We ordered beers and drank with gusto. The night was one of the best I ever had. No more talk of O'Halloran and the small-town bullshit antics that people seemed so obsessed with. Frankie was back to his brilliant best and held court in spectacular style. The craic flowed effortlessly. I told the story to all the boys about Frankie's prank on Elsie, with his consent, and got the biggest laugh of the night. Again, Frankie shared the limelight with me like he always had. Anyone else would retell the story themselves, but he had the self-assurance and humility to sit back and let his friends get the big laughs.

We drank on and broke into smaller groups as the night progressed. I sat in one of the booths with Nosey, Frankie and Ryan Byrne. Frankie, although quite drunk was his usual self-not the depressing drunk who had called me during the week those few times. Just as I was about to get up and head to get another round in for us, my uncle Willie appeared out of nowhere, sitting down beside us.

"What the fuck, John-Paul? You're in town and you couldn't have let you're aul uncle know?"

Before I could reply, Frankie shook hands with him.

"Willie! Good to see you man. What are ye drinkin'?"

I sat and shook my head in disbelief.

"Hold on. You two know each other?"

"Oh aye. Willie and I are good mates...aren't we Willie?"

"We are. Now...I'm getting this round. No questions asked. It's not every day I get to have a drink with my nephew."

He stood up and took our orders. Willie wasn't a man who would take no for an answer or indeed any bullshit or hesitation. When he went to the bar I turned to Frankie.

"How the hell do you know Willie?"

"We work together."

"In the meat packing factory? Since when? Sure, Willie's a painter and decorator."

"Yeah, in the factory. He said the painting was slow these days and he had to get a full-time job to pay the bills. We don't work on the same line, but we would go out for a smoke together at breaks. He's a mad bastid...some craic like, and he fuckin' loves you, man. You should feel privileged to have the love of so many people...don't *ever* take that shit for granted."

I nodded in agreement before a surge of panic took over. Nosey was a stoner, a harmless goon, but fond of the marijuana. He had a good lump of stuff on him and had went out the back a few times to smoke joints. He had offered some to Frankie and me, but we had declined, the beer and craic inside the pub trumped getting stoned any day.

"Listen…Nosey. Don't offer any of that dope to Willie. He's not a man who needs to know about drugs floating about the area."

"Willie's all right. He's a man of the world, he's not gonna get upset about a wee bit of hash for fuck sake.", Frankie butted in.

I shook my head in disdain; "Seriously Frankie. Believe me, don't mention drugs to Willie. He's my uncle and I know him a lot better than you…and he knows some dangerous people."

I was beginning to get angry now. Not at anyone in particular but at the situation and the inability to get my point across. Frankie sat coolly looking at me for a moment or so before continuing; "I agree with what you're saying. I'm not stupid. I'm fully aware of Willie's, let say social standing, around the area. *Believe* me, he's not gonna give two shits about a wee bit of hash. Him and his…friends, have much bigger issues to worry about than that. *Believe* me."

I took a sip of my drink and contemplated what Frankie had told me. I was surprised but knew by the way Frankie delivered the information with such confidence he knew something that maybe I didn't.

As We Sat Amongst the Sleeping Swans

Willie came back with the drinks. We drank and moved onto another few bars with the boys at the party. With both Frankie and Willie firing on all cylinders the craic was mighty. After the pubs closed, we got a carry out and went back to Willies house for a party along with half the town. I think Nosey was a little spooked at what I had said earlier, as the frequent "smoke" breaks stopped, and he didn't broadcast his stash to the people at the party. Even though I believed what Frankie told me, I still didn't think it would have been the best move Nosey would make by rolling joints and smoking dope in Willie's house.

At around 4.30 in the morning I walked out of the packed living room to go to the toilet. On the way past the kitchen I spotted Frankie and Willie in a quiet corner of the kitchen chatting. The conversation looked very intense and I didn't interrupt. I needed the toilet badly after all the beer I had drank during the night.

On the way back I popped my head into the kitchen. Frankie was sitting on the worktop beside the sink and Willie was standing in front of him, the intensity of their conversation in stark contrast to their earlier antics. The court jesters were having a brief and unexpected respite. When I walked in and tried to get up to speed with their conversation, I was surprised to hear them whispering to each other with such an intensity their whispers were more like hisses. When they noticed me, their manner suddenly became friendly and they both greeted me heartily with cheers and high fives.

I walked back to join the rest of the party, confused and anxious about what was going on with both men in the next room.

Months after that meeting between those two friends of mine, I couldn't help but wonder if it was then, at that moment, the wheels were put in motion that could not be stopped.

The wheels that would motion so much trouble and heartbreak.

I couldn't help but wonder.

CHAPTER 13

I woke up.

For a moment I felt OK.

Then I didn't.

Then I ran to the communal bathroom and thanked God there was no-one in the toilet cubicle. I vomited so much I thought I was going to die. I couldn't breathe because of the volume of liquid being expelled from my mouth . Finally, it stopped, and I sat exhausted on the floor. I wiped my brow and was amazed by the thick, cold residue of sweat that sat upon it. It took a minute or so for my heart to return to its normal rhythm, before the nausea took hold once more and I repeated the process, this time the ordeal not quite so bad as the first. The thought of my bed now seemed like a haven.

I crawled to it.

I lay and fought the nausea for ten minutes or so, an important fight as I simply didn't have the energy to get back to the toilet again. I very painfully won the battle and sleep took hold like a tender embrace. I dreamt strange dreams and was nudged awake by two formidable looking cleaning ladies. They stood glaring at me, obviously bewildered and angered in equal measures at my insolence. My head pounded so bad I thought I was going to be sick again.

"I can't...not well.", were the only words I could utter.

As We Sat Amongst the Sleeping Swans

They stood glaring at me still, neither moving. I didn't care what the consequences were. There was nothing anyone could do or say that could make me feel any worse than what I already did. I rolled over and lay facing the wall until I fell asleep a few seconds later.

When I woke again, I looked at my watch.

4:11.

My head still pounded but the nausea had subsided. I stumbled to the bathroom and put my head under the manky looking tap and drank deeply. At that moment I didn't care if there was no water in the tap, I would have drunk from the toilet itself, the intensity of the thirst that was upon me. Once satisfied I ran to my bed. The room was freezing, and the warmth of the bed offered a little luxury that was all consuming at that time. I lay and images of the night before began to seep into my mind. All were blurry like images taken from a poor camera, but none were pleasant. Suddenly a terror ran through me as I recalled buying a round of drinks for a group of old men in a bar. All drinking fucking stout *and* whiskey chasers.

I scavenged inside my jeans pockets to get my wallet. I was sweating again, this time the cold sweats replaced with an anxious hot and clammy perspiration; "Please Lord.", I begged and to my huge relief I noticed a wad of twenty's still in the wallet before I even opened it. There wasn't as many as yesterday, but at least there were still some. I was paid up in the hostel for another three nights and realised then that I wouldn't be able to afford another week with the money I had left. Blind panic ran through me. Today was gone, the next day being Wednesday, it was essential I found a job to pay the Jackeens something on Thursday to secure another week's lodgings. But where was I going to find a job that paid on a daily basis? Maybe I could pay them with what I had on me, work for a week and worry about food and supplies next week when I got paid.

Just as I played out the desperate scenes in my mind the door opened, and Canadian Clive entered the room.

"Clive!", I croaked; "What's happenin'?"

To my surprise he ignored me and sat on his bed, putting his headphones on and lying down to rest. Clive had always been a funny one, so I passed no remarks and lay once more dozing in the bed. Twenty minutes or so later, I was disturbed by his huffing and puffing, and knew he was trying to get my attention.

"You OK Clive?", I asked, giving him his platform to vent whatever was on his mind and get it over and done with. He could be as bad as a woman at times.

"Not really.", he petulantly replied.

"What's up now?", I asked, my levels of tolerance decreasing by the second.

"*What's up now*, he asks.", he replied sarcastically.

"Listen Clive, cut the crap. I'm obscenely hung over and you've come in here making a big song and dance about something I've done or said. Cut to the chase and tell me what I did so I can apologise.

As We Sat Amongst the Sleeping Swans

Honestly Clive, I think you're a top man and I'm sorry...genuinely sorry if I've done anything to offend you when I was off my fuckin' tits. I honestly can't remember a thing."

He sat for a few seconds in silence, my words obviously neutralising his reaction to whatever I'd done last night.

"You were a huge jerk last night...a *huge* jerk. I didn't think you were like that. I mean, I tried to get you a job, tried to help you and you came back last night and gave me the biggest load of shit I've ever had to listen to. You were nasty, man...*nasty*!"

I sat for a moment. Usually if someone had spoken like that to me, I would have jumped down their throat in defence whether they were right or wrong. But I sat, ashamed I had hurt someone as childlike and harmless as Canadian Clive. What the fuck was wrong with me?

"You woke Ger up too.", he continued, the anger in his voice now so deflated it seemed almost empathetic as he had read my features so well.

"Ah fuck! Did I insult him too?", I asked. My heart raced in fear at the prospect of an angry Ger coming back.

"Well, he was pretty pissed off this morning at you waking him up. Really not cool JP. I expected better from you."

His precision condescension worked, and I lay in bed like a child who had just been told off by a very disappointed parent. He turned his back and lay reading a book in the meantime. I didn't fight my corner anymore. Again, I dozed until I heard the distinctive accent of Ger in the room. I lay in bed, frozen with fear. Ger was a big, ignorant Kerry man...not the type of person one might insult without some severe, and most likely, violent repercussions. I was disappointed I had insulted him too, as I genuinely liked him, but fear overrode shame and I lay there not knowing how to deal with the situation. He mentioned to Canadian Clive that he was going for a shower and Clive replied that he was going out to the shops, asking in turn if he wanted anything back. When the door of the room closed, I waited for another half minute or so, checking they had both left. Then I rolled out of bed and began to dress. When I stood up to put my trousers on, I had to hold onto the closest wall for assistance due to the weakness the vomiting and fasting my body had endured. I spent a minute or so checking for my shoes. No matter how hard I looked I couldn't find them until I spotted one of them in the far corner of the room and the other sticking out from the top of a wardrobe on the other side of the room. I didn't even try to figure out how the hell they got there. Just as I was tying the laces and planning my swift exit, the door to the room opened and in walked Ger. Droplets of water dripped from his mullet onto his traps, and only then did I appreciate the sheer size of him. He had a neck like an award winning Belgian Blue bull and a powerful chest, adorned with necklaces that would have put Mr T to shame.

I thought I was going to throw up again...this time in fear.

He said nothing, sitting on his bed drying himself, his breathing laboured because of his immense size, the noise much like a bull grunting.

"Look Ger, Clive told me I was a complete prick last night and I insulted both of you after I woke yez up. I can't remember a thing. I know it's no excuse, but I'm very sorry. You boys have been nothing but good to me and I consider you both as friends. I'm sorry, but if you want to beat the fuck out of me, then do it."

My heart pounded as he sat with his head down, drying the mullet that he took so much pride in. Because of his huge size I was convinced he was on steroids and I had heard all about the violently unpredictable nature of those who used them, so called "roid rage."

To my surprise and momentary relief, he began shaking and I couldn't work out whether it was from laughing or crying. Then he lifted his head and I could see it was the former.

"Yea, you did wake me up…ye little prick. But luckily for ye, ye didn't insult *me*."

He stood and strolled around the room drying himself, breaking into more giggles every now and then. I found myself laughing along, half out of relief and the other half because of the *way* he laughed. For such a huge man, he had the strangest laugh. One would expect a great booming sound to emanate from his vast chest, but he tittered like a schoolgirl…it was the strangest thing.

As We Sat Amongst the Sleeping Swans

"You're a bad bastard, JP...but a funny bastard at that.", he continued when he had calmed down.

I shook my head. "Why, what did I say...what did I do? I can't remember a thing, Ger."

"Well, poor Clive got the brunt of it. You came back and tore into him. Some of it was pretty nasty, but you couldn't get your words out properly cos you were so drunk. To be fair, from the sounds of it he did write a few cheques that his ass couldn't cash...I could see how and why you were so mad at him."

I sat for a moment, relieved Ger didn't want to kill me, but ashamed and embarrassed about what I might have said to poor Canadian Clive.

"You kept on going on about his boss...Damo or Davo or whatever the fuck he's called. At the beginning you told Clive you took him by the throat and threw him out the window, then went on a rampage around Dublin, as you put it "like that Michael Douglas motherfucker from that film where he went apeshit". The story began to get more ridiculous as you went on, to the point where you "kicked the shit out of 4 China men" after they wouldn't serve you in the Chinese takeaway. What made it more ridiculous was the fact that they all jumped out from behind the counter with Nunchucks and knuckle dusters...as you do. You were so adamant and when into great graphic detail about how it happened."

What the hell was wrong with me. I didn't even remember telling this story to anyone.

"Did I do anything else, anything bad?"

As We Sat Amongst the Sleeping Swans

"You weren't too bad. You kept on going on about my fuckin' hairstyle which got a bit annoying. Kept sayin' you'd love to put "Soul glow" or whatever the fuck on it and rub oil all over me to shine me up like a Christmas turkey. Kept comparing me to some guy Henry Ramsay out of Neighbours...pretty gay stuff. You're not though...are ye?", he asked with searching concerned eyes.

I laughed, anxiously without humour; "No...of course not. I'm sorry about all that shit by the way. You must think I'm a complete bell end. It's just I'm going through a bit of a rough time and...", I stopped myself there, careful not to divulge anything further.

He sat and finished changing into his clothes for another few minutes in silence. Then, to my amazement he threw me a lifeline I wouldn't have seen coming in a hundred years.

"Look JP, I think you're a good kid. We all do...even poor aul Clive. He was only trying to help you but the whole thing went pear shaped and he feels really fuckin' bad about it today. Now, I'm not excusing what you did last night, because you were a right little prick, but I've been thinking about your situation all day, keeping my ear to the ground to see if there's anything I can get you in *my* work. Turns out one of the boy's grandfather died today. The funerals on Thursday. He's from up north too, Donegal or Derry direction, so he's goin' to the funeral on Thursday and stayin' up there for the weekend. This means we're a man down for 2 days. The work is hard, but the pay is good. Do you want me to put your name down to cover the two days tomorrow?"

For the first time that day, I had some energy and jumped from my bed onto the floor in excitement; "Ah that'd be great Ger. Fuckin' hell! Are you sure? I mean, what's the chances I'll get it?"

He let out a booming laugh; "In fairness to Clive, you're not dealing with *him* now. I wouldn't have mentioned this if I didn't think I could get you a few days' work. I just wanted to see if you were interested first. By the looks of it, I think you are. In this case, it's a promise."

I felt like rushing over and hugging him, but due to his recent comments questioning my sexuality, I deemed it wise not to. I sat on my bed and thanked God. I had a lifeline again.

At that moment the door opened, and Canadian Clive came moping into the room.

"Clive...my man", I cheerfully exclaimed, and he looked at me with a mixture of surprise and anger. He wasn't the angry type and I laughed at the silly expression he wore.

"Don't talk to me, man. Not after last night. In fact, I don't think I ever want to hear your silly voice ever again.", he replied and stomped to his bed like a petulant child. Both Ger and I laughed.

"You're *laughing* together? Ger, I didn't expect to see you joking around with *him* today. I'm sure you suffered on the sites today, much like I did.", he asked, incredulous.

Ger laughed. "Did ye suffer lying up in that bed of yours for half the day? Sure, you were off today, ye bluffer."

Canadian Clive sat on his bed, taking off his shoes, now red faced; "Well, that's beside the point. John-Paul wasn't to know that when he was running riot last night."

He looked like he was about to start crying, as if we were ganging up on him.

I felt sorry for him.

"Listen Clive, I'm really sorry about last night. I've apologised to Ger and he's very kindly accepted it. I'm hoping you can do the same and we can move on. I realise you took the brunt of my shit last night and I'm very sorry...genuinely. Come on aul friend, let's not fight.", I said and extended my hand in friendship.

He sat for a moment before a crooked smile brightened his features. He shook my hand heartily.

"All right then, you swine. Just don't make a habit of it."

"I won't. I promise."

"Listen, John-Paul.", he continued whilst looking very uncomfortable; "I feel bad you didn't get the job yesterday. I thought you would, I honestly did. Davo is a tough nut to crack at times. He likes to be pandered to. To tell you the truth he's an egotistical prick with severe small man syndrome. To be honest you probably had a lucky escape. You're a smart kid...aim to do something better than what a loser like me does."

He didn't deliver the last line seeking sympathy, like most do when they say something so scathing about themselves. The words and his expression were raw and real, forged by years of hurt and the put-downs of others. I felt ashamed I had treated someone as gentle and delicate so badly. A sudden act of kindness dawned upon me, attempting to make things better with both of them. Buoyed by my sudden ravenous hunger and the prospect of a few days of upcoming work, I announced; "Listen boys, I feel like shit about yesterday. I'm fuckin' starvin' and I'm gonna go and get some chips and shit. Now, I'm not taking no for an answer, so tell me what you want from the chippy...it's my way of apology.

As I expected, they both protested good naturedly, but I insisted and eventually took their orders. I made my way out into the cold, March evening and walked in search of a chip shop. The evening had turned dark and there were a lot of people around. The atmosphere seemed good, people coming home from work and heading out into the city to meet with friends and have fun, their breath visible in the neon streetlights of Dublin, confirming the coldness of the early spring air. I walked onwards, lightheaded, and heavy hearted. A sudden all-encompassing loneliness took hold of me at that moment and I had to stop and sit down on a nearby bench. I hadn't allowed myself to think of what had happened, but the weakness the hangover and non-deliberate fasting my body endured that day stripped me of any self-control. Images of the night flooded my brain and I felt my breathing getting quicker, anxiety taking hold, so much I began to think I was having a heart attack. Just at that moment, to my great relief, a familiar voice dragged me from the depths.

"G'day ya glum lookin' fucka.".

Kurt.

"Charming as usual, Kurt. How's things?"

"Good. Last night in Dublin. Heading to Galway in the morning for a week or so."

Even though he could be a major prick at times, I felt sad that another acquaintance was moving on. People were moving on with their lives and I remained in limbo.

"A few of my mates are heading out on the town tonight for one last hurrah. If you're interested, you're more than welcome to tag along."

I thought for a moment before replying. Even though I remained severely hungover, I knew I would feel better after eating something, and sure why not? I had nothing to do the next day, I could rest then for the two days of work Ger was getting me.

"Yeah, why not?"

"Great. Be outside my hostel at 8pm. See ya then.", he replied and made his way back.

Invigorated at the prospect of a good night on the town, I had a spring in my step as I went to the chip shop. I felt like part of the city once more, not like the lonely outsider I had been. It was amazing the impact one familiar (if not slightly annoying) face could make whilst in a city of strangers. Back in the hostel, Ger, Canadian Clive and myself ate the food with gusto and it seemed the mayhem of the night before had never happened. Very tepidly I asked if either of them was interested in coming out that night. As expected, none of them were interested and I assured both there would be no repeat of the night before as I didn't plan to drink a lot. They both laughed and told me I had a problem. Even though I laughed and joined in the jest, deep down I worried if they were right. I had never been a big drinker, only ever drinking for social purposes and mostly with Frankie in the past, the alcohol only fuelling the fun and good times even further. Now I found myself drinking constantly. When I drank, the memories and feelings I carried with me during the days, during those lonely times walking the cold streets of Dublin, thronged by a million strangers, was dampened, extinguished by the alcohol. I would get my act together the next day in anticipation for the work on the sites.

One more night on the drink.

I changed into a shirt and sweet-talked Ger into letting me wear some of his fancy aftershave. Then I bid my friends farewell and went out to meet with Kurt. I was slightly early for a change and when he arrived, true to form, he made a comment about it and told the story to his two friends about my sleeping in a few mornings earlier. He was annoying me already and I regretted agreeing to come out with him. I could have done with staying in and having an early night like what Ger and Canadian Clive were doing, but I just couldn't help myself. The allure of alcohol, adventure and girls outweighed an early night, hands down.

I shook hands with his two friends, noticing how limp both were. They were Frenchmen so maybe they were more accustomed to hugs and kisses I reasoned. I had always subconsciously judged a man on the strength of his handshake (my fathers had been like a vice!) so made a mental note of the limited trust I should invest in both. Kurt told me their names, one of them easy to remember, Pierre, but the other I swear he had said Beetlebum. I laughed and asked him to repeat the name and he replied with the same name. I asked the man himself to repeat the name and he replied the same. I didn't refer to the man as his name, not wanting to offend him (when I had been sober). Pierre was very tall, good looking and charismatic...very French. Beetlebum however looked like a man called Beetlebum.

Sleazy, dirty, and dodgy.

I would keep an eye on him throughout the night I promised myself.

We headed into the city and I made my excuses to slip into an off licence to buy cigarettes. I also bought a half bottle of vodka on the sly and snuck it inside my jacket pocket. I couldn't afford to be drinking in bars.

When we got inside the first pub, everyone ordered pints and paid for their own. Perhaps it was a French custom to not enter rounds, but I couldn't have been happier. I didn't have the money to be buying rounds and had a plan for a cheap night. I ordered a Coke. I took the bottle and the glass to the table where we sat and put a good dash of the vodka into the glass under the table with a smaller dash of coke on top of it. I worked out I could get three good drinks from one bottle of coke. I sat very pleased with my ingenuity when Pierre began speaking to me. His English was very good, and he seemed like a nice enough guy. We talked about football, Eric Cantona mostly. Kurt and Beetlebum were more suited to each other's company...two pricks, and I was glad of Pierre's company and his friendliness. The night drew on and I had just finished my third vodka from the one Coke bottle when Kurt suggested we go to a nightclub to see what girls were around. Beetlebum's features drew more lecherous at the mention of females and my stomach almost done a somersault. We headed out into the cold night air, the city alive and inviting. It was hard to believe it was a Tuesday night. To walk the city alone during the day was bleak as a winter moor, but to be with company enjoying some drinks, oh, such a contrast...like two entirely different places.

We got into the first nightclub we found. The vodka had bestowed a confidence usually alien to me and the bouncers obviously mistook it for a more mature demeanour. The place was full of girls, again I wondered if it was the vodka in my system working its dark magic, as the girls all seemed stunningly beautiful. The music pumped from the speakers and the UV lighting accentuated everyone's teeth and clothes. I broke into a little dance as I strutted towards the bar to buy another Coke. A few girls giggled as I made my way past. If I had been sober, I would have stopped my dance/strut to burn with embarrassment, the vodka once more fuelling me to step it up and wink and smile at them as I made my way past. I would come back for them later. We got our drinks and made our way to a vacant patch of sticky carpet overlooking the dance floor. Two blondes dancing below us began making eyes, and the world seemed to be perfect at that moment. Again, I'm sure they were making eyes at the tall and handsome Frenchman who stood beside me, but the vodka fuelled my ego to let me believe I was the focal point of their admiration. I waved at them and they giggled and came up to talk to us. They were students from Longford, and they were definitely up for a bit of craic.

"Hey girls. Can we get you a drink?", I asked, the vodka unaware of my ever-dwindling funds. They accepted my offer and I asked them to mind my drink when I went to the bar. As I got halfway to the bar, Pierre tapped me on the shoulder, grinning.

"I know.", I said, high fiving him. "Couple of quare ones, eh? We've struck gold my friend."

Pierre nodded and when we got to the bar, he tapped me on the shoulder, telling me to look directly across at the girls on the other side of the dancefloor. "Look what those bitches are doing."

I looked over and spotted the two girls taking turns finishing my drink between them.

"What the...?", I asked Pierre as he laughed, raising his glass towards me.

As We Sat Amongst the Sleeping Swans

"I didn't leave my drink with them. The moment you go back with those drinks and look for your own, they will say someone spilled it accidently. They will probably talk to us for five more minutes before excusing themselves to go to the ladies, then they will disappear and find another couple of generous willing fools. I've seen it all before. Get yourself a drink, never mind those bitches. We will play them at their own game.", he said and gave me a hearty slap on the shoulder.

I felt disappointment at their duplicity and frustrated at not getting a chance to be with one of them, but I was glad Pierre had warned me. My wallet could certainly do with the break. It was my turn to smile and return the slap to his shoulder as I showed him the half bottle of vodka in my pocket and promised to split the rest of it with him. Decently, Pierre bought the two Cokes and I honoured my promise to him by splashing a generous dollop of vodka into his glass. We walked around the nightclub and after I went to the toilet, I came back to see Pierre getting off with some dark haired lovely. He didn't mess around like me and I admired and envied him in equal measure. I looked around the club and caught the eye of Beetlebum. He winked at me and I acknowledged him with a half-hearted wave. He was standing beside Kurt who was mirroring what Pierre was doing. The high the vodka had given me was blunted by the thought I was the Beetlebum between myself and Pierre. I wondered how Frankie would describe all these weird and wonderful characters, and the mere thought of him plunged me into a state of depression, so strong and debilitating that I had to take a seat in the corner, to

As We Sat Amongst the Sleeping Swans

drink the remaining vodka left in the glass. Just as I was about to get up and leave the club to go back to the hostel, Beetlebum appeared from nowhere and sat beside me. Unlike Pierre, his English was terrible, and he stank only like someone called Beetlebum could. I had a bad feeling about the fucker and wanted to run but was too drunk to do so. He pointed at girls walking past and made gestures as to what he'd like to do. Unlike myself and my friends who would have done similar actions in jest, his eyes were wolf-like and intense, there was no humour in his actions.

"Listen, man (I didn't know how to pronounce his name and didn't want to call him Beetlebum for fear of an adverse response), I'm wrecked…gonna head back. You fella's have a good time."

Before I could get past him, he reached into his pocket and brought out a joint; "You want…outside?", he asked.

The thought of Frankie had nullified the effects the alcohol had earlier rendered upon me and attempting to escape my thoughts, I agreed to go outside and smoke the joint with him. If anything, I thought, it would help me sleep. Outside, we took a turn to the left and slipped down an alleyway. I was wary of Beetlebum and knew that if he tried anything with me, I would have a good chance of beating him if it came to blows. He took a lighter out of his pocket and lit it. His face took on an eerie red glow every time he pulled on the spliff and I regretted joining him. He didn't speak until he handed it to me and said the generic and universal; "Its good shit.", in his strong and creepy French tone. I took a pull on it and felt instantly dizzy and light-headed. He cackled with laughter and encouraged me further; "Come on meng, hit it meng...good shit, ah?"

I nodded my head against my better judgement. I should have rammed it up his ass and ran, got the hell away from the creepy little prick, but I pulled on it again. Shit, I had dabbled a little in the past with the boys from back home, usually sitting in someone's car on a boring Friday night listening to music, but this was different level stuff. My mouth felt dry and the alleyway became longer whilst Beetlebum decreased in size to that of a dwarf.

I could only point towards it, asking him; "What's in this shit? This is not good.". My words were drawn out and it seemed to have taken an eternity to deliver them, whilst Beetlebum was now hopping from leg to leg, gleefully cackling; "I told you. Its good shit meng...good *French* shit. You like?"

"No, I fuckin' don't like, you creepy little bastard.", I replied and handed it back to him before trying to get past him and out into the safety of the street.

"Not cool meng. I give you good shit and you give me *shit*.", he replied, his features beginning to grow cruel.

"Fuck off.", I shouted and tried to nudge past him with my raised elbows. Seemingly out of nowhere, Pierre arrived behind him. I smiled at him, glad of a friendly face, and quick as a flash he struck me on the jaw. I looked up at the Dublin night sky and fell to the floor, hitting the back of my head as I landed on the cold, unforgiving alleyway ground.

As We Sat Amongst the Sleeping Swans

I didn't feel any pain.

The two Frenchmen stood over me and I expected the onslaught to begin.

I didn't care.

Then they did something far worse than beat me or kill me.

They robbed me and left me alone.

CHAPTER 14

Christmas came and went and my workload in school ramped up ten-fold with the exams rapidly approaching in the summertime. Evenings were spent in my room, studying until 11pm most nights, the long-term goal of university and short-term goal of a Saturday night on the piss, keeping me motivated and sane in equal measures.

We had a new member of our gang now.

My uncle Willie.

Wild Willie.

I hadn't told my mother, as I knew she wouldn't approve, but Willie's house was used as a drinking den after most Saturday nights on the town. He was calming down. He had met a woman, got himself a girlfriend. She was called Kate, a woman he worked with in the factory. She was surprisingly very pretty (way out of Willie's league) and even nicer as a person. He didn't drink as much and was more content to sit in with Kate and enjoy quieter nights. He was doing well in work and was recently made a supervisor. It was good to see; I was glad for him. Frankie, I, and any others in our group on any particular night would phone and ask him if we could come around. He always agreed and the night would be even better than what it had been in the pubs and nightclubs. Eventually we would arrive earlier and earlier to his house, until there came a time when we wouldn't even bother going to a pub or

As We Sat Amongst the Sleeping Swans

nightclub-his house becoming the main event on a Saturday night.

Some nights Kate would cook dinner for Frankie, Willie, and me. Some nights Frankie would bring Dawn around (who was very beautiful and very down to earth-a trait not commonly found in beautiful women) and Kate and Dawn would drink wine and chat whilst we all tore into beer and laughed and joked the night away. Those nights were tamer but just as enjoyable as the wilder nights when the house would be packed. Dawn and Kate would turn their attention to me from time to time asking why I didn't have a girlfriend as I was "quite" handsome (the "quite" used as a huge disclaimer and with great generosity to my bland features). Frankie and Willie would joke as to why I wouldn't or couldn't get a girlfriend and I would sit silently blushing and hoping the conversation would take another conjecture.

They were good times. The people we associated with were kindred spirits. People always up for a laugh, unconcerned about the small town, small time idols of the local area. If anyone from that demographic was mentioned in a conversation, a withering comment would be delivered from someone in the group to totally discredit them. These were people I longed to associate with-people whose minds were open and not closed in-to house only the immediate people and issues from where they were based.

My social circle increased also from my association with Nosey. Some nights during the week I would drive to his house and sit watching television with him. He would sit smoking weed and most nights he would have other friends from all around Ireland at his place. There were some nights, even weeknights, that there had been an abundance of girls at his place and I got lucky, getting off with a few of them over a period of months. Frankie remained elusive at times, but at least I had Nosey and Willie to hang out with in his absence.

They were good times, and ironically, trying so hard as I had to leave the area to go to University, I now began to think staying at home and getting a job locally wouldn't have been the worst thing in the world. That was typical of me. I was the type who would give up drinking for three months in preparation of an exam, only to go out the night before it and get completely hammered.

I could be a complete gobshite at times!

But, the craic from the beginning of the year had been so good. The people I was associating with were nice, cool. I felt like I was beginning to fit in. The whole Frankie, Nosey and Willie gang with everyone who they brought to the parties offered a new perspective to my views on living in the area. Nosey knew everyone. All his acquaintances were extremely cool, and I was becoming part of the whole thing. I knew when I moved to University, I would be back to square one, trying to make new friends when I had the coolest friends to call upon at any time, at home. It made it hard to get motivated to study, now I seemed to study for my parent's sake more than my own.

Every Saturday night would provide some sort of glorious nugget of conversation and rumour for the people not privileged enough to join the parties to speculate and gossip about for the rest of the week. When Frankie and Willie were firing on all cylinders, it was magical.

Another character I was introduced to in January was a man called Wolfe. Wolfe was his nickname. His real name was Rodney Wright. He was a Protestant from outside Ballymoy in the south. He was very good friends with Willie and the two of them had spent time in prison together for smuggling offences a few years before, when there was money to be made in that profession. He got the nickname from the comparisons he drew from Wolfe Tone. Like Wolfe Tone he had French ancestry through his mother and more importantly, he drew the unusual association of being a Protestant living in Ireland who was a staunch nationalist. He embraced the nickname of Wolfe and commonly joked that the Catholics referred to him with affection whilst some of the Protestant community thought the nickname meant "a wolf in sheep's clothing" because of his perceived turn coat nature.

Wolfe didn't give a shit. He spoke his mind and didn't care what anyone thought.

He was also one of the maddest bastards I had ever met in my life.

The first time I met him, I had to do a double take. He was huge, big in every way, both physically and in character. He must have been 6'4-6'5 and surely weighed well over twenty stone. Not fat, just big in all areas of his body. Barrel chested, arms and legs like tree trunks and a big generous belly-he was solid and very daunting looking. His head was completely bald, and he had a black goatee beard on a face that was so red, it looked like he was wearing blusher. He usually wore blue jeans, dealer boots and a lumberjack shirt that he always seemed to be bursting out of. The first time we met, he immediately insulted me and endeared himself to Frankie simultaneously.

Willie had introduced us all to him. When he heard my name, his eyes locked on me and he continued to shake hands with everyone whilst still looking at me.

"John-Paul? Born in '79?"

"Oh fuck.", cried Willie, beginning to laugh.

"Yep.", I replied.

"Named after the Pope?", Wolfe probed further.

"Yep"

He shook his head and began laughing. "You stupid fuckin' Catholic assholes."

I was stunned. He had boomed the last sentence without any thought for consequence. A man of his size probably didn't care, but there were a lot of people at the party who could have taken umbrage to that last statement.

I could see Frankie's curiosity peaked at that moment. He came and stood beside me looking at Wolfe.

"Why do you say this?", he asked Wolfe.

As We Sat Amongst the Sleeping Swans

"Why? Because of this fascination with the Pope you all have. "The Holy Father" What a crock of shit. Some aul prick sitting up in his ivory tower thinking he's God almighty. Living the life of luxury and preaching humility and sacrifice when there's millions of people in the world starving. Don't get me started on that fucker."

Frankie's face lit up in glee.

"Ach now.", Willie interjected, "Sure he's still not as bad as those fuckin' Royals of yours now, Wolfe."

Wolfe took a sip of his drink and shook his head, smiling. "Now this fucker Willie is trying to wind me up. The Royals. *My* Royals indeed. Do not get me started on that shower...Holy good God!"

Willie burst into laughter and gave Wolfe a big slap on the back. "You are some boy Wolfe...some boy altogether"

Willie was right. He *was* some boy.

Two weeks later, the party was in full swing and the numbers in Willies house had swelled as the evening grew into night and early morning. Frankie declared he was going to do a beer run and took the orders of some of the party goers. After half an hour or so, I was sitting talking to Willie and Kate in the sitting room when I heard much laughter and commotion coming from outside the house. We went out to look at what was going on and heard only the distinct sound of a horse's hooves.

It was Frankie, riding a horse up the street.

As We Sat Amongst the Sleeping Swans

We fell about laughing at the image, wondering where the hell he'd gotten a horse. It turned out he had bought it from an elderly man he worked with in the factory. The man had recently hurt his shoulder in work and was unable to look after the horse anymore. Frankie agreed to buy it for a small fee and was permitted to keep it on the man's land, providing he looked after it well. Dawn was a keen rider and took care of the horse mostly, so it had been a win-win deal for all.

Frankie tied the horse up and it became the main attraction of the night, as one would expect.

Later, in the wee hours of the morning, when the usual lull one would expect at that time after much merriment had taken its effect on the party, another surge in activity became apparent. I looked across the room and caught Frankie's eye as he sat at the kitchen table speaking with Nosey. He shrugged his shoulders, reading my curiosity and we all made our way out onto the street.

The image I saw will never leave my mind.

Atop that poor horse sat a man. A man so large the horse seemed to decrease in comparison to his sheer size. Maybe it was my imagination, but the horse appeared to grimace in reaction to the man's weight. It was clear to me then that the man was no other than Wolfe.

Wolfe was completely naked as he rode the horse.

Girls shrieked and men laughed.

As We Sat Amongst the Sleeping Swans

To see a giant man, ride naked on a horse, in the pale streetlights of the small hours of a Dunbay morning, was an event I was pretty sure I would never witness again. We laughed and enjoyed the insanity of the situation. Thankfully the horse returned to Frankie's colleagues' field and came to no harm.

Those were the type of character's we associated with. No wonder I wasn't as keen to leave for University as I once had been.

Of course, the good times couldn't last forever.

The problem with living in a bubble, in an ocean of bullshit, was that eventually the bullshit erodes that beautiful little bubble and floods in with great destructive force...sooner rather than later.

Our bubble burst the day the news broke of a teenager in a coma after taking drugs in Ballymoy. I didn't know the boy, but from all accounts he was a good, normal guy who worked in a supermarket in the town. He had gone to a nightclub in the area and was sold a dodgy drug and was currently in hospital fighting for his life.

The news spread like wildfire and my anxiety levels about Frankie's past convictions and my association with him went into hyperdrive. Reality hit when I came home from school one day and overheard my parents talking about it at the kitchen table.

"That poor family.", my mother said. "I know the lad's mother, Sylvia. A lovely lady who volunteers a lot in the church in Ballymoy. The poor dear. Having that to deal with, not to mention the stigma of all that goes with the whole sorry situation."

The word "stigma" stung me like a bee. That word would haunt my family if Frankie's secret was ever brought to the light of day. Especially now, especially with tensions running high in the area about drugs and the devastating affect it had on families. The poor kid fighting for his life *and* his families name, was now in the dirt. There were many busybodies around the area, the likes of Elsie in the shop and her cronies who would badmouth and exaggerate every detail of the sorry incident. If that was the fate a family suffered because of one of its members being known to take drugs, what kind of treatment could a convicted dealer (and his friends) expect?

I now depended on the goodwill and discretion of O'Halloran. I depended on him...and Frankie, to shut their mouths.

My kingdom was literally laid atop a foundation of sand.

If word got around what Frankie had done, then he would be automatically implicated in the boy's demise. Then they would come for Frankie's friends. Then they would come for the friend's families. My parents were too proud to endure that ridicule. They would sell up and move overnight, moving from a home and a community that they had built up friendships and respect over a period of years, not to mention the many generations of family who had lived there before them. All because of a relationship their son had with a boy with a questionable past.

As We Sat Amongst the Sleeping Swans

Those were the very real threats that lay ahead. That was the very unstable nature of country living. Respect was earned with great difficulty but lost in a fleeting experience. A sixteen-year-old girl from Dunbay a few years back had fallen pregnant and her family, a well-respected one at that, packed up and shipped out within the month. Events that happened within a city were diluted by its vastness and soon forgotten. In small towns and rural areas in Ireland, any scandal was condensed, the taste of any scandal made sweeter by its absence, the hounds feasting upon it down to the marrow.

I phoned Frankie that night.

"What's up Moz?", Frankie cheerily asked.

"Did ye hear the news…about the boy in Ballymoy?"

"Yeah, heard that today. Poor bastard. Hope he'll be OK?"

"Yeah, you and me both. Have you…had you any dealings at all with him?", I asked and instantly cringed, regretting the question immediately…but I felt I had to ask. There was a long uncomfortable silence.

"Dealings?", Frankie asked, his tone holding back a wave of anger.

"Sorry, didn't mean dealings…I meant did you know him. Him being from Ballymoy and all?"

"No. Don't know him, but if you ask me, I think he's a dumb fuck for putting that shit in his body. Alcohol and weed are bad enough, but at least we know where it comes from, that shit he was doing is dangerous. Hope the guy will be OK, but he should have known better. Is that enough for you Moz, as you seem to be very interested on my opinion on the matter."

"Yeah, yeah...I mean I just wanted to see what you thought and if you'd heard anything, that's all.", I replied, my voice small and pathetic.

Frankie was my best friend, but this was an issue that our friendship would not let us discuss openly.

"I have to go. Bye.", Frankie bluntly replied, and I lay back on the bed, kicking myself that I had even called him.

I didn't see Frankie again until the following Saturday night when we arrived at Willies house with a hefty carryout. We didn't discuss the matter and the craic was good. He was relaxed and in good form.

After a drink or two, I commented to him; "You're in some form tonight Frankie. Good to see it. What's up."

He took me by the arm and led me outside. He beamed from ear to ear.

"Got some good news the other day Moz. Really fuckin' good news."

My heart soared. It was great to see him with a smile on his face.

"Well, spill the fuckin' beans then. What is it?"

"I got a phone call the other day, from an old friend of my grandads. I got talking to her about a few things that were goin' on in my life.", he hesitated and looked me in the eye, before continuing. "You see, this lady was a trusted friend of my grandads and was there for us after my dad died. She's a saint this lady...a true saint."

He hesitated once more, took a drink, and continued; "Well, after talkin' to her for a while she persuaded me to go back to school and get my A Levels."

I raised my can in celebration. "Ah, Frankie that's great. We could end up goin' to the same university after all. How good would that be?"

His features darkened with worry before he continued. "Well...that could still happen, but the thing is. Well, here's the thing...this lady has offered to let me live with her for a few years until I get my exams."

Again, I raised my can. "Nice one. Jeez, you have landed on your feet there. You get to go back to school and get the hell away from that bastard Quinn into the bargain. Fair play to ye man.", I gleefully replied and high fived him in the process.

"Cheers Moz. Only thing is, this college I'm enrolling in is in England."

It took a moment for the penny to drop with me.

"In England? Does that mean that you will be living and moving to...?"

"England.", Frankie finished on my behalf.

We stood in silence for a while, drinking from our cans.

"Is it that bad over here?", I asked.

I looked at him, he drank from his can and looked at the ground.

"It is…isn't it?". I continued after reading his features.

He nodded.

I shook my head; "Fuck sake. I hope it works out for ye, but Jeez…I'm gonna miss ye. What am I gonna do without ye?"

He swigged from his can again before punching me playfully on the arm. "You'll be fine. You can come visit me. I'll come visit you in Belfast or Dublin or wherever the fuck you'll end up. It's good for us…great for us. Finally, both of us will escape this shithole, it will soon become a distant memory."

I thought for a moment before agreeing with him. My resolve to go to University that had recently been waning, suddenly became bolstered. Just as I went to say something to him, a giant arm appeared around his shoulders and Wolfe drew him away to join another group. The rest of the evening I drank more than ever before. I didn't feel great, so many things were festering in my mind, and I was trying to drown them all out. The craic was good, but I wasn't enjoying it.

Then the subject of the boy in hospital arose.

I wished to fuck it hadn't.

As We Sat Amongst the Sleeping Swans

Wolfe brought it up in the early hours and everyone had their say on the matter. Mostly the girls were sympathetic and most of the men commented on how much of a "stupid wee cunt" he was. Wolfe made a menacing comment about weeding out the suppliers rather than witch hunting the users or victims, which was greeted with a chorus of approval from all in the room. The hairs on the back of my neck stood on end in anxiety and I looked over at Frankie who remained calm, sipping from his can. One of the girls mentioned that her uncle, one of the teachers at the school, was planning a town hall crisis meeting to get everyone in the communities together. The drugs in the area was reaching epidemic levels and the community leaders were having to act.

Looking around the room, I was thinking the likes of Willie, Wolfe and a few other boys would be actioning the main event.

I felt queasy from the topic and prayed that it ended…quickly.

The hard men in the room, men like Willie and Wolfe, sat like Frankie, sipping from their drinks, not really partaking in the conversation. One loudmouth from around the town who was making a debut at the party, a co-worker of Frankie and Willies, Adrian Mackey, began shooting his mouth off; "I tell ye, if I ever seen one of them boyos out pushing drugs to the kids in the area, I'd fuckin' do time over the bastards."

As We Sat Amongst the Sleeping Swans

There was a chorus of cheers from the others, before, to my great surprise, Frankie snarled in his direction; "You would on your shite Mackey"

There was a stunned silence in the room. Mackey laughed an awkward laugh.

"What do ye mean Frank?", he asked

"What do I mean?", Frankie replied, "I mean you'd do the same thing as most of the other assholes in this country...walk past and look the other way. Fuckin' gobshite."

"Gobshite, eh? You may watch who your fuckin' talkin' to kid.", Mackey replied. He had a reputation as a loudmouth around the town, but he got away with it mostly as he was also known as a hard cunt.

Frankie walked up to him, smirking. He stood across from Mackey and gazed into his eyes.

"Who you calling kid?"

The two of them stood eying each other up for about half a minute or so. Mackey didn't respond to Frankie's question and the tension in the room was palpable.

"Catch yourselves on...pair of pricks.", Wolfe butted in and stood between them, for once laughing nervously, his size dwarfing both potential combatants. Mackey turned and went back to where his drink was, and Frankie did the same. For ten minutes or so the tension in the room hung like a cloud but dispersed when both men held court once more with their respective groups, laughing and joking.

As We Sat Amongst the Sleeping Swans

I remained worried about Frankie. The laughing and joking didn't come as naturally to him as usual, it seemed almost forced. The acts of impulsive aggression were not in his nature either. Yes, he could handle himself, but it was always in self-defence, he never went looking for trouble. I approached him a few minutes after everything had calmed down.

"The fuck was that all about?", I asked, my lack of tact once more evident.

"What was what all about?", he asked, obviously knowing what I was talking about. I dropped it and changed the subject. I was drunk, but Frankie was very drunk. He put his arm around me and declared to the room I was his best friend. Everyone in the room cheered, including Mackey.

We drank into the night and all was good with the world once more.

Around 2.30 a.m., the rooms energy sapping and a tired, smoky haze hanging low in the air like a blanket ready to cover many of its sleeping inhabitants, I sat talking to Willie and Wolfe. Frankie came over and tapped me on the shoulder; "Come out here a wee second Moz...need a word." Willie began singing YMCA and Frankie danced out of the room, performing all the moves from the famous video.

The cold night air hit me hard when I was outside, and I stood shivering as Frankie lit two cigarettes and gave me one. We inhaled deeply and I hoped the fiery weed would warm me up. It didn't. Frankie stood smoking, wearing a smile he had put to one side for a long time. My heart soared at the sight of it and I couldn't help but ask; "The fuck you look so pleased with yourself for?"

"Ah, things are startin' to go my way Moz."

I smiled too, as his was so infectious. I was happy for him and interested in why his fortunes were changing.

"What's happened? Tell me...motherfuck.", I joked.

He took another drag before continuing; "Remember earlier I was telling ye about moving over to England to live with my granddads friend and finish my A levels?"

I shrugged my shoulders. "It was like a few hours ago...what am I a fuckin' goldfish?"

He laughed.

"Yeah, well what I didn't tell you was that I called my ma just after I told ye. I was waiting on something...and it's came through."

My heart soared in anticipation of his good news.

"You see, my friend in England has a nephew who is management level in a meat packing factory. She said she would put in a good word for me and what with my experience over here, I landed the job."

I high fived him and we both cheered and laughed.

"When do you start?", I asked.

He took a drag of his cigarette, looking up at me from below heavy eyebrows.

"The first week of April"

"The first week of April?", I asked incredulously, my heart sinking.

"Yea"

I shook my head, not that I didn't believe but more I didn't want to.

"Sure, that's only a lock of weeks away. Fuckin' hell Frankie...April?"

Once more he stood and wore an expression of sorrow.

"What can I do Moz? I have no chance over here. I'll end up like my father, dead and remembered by all as a..."

He couldn't finish the sentence and took a pull on his cigarette to compose himself.

We stood in silence for a few moments. I felt a selfish anger, at that point unable to comprehend the domestic circumstances Frankie had to endure.

I don't know if it was my lack of tact or a passive aggressive anger that had built within me over the past while, but I wished to fuck I never said what I was about to utter. Just as we were finishing our smokes, Frankie patted me on the shoulder and began to encourage me; "Listen Moz, your almost home and dried. Get the exams, get to Uni and we can visit each other all the time. Can you imagine the parties we're gonna have?"

I disregarded his kind words of encouragement immediately by hitting him hard with my horrible and petulant mouth.

"S'pose it's come at a good time, all of this. Perfect timing for you to make your escape...isn't it?"

He had been walking back to the party when I had spoken, my words seemed to physically turn him around like a strong hand on the shoulder. He had a glint in his eye...not a good one.

"Whats that Moz?"

"You know what I mean. It's a good time for you to get the hell outta the country. I'm on high alert every time some prick mentions the whole drugs thing in there. If word got out, you...and I are finished...forget about it."

He stood in silence for a moment, before asking in a very low voice; "Why would we be finished? What's any of this got to do with *us?*"

I laughed, surprising myself at how bitter it sounded.

"What's any of this got to do with you? Are you fuckin' stupid? You do realise if your past exploits are made known, if the likes of O'Halloran let's his mouth run, then you are fucked...*truly* fucked?"

Again, he stood silent, not moving a muscle.

"Maybe I'm stupid, but please enlighten me...genius, what my past exploits are?"

I shook my head in confusion. Whispering through gritted teeth as I was beginning to become angry, I replied, "Frankie, the fuckin' drug dealing past. Remember…O'Halloran caught you…Jeez…"

Before I finished the last sentence, I was astonished to find myself rammed up against the wall, Frankie's hands clasped tight around my throat.

"You little fuck.", he hissed, droplets of spittle arrowing into my eyes; "How many times? You really don't think much of me, do you? I thought you understood. I should smash your fuckin' face in for you…do us both a favour."

His grip tightened and he pulled his arm back, preparing a punch. His eyes roared with a manic intensity and I feared for myself at that moment. To my great relief he released his grip and put his other arm down. As he walked back to the house, he turned and spoke over his shoulder.

"Morrissey…never call my house again or come near me. If I see you again, I'll kick ten bells of shite out of you. Count yourself lucky I didn't do it tonight, I didn't want to do it on your uncles' property, ye can thank him. Now, go to hell like the rest of them…fuckin' gobshite."

When he went back to the house, I made a quick exit out the back gate and walked towards the taxi office. I wept the whole way there. To be spoken to like that by my best friend in the world, the only person in the world who understood me, had broken my heart into pieces. As usual, full of self-pity, I sat silently in the taxi worrying about how I came across to other people, trying to work out what my problem was…with no real thought for how Frankie was feeling.

Then, just before the taxi took the turn off to Lisnaderry, I saw the sign. Hanging on a streetlight, the sign read;

"Due to recent incidents in the local community, a crisis meeting will be held in Ballymoy Community Centre on Wednesday 4th March at 8pm."

A shiver ran down my spine. A crisis meeting only a few weeks away. I prayed Frankie would be long gone, but then remembered he said he would be leaving around the first week of *April*, not *March*.

When the taxi dropped me off at my house, I rushed to the toilet and threw up. It was then I began to realise that the local plot was only beginning to thicken.

As We Sat Amongst the Sleeping Swans

CHAPTER 15

I don't know how I made it back, but I awoke the next morning in my hostel bed. Again, there was no one around and I sat on the edge of the bed, head pounding wondering what the hell to do. Most of the night appeared to be a blur, the only vivid image in my mind was the sight of Pierre's fist coming hard into my face. Although the strike had come like a bolt from the blue, my memory seemed to be punishing me for not seeing it coming in real time, as I could remember it coming towards my jaw in slow motion. I rubbed my jaw instinctively and felt no pain. The impact hadn't been hard, the shock of being hit most likely knocking me to the ground, that, and the trippy fucking drugs Beetlebum had given me.

I didn't bother checking my clothes for money. I had always kept money in my wallet, and they had emptied it the night before, throwing it back to me like a discarded carcass. A wave of panic spread through me and again I rushed to the toilet and threw up nothing but yellow bile. Normally I would have worried about my health, and the consequences all the vomiting on an empty stomach would incur, but at that moment I would have gladly choked and died.

I went back and sat on the edge of the bed once more. I remembered when I used to play chess with my father. He was a very good player, never one for letting his son win a handy game against him. I remember the feeling of being completely checkmated, a position where there was nothing else to do but concede. I knew I was in a similar futile position now.

I considered a shower but couldn't muster the energy. I sat ruffling my hair reflexively, my mind a void. Just when I thought things couldn't get any worse, one of the surly cleaning ladies entered the room and disappeared immediately. I heard accented ranting coming from outside the room, then silence. I dressed quickly as I sensed what was coming. Just as I had finished, I began packing my stuff.

The two Jackeens swaggered into the room, grinning from ear to ear.

They both sat down menacingly on either side of me. I felt I was in a lucid dream at that moment but felt no intimidation after what I had endured in the alleyway the night before. If they intended to harm or even kill me, I couldn't have cared less at that moment. It would have solved a huge problem I was struggling to deal with, so they'd be doing me a favour.

"We've had some complaints about you.", said the ferrety looking one. The baby looking one sat in silence, only for the sound of a few tut-tuts.

"Yeah.", I replied, "And what?"

Both laughed; "And what, eh? These fuckin' nordies and their quick mouths.", replied the ferrety looking one. The baby looking one shook his head and laughed without any humour.

"You've been breaking the rules fella. Cleaning ladies aren't happy with ye. You know how it is, we need to keep these women happy to have a good business. They want you out...sorry fella, but you need to leave...now."

I knew it was coming so stood and packed the remaining few things into the bag.

"OK-I'll leave now. However, you owe me some money."

The two of them sat in mock surprise.

"Oh no, we owe ye money. Had forgotten all about that...sorry.", said the ferrety looking one. The baby looking one put his hands in the air in mock horror. "How much do we owe you sir?", the ferrety looking one continued.

I feared from their sarcastic words that things were not going to work out too well in this particular transaction.

"Well, I paid for seven nights and you're kicking me out after five, so you owe me for two nights. So, can you give me thirty punts back then please?"

They both sat and rubbed their chins in mock confusion. This was getting tiresome and I wished that they would just pay up so I could get the hell out of there, and more importantly get the hell away from them.

"Jeez, thirty punts. That's quite a bit...wouldn't have that amount on me. What do you have on ye?", the ferrety looking one said to the baby looking one. The baby looking one emptied his pockets of a few used tissues, a fiver, and a few coins.

"Hmm, not much. Let me see. Emm, seven punts and sixty-four pence."

He looked up at me; "That do ye?"

Before I could answer, the ferrety looking one replied; "Coz it'll fuckin' have to. You're lucky to get anything back. You broke the rules and we have every right to evict you without giving you anything. So, I suggest very strongly that you take this few quid and get the fuck out of here...before we *kick* ye out."

I stood with rage flooding my veins. Again, another check-mate position facing me. I walked towards the baby looking one and before I took the money, he stood, and the money fell from his lap onto the floor. I crouched and gathered up the coins. Just then, the baby looking one put his foot on my right hand. I swore I heard bones cracking and the searing pain shot up my right arm. The ferrety looking one bent down and hissed into my face;

"Now, get the fuck outta here and never let us see you again. We never liked you. We've seen your type a thousand times before. Troublemaker with a smart mouth. So, I suggest you leave now before we break your fuckin' teeth too."

I stood and massaged my hands. I had an almost uncontrollable urge to lunge at them and unleash hell on the bastards. I wanted to pay back some pain but composed myself and turned to go, as I simply couldn't summon the energy.

As We Sat Amongst the Sleeping Swans

Just as I went to open the door, one of the Jackeens called after me. I turned to see what he wanted.

"You need to sort yerself out fella. You're a mess.", said the ferrety looking one. I looked at him. He was the type one would cross the road to avoid, he looked wrong in every way, yet he was the one giving me life advice. I let out a little chuckle at the irony of it all, much to their confusion and left that place with the loose change jangling in my pocket sounding in my head like the clanging bells of doom.

The early afternoon was cold once more, colder than what it had been. I walked aimlessly once more around Dublin's streets. I had no more direction left. I almost laughed at how much of a useless prick I had turned out to be. When my father had been my age he had been working in England as an apprentice electrician, living in digs and making his way in the world without a penny in his pocket apart from the little he earned. Here I was, not being able to survive a week on my own. I had my grandfather's inheritance in my back pocket, a plan and a relatively clear head and I completely fucked everything up...royally! I had always thought I was smarter than what I was. Book smart, yes, but when it came to life, I proved to be what I always suspected Frankie thought of me, that being a silly little boy who relied upon his parents for everything.

I was an embarrassment.

Just as I had that moment of clarity and my defences and ego were completely immobilised, I had my revelation. I had a direction once more, this time it was a completely selfless one. The feeling was completely alien to me and I walked with purpose once more to a friendly face in a city where they were few and far between.

It took me a few hours due to my poor sense of direction, but when I got there, I smiled for the first time in days. I walked into the smoky pub and tried to pick her out from behind the bar. There was no sign of her, and I panicked a little, quickening my pace towards the bar. A large old lady stood behind it, conversing with some of the barflies.

"Is Hilda around?", I interrupted as I grew impatient waiting for the lady to turn her attention towards me.

"Who's asking?", came a gruff response from a gruffer voice. I knew she was a smoker from the lines around her mouth and the growl from her throat. She confirmed my suspicions by lighting one up, drawing deep on it and gazing at me with steely eyes awaiting an answer.

"I'm a friend. She told me to drop by the next time I was in the area for a catch-up. Is she around?"

My heart was beating in anticipation of her response. She seemed to realise and relish this as she drew out her response a little further, so much that she took an order from one of the punters in the time it took her to respond. As she poured a slow pint of Guinness, she pondered me once more.

"Are you a relative?", she asked.

As We Sat Amongst the Sleeping Swans

"No...I'm not a fucking...sorry, no. I'm a friend...like I just said."

This bitch was really trying my patience now and I was disappointed I lost my temper with her. She smirked and on-cue the punter who was waiting on his pint, scolded me for my petulance towards her; "Mind yer fuckin' language ye pup. Don't speak to Paula like that."

I nodded my head and apologised. "Listen Paula...I was in here last week and Hilda and I seemed to hit it off...in a friendship way. She told me to drop by for a chat the next time I was in the area."

"Friendship, eh? You know Hilda is a married woman with a couple of children...don't you?"

"Yes, yes...of course. Look Paula, I have no romantic interests in Hilda if that's what you think. Look at her, look at me. I'm a friggin' boy for God's sake."

She nodded her head in agreement. "Yes...yes you are. A little boy. I was only pulling yer leg by the way. As if Hilda would be interested in the likes of you."

She smiled for the first time, her teeth stumpy and yellow and I was glad then of her surly demeanour, as it at least saved mankind the horror of those teeth.

"Hilda is off today; she won't be back until Friday. Now, do you want a drink?"

My heart sank.

"Can I have an orange please?"

As We Sat Amongst the Sleeping Swans

She poured a bottle of fizzy orange juice into a glass with ice in it. I gave her two punts and she didn't give me any change from it. Dublin was an expensive hole I thought as I took a sip. It was the first little bit of pleasure I had in days as the fizzy orange tasted so good it took me by surprise and I had to stop myself from drinking it all down in one go. I found a corner of the pub and sat there for a while thinking. I knew it was ending. I considered my two options. The first was most appealing. Walk around Dublin until I found a busy road with cars driving very fast along it. Step out and lights out, the blissful feeling of being no more, a permanent sleep offering a permanent peace with no more world worries...and memories. Option two was worse. Phone home and go back to Lisnaderry, face it all and take the consequences. I felt dizzy at the thought and took another small sip.

But I had to do it...for Frankie...and his mum.

I spotted one of the old regulars at the jukebox and had to endure some terrible old song for a few minutes before I got up and went to it. I hoked in my pockets and put some coins in the jukebox. Once more I selected "The Lonesome Boatman" and retired back to the solace of the corner. I took another sip, closed my eyes, and listened to the magical sound of that song. I remembered the last day I heard it. I had been broken but had been full of a strange kind of hope that I could start my life all over again. This time, I was *more* broken and devoid of any hope. It was all too much and the beauty of the music made me cry in that corner, anonymous and quite pathetic.

As We Sat Amongst the Sleeping Swans

An hour or so later, the surly barmaid came over to where I sat. I still had half a glass left and was glad I did. Surely, she couldn't kick out a paying customer who hadn't done anything wrong nor finished their drink. She hovered above me and considered my glass.

"This dead?", she asked and was about to lift it and take it away.

"No, I'm still drinking it.", I answered trying not to let my irritation spill over. She tutted and said something under her breath before finally walking off.

"Fuckin' hell", I hissed under *my* breath and felt like punching the wall in anger. I restrained myself with all my strength as surely that would have given her excuse to expel me from the pub.

I got up from where I sat to go to the toilet and as I walked past the door of the pub, I realised it was dark outside once more. A man walked into the pub at that point and I could feel the cold air follow in behind him. I smiled to myself, very ironically.

My bed would be cold tonight I thought.

I came back to the corner when finished in the toilet and sat for a few minutes. I shivered, even though it was warm and cosy. It seemed to be a reflexive response to what I was planning to do. Once more I felt nauseous and had to use all the little strength I had left in my body to refrain from vomiting once more.

That would surely give her the excuse to kick me out.

I took a deep breath, went to the jukebox, fished out one of my last coins and let "The Lonesome Boatman" play once more. I went up to the bar.

"Are ye finally finished with that drink? Ye want another?", the barmaid asked as surly as ever.

"No, I'm OK", I responded.

She put her hands up in confusion; "What do ye want then?"

I took a deep breath and felt like crying. The enormity of what I was about to do mixed with hunger and the beautifully haunting music were drawing out emotions I never realised were there before.

I held it together.

"Could I use your phone please?

Again, she stood considering me for a few moments. She really loved the power plays!

"Where are ye calling?"

"Just up north. It will be a very quick call."

Once more she considered my question.

"OK-two minutes, two punts."

It was an unusually fair offer from her, and I handed her the last fiver. "Might as well give me another orange too."

She poured the orange drink, directing me to the phone in a little hallway behind the bar.

"Two minutes. Anymore and I'll charge you a fiver a minute.", she scolded as I lifted the phone.

I almost laughed. If only she knew I had given her the last money I had in the world.

I had to think for a moment before dialling the number and needed to input it twice as I had forgotten the code. Finally, it began to ring. My heart pumped so hard, I thought I was going to faint, and my mouth was so dry I wondered how I would even speak. The phone rang...and rang...and rang. I half hoped he wouldn't pick up, but desperately needed him to. Then, just as I was about to hang up; "Hello"

My heart pumped even faster and I could feel drops of sweat fall onto my side from underneath my armpits. I thought I was going to be sick but licked my lips and took a huge breath to compose myself.

"It's me...John-Paul."

A few seconds of silence, before he replied; "Where are ye?"

"Dublin."

"Whereabouts?"

I told him the name of the bar and gave him the address that was printed on a notice, on a noticeboard.

"Are ye OK?"

"Yes. Listen…I'm in big shit here. I know I'm in big shit at home, but I need to…"

"Do you need me to come and get ye?"

"Can ye?"

"Yes, definitely. I have drink on me, but I'll get one of the boys to give me a lift down. Stay where you are. I should be about two hours…don't go anywhere…do ye hear me?"

I nodded and from the corner of my eye I could see the barmaid tapping her watch aggressively.

"I'll be here. Bye."

He hung up before I did.

I walked past the barmaid; "I should charge you extra…you were pushing it."

It took all my reserves of strength not to tell her to go and fuck herself. I managed to control myself somehow. I took my drink and headed back to the corner where I had previously sat. I would have to make it last a few hours and keep out of her way until he arrived.

CHAPTER 16

On the morning of the community crisis meeting I sat on the bus alone with my thoughts. I hadn't slept well for a few weeks and felt exhausted. My study regime had gone to the dogs and the exams were fast approaching in June. It was hard to get motivated for exams I didn't even know I would sit. If mudslinging began at the meeting and Frankie's name was mentioned in the same breath as drug dealing, we were finished in the area.

I broke into a cold sweat just thinking about it.

No one talked about it on the bus or in school. I found it baffling, but at the same time I understood. No one was as invested in it as I was, and it was just another boring issue the adults in the area were making a big deal of. I skived off school early and went home. There was no one in the house and I called Frankie's number. I hadn't spoken to him since the night he took me by the throat, but I *needed* to speak to him. I didn't know what I would say, if he even agreed to speak to me, but hoped the right words would flow in the moment.

His mother answered. She said he was at work and wouldn't be home until late. The word "late" gave me hope. Both he and Willie would work longer hours regularly to keep up with large orders from time to time and reaped good overtime pay from it. I relaxed a little as I figured Frankie wouldn't make an appearance at the meeting.

Out of sight, out of mind.

As We Sat Amongst the Sleeping Swans

I went to bed and slept fitfully for a few hours. When I awoke the house was full of activity and I got up, showered, and changed. I made an excuse to my mum that I hadn't been feeling well and she bought it with no further questions, to my great relief. The hot topic of conversation was the crisis meeting. My stomach was in knots and I couldn't eat.

"Are you sure your OK sweetheart?", my mum asked placing her hand on my forehead. "It's not like you to go off your food."

I felt even sicker. My poor mum. In a few hours word may have leaked about Frankie's past and the witch hunt would begin...and my poor family would become the prey.

"I'm fine mum, just a bit tired with all the studying these days.", I lied, feeling like the worst person in the world. I forced myself to eat a little to relieve any suspicion. I helped with the washing up to take my mind off the meeting, then I went to my room and said a prayer that everything would work out. My faith had never been the strongest, but channelling Frankie's inspirational talks, I prayed like my life depended on it (which it did) and felt a certain comfort in it. Just then there was a knock at my door. My mum entered.

"John-Paul, your father is dropping me off at work. Then him and the twins are heading to that meeting in Ballymoy. Just thought I'd ask if you wanted to come with us. I know your busy son, but it might be good to get out of this bedroom for a few hours."

As We Sat Amongst the Sleeping Swans

I feigned disinterest and told her I would think about it. I asked if I could bring my dad's van later if I decided on going. She shouted down the stairs to ask him. He said it was OK and he would leave the keys on the kitchen table. She kissed me on the head and before she left, I called her name.

"Yes, son. What is it?"

"I love you mum. Been a while since I told you...but I really do."

She stood at the door and looked at me. "Oh, John-Paul I know. I love you too, so much. Now, finish up and join them later. They might just stop in for ice-cream on the way home.", she smiled.

"OK mum."

That was the last time I saw her.

When the house was empty, I sat in the living room and tried to calm myself. However, looking around at the photographs on the wall made me almost break down and cry. The life my parents had built could soon come crumbling down around us all...because of me. I had to get out. I had to face the music. Then I left the house and took my dad's van to Ballymoy.

I got there ten minutes early and had to drive around for a while to get a parking space. That was an indicator of the interest and concern generated by the local communities and it didn't do my nerves any favours. I finally got parked on the outskirts of town and had a five-minute walk to get to the meeting. When I got there, it was standing room only. I stood at the back of the building and after a few minutes I could see that there was a crowd of people gathered outside the building too. I spotted my dad and the twins sitting in a row in the middle of the hall, but there was no sign of Frankie...thank God.

At the top of the hall sat the panel of five. The so-called pillars of society. The panel was made up of the parish priest of Ballymoy Father O'Shaughnessy, the principal of Dunbay tech Mr Kennedy, the principal of Ballymoy High School Mrs Hagan, Tom Bennett a local building contractor and big shot of the area, and of course the much deified Pat Joe O'Halloran.

O'Halloran stood and asked for silence to commence the meeting. He looked the part of the local hero and golden boy. He walked along the stage and lit a cigarette whilst doing so. He wore a light blue shirt with beige trousers. Compared to the others who were mostly tired, old, and bloated, he looked like a film star. Tall, muscular with bags of charisma, he strutted the stage and took ownership of the meeting. The women in the audience seemed to melt and the men gazed in admiration at the alpha male of the community. He took over MC duties and introduced the others who spoke for about five minutes each, rolling out tired old clichés about family values and respect in the parish. It had a school assembly feeling and I actually looked forward to O'Halloran's parts as he had at least something to say, delivered with more charisma than all of them put together. I began to relax and was disappointed I

As We Sat Amongst the Sleeping Swans

had worried so much about this in the past few weeks. It was a box ticking exercise, the audience were being bored to death. Nothing was going to happen, and I had nothing to worry about. I relaxed so much I began to laugh at some of O'Halloran's witticisms, much to my annoyance. Half an hour in and I was contemplating leaving, the thought of going for ice cream with my dad and the twins now very appealing as my appetite was returning. I decided to stay on because of that and wait on my family. The usual clichés continued to flow like shit from the mouths of the panel and the audience clapped politely playing along with the charade. O'Halloran strutted the stage like it was his own one man show, saying a lot but giving little away at the same time. We knew the meeting was closing when O'Halloran called Father O'Shaughnessy to lead the prayers.

"Can I ask a question please Mr O'Halloran?", an audience member asked. The hairs on the back of my neck stood on end and I almost shouted out to stop the scene from unfolding.

It was Frankie!

Where the fuck had *he* come from?

What the fuck was he *doing*?

O'Halloran squinted, putting his hand over his brow to see who asked the question. When he realised it was Frankie, a little smirk donned his features.

"Ah, Mr Harris. Fire away."

"Well, just before the priest starts with the prayers I was wondering if you have a plan to catch the scumbags who sold that poor kid drugs. The scumbags who almost killed him."

O'Halloran laughed and once more prowled the stage.

"You must have missed the meeting, or you haven't been listening, as this is what we have been discussing all evening. By the way, "The Priest" has a name and its Father O'Shaughnessy. I'd advise you to have some respect."

"*You* can call him that, but *I* won't. Did our Lord not say in the Bible to never call any man in this world "Father" apart from our Father in heaven? But sure, who cares about what's written in the bible when the catholic church says otherwise?"

There was a gasp from the audience.

"And what are we gonna do? Chant a whole raft of Hail Mary's when again it states in the bible not to pray that way...and especially not to Mary and saints...dead men. This church has completely bastardised pagan ways to pacify the pagans of this country. Men like you and the priest who ravage widows' homes like they did my mothers, saying lengthy prayers and taking pride of place at social gatherings like this, like ye are gods amongst us. Please excuse me if I don't have as much respect as I should. Especially not to a man who turned me away from the church when I was a child wanting to become an altar boy, because of the fact I came from a broken home and my mother's colourful history...a history you know all about Pat Joe O'Halloran. This is despicable…"

"Shut your mouth ye tramp.", Tom Bennett roared from the stage and many others in the crowd joined in. I never saw a response like it, the vitriol aimed at Frankie from most of the crowd was nothing like I had ever seen. I didn't know what to do. Fight or flight kicked in and I made my way to the door like the coward I was.

O'Halloran called for calm and eventually calmed the audience down. Even from the back of the hall I could see the foam from Bennetts mouth. Frankie stood his ground and awaited a response.

Before O'Halloran could answer, Frankie spoke again; "Are ye going to answer my question. What are you going to do about this?"

O'Halloran smirked; "I'm going to do plenty Frankie Harris. Whilst we are washing our dirty linen here, I'd like to ask what *you* were doing the night the lad was sold the drugs?"

"And what is that supposed to mean?", Frankie answered.

"Well, are we going down this road here…now…really? Let's just say we have a list of suspects we have reason to believe…."

At that, the crowd started up again.

"Bastard…you hateful lying, vindictive bastard.", Frankie roared and bolted out of the hall. The crowd was going mad and O'Halloran had to work twice as hard this time to calm them down.

I slipped out too and had to prop myself up against the wall for fear of falling over. I couldn't stay in there and listen to the rest of it. It was all over for me and my family now. The eyes of the country would now be turning on my dad and twins once the penny slowly dropped and the chit-chat began amongst the people.

The local drug-dealer Frankie Harris who bad mouthed the parish priest in front of the whole country like the devil himself. Never would anyone have seen the likes of it. The local drug dealer and his best friend…John-Paul Morrissey.

No smoke without fire.

I ran as fast as my legs could take me to my dad's van.

I had to speak to him. I needed to see why he had done that. I knew where he would be and headed there straight away.

I drove for five minutes or so and parked the van up on the grass verge, walking for a few minutes until I got to the lake. As expected, I saw him in the distance sitting on his haunches at the lakeside. I walked tentatively up to him.

"The fuck you want?", he asked. I couldn't work his tone out. It was neither angry nor sad. He seemed defeated; it was worrying.

"What do *I* want? Fuckin' hell Frankie…what have you done? Why did you do that?", I asked and realised my voice was cracking with emotion. I was scared. Not scared of him or O'Halloran, but of the response from the people of the country. To my great surprise, he began to laugh.

"What have I done? Why did I do that? I did that because those fuckheads were sitting up there lapping up the adulation from that dumb crowd, rolling out clichés and talking absolute shite. O'Halloran poncing round like he's Dirty Harry and all the aul housewives creaming themselves over him. Somebody had to say something. They have no intention of catching the fuckers pushing drugs to the kids in the town. There's a poor bastard lying up in hospital half dead and these cunt's are wasting peoples time by ticking boxes. Fuckin' bullshit man. No other fucker had the balls to speak up only me."

"What about all the anti-Catholic stuff? Holy shit...you were lucky ye didn't get lynched."

"Again, I spoke my mind. That fuckin' priest sittin' up there lording it over the people. That bastard knows all about O'Halloran shagging my ma behind my da's back. Now he's dead and gone and those scumbags are sitting up like they're saints, praying and getting on like they're God almighty. I've told you in the past about the whole Catholic thing and why I'm so against it. Just thought I'd tell it to them straight."

"OK-if you are so against it, why don't you just go to a Protestant church then? Just let it go.", I pleaded.

He let out a belt of laughter.

As We Sat Amongst the Sleeping Swans

"We have *some* issues over here with regards Protestants and Catholics Moz. Don't think someone with my nationalist views would be too welcome worshiping in a place beside a bunch of Orangemen. This fuckin' country man. Can't wait to get back to England away from this shite."

"OK, fair enough. But what you are doing could break people's faith. People need something to believe in. The church is all some poor souls have. My parents, grandparents...so many good people. Are you saying they are all stupid and going to hell? I don't know much Frankie, but what I do know is forgiveness, especially from God. It's his thing after all, is it not? Are you saying that my grandparents are standing before God, after having a relationship and putting all their faith in him and Christ, only to be turned away because they were part of the wrong church? That seems pretty fucked up Frankie. Sorry to say it but I have listened to what you say on many occasions and I think you're wrong. You shouldn't have said that down there...you have no right to break peoples hope...no right."

I surprised myself at how angry and passionate I was getting. Frankie sat sombre and to my surprise, nodded his head. In a small, hoarse voice, he continued; "I don't want to break peoples hope or their faith. You're right. It's the system, the machine. Rome and its rules and hypocrisy. People are people. Our Lord moves in mysterious ways and I'm not sayin' Catholics are doomed. Who am I, or anyone to say that? I have nothing against the people...half of my family are Catholics who I believe are in heaven. Its people like that priest I have a problem with. If I'm misunderstood, I'm misunderstood. No change there."

I felt bad. He had been hurt badly in life, let down by people. He looked utterly broken. I sat beside him and put my arm around him.

"I'm sorry. I know. I'm your friend. We will both go down together. I love you and I'd die for ye…and it looks like I might have to now."

To my surprise, he shrugged his shoulders away from me.

"What do you mean by that?"

"What do I mean? Fuck sake Frankie you've signed both our death warrants around here. Not only your own, but my families too."

He let out a snort of laughter.

"How in the name of fuck are your *family* affected by this?"

I mimicked his response, letting out a bigger snort.

"Frankie, you just kicked the hornet's nest tonight. You saw what was happening there, they were goin' through the motions. It was much ado about nothing for fuck sake. I bet after we left, O'Halloran has spilled the beans on your past, completely throwing you under the bus for this. My family will suffer the consequences for this now, believe me. Mud sticks, especially around these parts."

As I finished the sentence I almost began crying, the enormity of what just happened kicking in. How was my dad and the twins reacting to this? Would they be OK tonight?

Frankie stood over me.

"What can O'Halloran say about me? Whatever he says is lies. You know that, right?"

I hesitated before replying; "Yeah...of course. But everyone else is gonna believe O'Halloran. The small-town mentality all these fuckers around here have means my family and I are guilty by association...we're finished around here man."

He shook his head in disappointment; "Bet you wished you never met me, eh...sayin' as I've ruined your fuckin' life?"

I stood, shaking with rage. "To be honest, yes. You are a fuckin' loose cannon. You went barging in there without thought or consequence for anyone. Your hatred for O'Halloran clouded everything. You have fucked everything you prick..."

Just then, I found myself looking up at the stars in the night sky. He had punched me on the jaw and knocked me down. In a dreamlike stance, he stood over me, hissing into my face.

"Don't you fuckin' dare. This has been coming your way. I should beat the shit out of you, I really should. I have to expose him for what he is, he needs stopping. He's a scumbag and I will expose him for..."

"For what?", came a booming voice from behind him.

As We Sat Amongst the Sleeping Swans

It was O'Halloran.

He must have been watching us, waiting for an opportunity to sneak up unannounced. I could see Frankie was totally in shock, then I heard the sickening crack of Frankie's jaw.

O'Halloran hit him that hard, he lifted him off his feet. Frankie lay beside me, motionless and even in the darkness of the night I could see blood pour from his nose and mouth. O'Halloran lifted me straight off the ground by my collar, his power terrifying.

"I told you, Morrissey. Stay away from this piece of shit…I told you, but you wouldn't listen."

He threw me to the ground again. I couldn't breathe. He walked over to Frankie and kicked him a few times on the ribs. I tried screaming to get him to stop, but no sound came out. It took a minute or so to catch my breath again.

"Leave him alone.", the words finally came out.

He walked over and repeated the act of dragging me to my feet. He gritted his teeth and took me by the collar. I could smell his breath, a mixture of cigarette smoke and coffee.

"Only I have so much time for your parents and your brother, you'd be getting the same treatment as this scumbag. I warned you to stay away…I fucking warned you. Here's what's gonna happen. This bastard is going to disappear tonight, and you disappear tomorrow. Believe me, you are very lucky you don't join him where he is going."

"Where is he going?", I asked.

As We Sat Amongst the Sleeping Swans

O'Halloran smirked and looked across at Frankie's prostrate body lying by the shore; "Where I should have put the bastard years ago."

"You're not goin' to get away with this, you psycho motherfucker."

He took me by the throat and squeezed hard. I couldn't breathe. Is this how it was going to end I wondered? Behind him I saw a beautiful white swan sitting on the grass beside the water, a group of ducks sitting alongside it. Such peace, such serenity co-existing with such violence. Did they know what was happening, they seemed blissfully unaware.

He let go of my throat and the air gushed back into my lungs making them feel like they were on fire.

"Get lost. Go. But before you do, here is a warning. If you mention a word of this to anyone or I see you again, you are dead. But...and please listen carefully as you have a habit of not listening to me, before I kill *you*, I will kill a random member of your family...the first one I come across. Could be that great little brother of yours, or your father. Be a shame to lose one of them over a scumbag like that lying over there."

I burst into tears. How the hell had it come to this? Behind him, another swan emerged from the water and sat with the ducks and its comrade.

"Now, leave. Run as fast as you can before I change my mind. And remember, if you don't leave this country you will have blood on *your* hands."

As We Sat Amongst the Sleeping Swans

He grabbed me by the scruff and threw me with such force I stumbled twenty yards or so before falling and quickly getting up. As I ran towards the road, I looked back to see him standing over Frankie, the swans sitting like statues of peace in contrast to the brutal violence that was surely about to ensue.

CHAPTER 17

I had fallen asleep in the corner of the bar where I sat. The nightmares had visited once more. When I awoke, the nightmare continued.

He sat across from me; arms folded.

Full of menace.

Willie.

I rubbed my eyes as if he were a mirage sitting there. I had rung him after all, but it was a shock to see him sitting there. He sat, staring.

"Willie.", I said, my voice croaky; "Thanks for coming."

He took a sip from his pint and I noticed the empty pint glass sitting alongside it.

"Fuck me-how long was I sleeping for?"

He took a long drink; "A good while."

We sat in silence for a few moments.

"How is everyone?"

He let out a little bitter laugh, before setting steely eyes upon me; "How do you think? Your mother has been drinking and poppin' sleeping pills…she's out of her head with worry. Your father has gone into himself, stuck his head in the sand. Susan had to come home from university to look after the twins, the poor children are tormented. Apart from that, everything's hunky fuckin' dory.", he replied with a good dose of sarcasm.

I felt like crying; "What about Frankie?"

Again, he took a drink, wiped his mouth, and stared at me, this time with a certain disgust. He shrugged his shoulders; "What about him? You tell *me* about him."

I felt sick. Why was I here talking to him? I should have been in England, Australia, America...anywhere apart from here face to face with him.

"I don't know what you mean. Now tell me is Frankie still...around?"

My heart was pumping so hard I could hear it in my ears. I knew what his fate had been but didn't have the stomach to hear it confirmed. I was perhaps like my dad in that regard, happy to bury my head in the sand.

"He's went missing. We thought the both of you had done a runner together. Have you not seen him?"

That bastard O'Halloran had done it...killed him.

"No, he's not with me. Willie, I think he...well...I'm almost 100% sure he's...dead."

Willie didn't flinch. He played with a beermat for a few seconds before lifting his head and responding; "Good"

It was the coldest response I had ever seen from anyone in my life. They had been friends for Christ's sake.

"*Good*? Are you serious?"

He looked me in the eye and continued; "He was a drug dealing scumbag. How did you not know that? Are you stupid? He was a dog and whoever put him down deserves a medal. Do you realise the trouble you've brought to your family...and to me? So, yes...I'm serious when I say good riddance to the cunt."

I sat and again fought back the tears. Frankie had always denied any wrongdoings, vehemently. If he had been lying, so what. He had the hardest life of anyone I had ever known, but he was the kindest spirit I had ever encountered. He was a poor mixed up kid who never got a chance in life. He didn't deserve what he got. I loved him like a brother and my heart was broken over him. As usual, not being able to express my emotions properly, rage took over instead of sorrow.

"How fuckin' dare you! You don't know jack shit. I can't believe you said that, you were his friend for fuck sake. He had nothing to do with drugs...nothing. O'Halloran had a spite against him. What about that scumbag who's living with his mother? Why is he not under any suspicion instead of poor Frankie?"

Willie rammed his fist into the table, before looking around not to arouse any suspicion.

"I'm not the stupid fuck who got himself involved with a drug dealer, an unstable and dangerous one at that. He pulled the wool over all our eyes, but you fuckin' *knew* about his past, *we* didn't. I thought you were a smart kid...obviously not."

I put my head in my hands. My head swirled so much I felt I had to physically stabilise it.

"Wait a minute. How do you know I knew about it? I never told you that."

He took another swig of his pint.

"O'Halloran released the details this week. Harris has went missing and the Guards are searching for him. O'Halloran has been to visit your parents this week-told them the whole thing. He also told them he warned you to stay away from him, but of course ye didn't listen."

Again, I sat, head in hands. My worst nightmare was unfolding. Why didn't I listen to O'Halloran, tell Frankie to sling his hook?

Because he was my friend, and I believed in him.

What a fool I was.

"What way are mum and dad taking this? I suppose we're the talk of the country?"

Willie nodded sombrely.

"Listen, this can be fixed. You come home tonight with me; deny everything. Play stupid...shouldn't be that hard for you.", he stopped and finished his pint. The surly barmaid interrupted us by lifting the empties at our table. She smiled at Willie; her demeanour completely changed.

"Like another, darlin'?", she asked.

Darling?

Willie returned the smile, then turned to me. "Want a drink?"

"I could murder a whiskey. Double. I need it."

"Two double Jameson's please.", he confirmed. She looked at me, a mixture of contempt and suspicion.

"He old enough?"

"He is.", confirmed Willie. That being enough for her she went to get them. We sat in silence until she returned. Willie gave her a hefty tip and she beamed from ear to ear before skipping back to the bar.

The dark magic of money.

We clinked glasses and took a sip. Whiskey on an empty and upset stomach was not a great concoction, but my nerves cried out for it.

"Willie, I can't go home. Can you sub me a few quid and I'll pay ye back when I get on my feet?"

"Absolutely not. You're coming home with me tonight, even if I have to drag ye back. You may be a lot of things, but I never put you down as a coward. If you don't come back, it'll kill your poor mother."

I took a drink and tried to compose myself. It didn't work. I burst into tears and cried like a baby.

"Willie, please...ye don't understand. If I come home, somebody in my family is gonna get killed anyway. Why wouldn't I want to go back home? I'm no coward...it's killing me not to be with them. Do you not see this?"

As We Sat Amongst the Sleeping Swans

Again, I put my head in my hands, my body rocking from the deep sobs. To my surprise, Willie put a strong hand on my shoulders.

"Come on, it's not the end of the world. We'll get through this. And what's all this talk about someone getting killed? Ye need to get your head together."

I composed myself and took another sip of the whiskey.

"Listen to me Willie. This is the truth and you need to believe me. O'Halloran killed Frankie. He followed us down to the lake the night Frankie kicked off at the community centre. He fuckin' killed him and he told me to disappear or he'd kill someone in my family. That's the truth. Now how can I go back home and let that psycho do that. How could I live with myself...how could *you* live with yourself?"

Willie gave me the steely eyed treatment. He then took a sip of his drink before he replied; "If Frankie's dead, then where's the body? Nothing has been found. I don't think O'Halloran's a murderer. A prick- yes...but hardly a murderer. And what would his incentive be?"

"Willie, I seen what he did. He knocked Frankie off his feet with a punch so savage I'm sure it broke his jaw. He kicked him to death, and I'd be almost certain he done the same to Frankie's father years ago. As for incentive, Frankie was goin' to expose him for having an affair with his mother. The great O'Halloran, sporting hero known all over Ireland, top Guard and respected everywhere. A guy with an ego like that is not gonna let some fuckin' kid tell the

As We Sat Amongst the Sleeping Swans

truth and bring his kingdom crumbling down around him. Come on Willie...why would I lie? You know me, I'm more like you than I am to my dad. You know I'm no liar and certainly no coward."

To my surprise he once more angrily thumped his fist on the table. "We're nothing alike. This is all bullshit. Harris was seen the next morning, there are at least two eyewitnesses. He was seen in the town and there was fuck all wrong with him. He left, just like you and hasn't been seen since.

My head swirled. It couldn't be true...it couldn't. Had O'Halloran bluffed me into leaving and done the same to Frankie?

But why?

"The only reason a missing person's report wasn't sent in for you was because you called your mother one night. Sure, she went to the police, but she had been honest, telling them when asked if she had spoken with you. You are over the age of eighteen and there was a record of contact, so no case could be opened."

He stopped and looked at me with a glint in his eye; "Ye knew what you were doing alright, ye cute wee hoor ye."

We both took a sip before he went on; "Harris had the same idea. Come on now, you've been in Dublin a week. Don't you think if he was missing...or dead, there wouldn't be a missing persons case?"

He had a point. I had kept an eye on the papers and television over the week to see if there had been anything, primarily about me, but it had also registered why there was nothing about Frankie.

"This doesn't make sense. I'm telling the full truth about everything Willie. You need to believe me. The madness and violence I seen in O'Halloran that night was terrifying. He meant to kill Frankie that night, there's nothing surer. I don't see how he just let him go. When I saw Frankie, he was unconscious, blood poured from him…and that was before O'Halloran laid into him with his boots. I experienced that fucker's power that night…he literally wouldn't know where to hit you to save ye, and he hit Frankie with full force."

"Well, Harris is obviously stronger than what you thought. He isn't dead, let me assure you of that. Now, drink up. You are coming with me."

My mind raced. Willie was convincing in his manner. It didn't make sense though. I resolved in my mind what my plan would be. Under the cover of darkness, I would speak to my family and we would arrange to move somewhere and start over our lives. O'Halloran would never know, and they would be safe.

It was all I could do. I finished my drink and followed Willie out to the car. When we got outside, I noticed the huge figure of Wolfe sitting in the driver seat. He didn't say a word to me.

When on the motorway, we drove for about an hour in total silence. Willie only spoke to me twice, when he offered me a cigarette and then asked if I needed a light. I didn't want the journey to end, the awkward silence in the car nothing in comparison to what I would inevitably face when I got home. I was drifting off to sleep when I heard Wolfe putting on the indicator and noticed we were turning off the motorway earlier than expected. I sat upright in the seat and tried to get my bearings. We seemed to be heading towards Dundalk. I reasoned we were detouring to fuel up but when I took a glance at the fuel gauze and seen it was at three quarters full, panic began to set in.

"Why have we exited here? I would have thought we'd exit a bit further up, no?"

"No", Wolfe growled.

We drove for another ten or fifteen minutes until I completely lost my bearings. When we began driving down country roads, I began to panic…big time.

"Where are we going boys? We're not heading home. What the hell's going on here?"

Willie turned his head around to look at me; "Don't worry. Just a wee detour. We have to quickly visit a friend…won't be long."

My mouth was so dry I couldn't even respond. Surely, they weren't bringing me to a kneecapping…or worse. I was his nephew, his flesh and blood. Surely, he couldn't be that ruthless.

Could he?

My mind raced as we headed towards a house at the bottom of a long lane. When we arrived, Wolfe and Willie got out of the car, Willie opened the back door for me; "Come on in. It'll be a quick visit."

He must have noticed the panic on my face, as he continued; "Don't look so worried John-Paul. It's OK- there's nothing to worry about. We are trying to make things better here."

He put his hand reassuringly on my shoulder and guided me towards a large out-house that sat beside the farmhouse. There was a light on inside it. When we opened the sliding door, I was surprised to see how well furnished it was. The floor was carpeted, and a snooker table sat in the middle of it. There was a door at the back of the room, and we headed towards it. I stopped short of it, frozen stiff with fear. I knew there was something sinister laying behind it. I couldn't tell for sure what it was, but my sixth sense was in overdrive, my skin goose bumped and the hairs on my neck erected.

"Boys, where are we goin'? Where are yis takin' me. Fuck sake Willie...has it come to this?"

Willie put his hand on my shoulder; "I told ye-you have nothing to worry about. Trust me...*please.*"

I searched his features and couldn't see any hint of deception. I complied with their request and followed them through the door. The room was like the one we had entered. It was carpeted and decorated tastefully; a desk sat were the snooker table resided in the first room. The three of us stood in the middle of the room for a few minutes. No-one spoke and my anxiety levels were approaching fever point. Then I heard a motor outside.

Next, I heard the front door of the building open and then footsteps. I waited to see who was going to enter. The person seemed to pause before entering the room and then the door slowly opened.

When I saw who it was, the room began to swirl, once more fight or flight kicked in. I don't know which instinct won as I began to bolt towards him, not knowing myself if I was directed at him or the door.

A strong arm belonging to Wolfe restrained me before my legs had taken my brains cue. I struggled with no success. Wolfe had taken me in a headlock and my oxygen levels were so reduced I fought for consciousness. Willie kneeled in front of me; "Take it easy John-Paul. It's OK. I told you nothing bad is gonna happen. Chill. We just want to talk."

Wolfe released me but still restrained me at the shoulders with his strong grip.

"Talk with *him?* Ye must be fuckin' kidding me-the mans a psycho."

O'Halloran had taken a seat at the table. It looked like he was trying to hide a smirk.

I was check-mated once more.

"Listen John-Paul.", Willie continued; "Mr O'Halloran just wants to have a chat with ye. We are workin' with him...very much off the record to try and resolve the drugs issue in the area. You...or Frankie are in no trouble, we just need to talk with you and get a fuller picture before any action is taken."

As We Sat Amongst the Sleeping Swans

I looked over at O'Halloran. I swore I could see a hint of confusion in his features which confused me further.

"This bastard is a murderer, a psychopath, believe me. He killed Frankie and most likely killed his father too. Willie...Wolfe, please believe me. Don't trust him."

O'Halloran let out a belt of laughter, stood and lit a cigarette and paced the room.

"I may be a lot of things, but hardly a murderer. Harris is alive and well. Now, John-Paul, please calm down and help us with this."

"Well if you're not a murderer, did you not threaten to kill one of my family if I ever returned? Ye gonna deny that too?"

Again, he laughed; "I'm a right bogeyman, aren't I? I think you've had a rough week son and your minds been playing tricks on you. Now let's stop this nonsense and settle down. We just need a quick chat and then you can go home to see your family. Nobody's going to get killed, so enough now."

He was so convincing I even began to doubt myself.

He sat down at the desk and Wolfe instructed me to sit down in front of him. It felt now like a full interrogation and he was truly relishing it.

"Now, John-Paul. As you were fully aware, Harris had a record for dealing drugs in the area."

He sat back and awaited my response. I couldn't deny it.

As We Sat Amongst the Sleeping Swans

"Yes, but…"

"But nothing.", Willie interjected, anger in his tone.

I turned to look at him; "Willie, you're not getting the full story here. Please listen to me."

"Enough John-Paul.", O'Halloran this time interjected; "You can't deny the facts here. The boy was a danger to the area and had history. Did he or did he not also come to my house shouting the odds at me and my family? What kind of person does that?"

"Yes, but…"

"But…but. Excuses, excuses.", O'Halloran continued; "He pulled the wool over your eyes and everyone else's. He was a charismatic and an expert in deception. You have no argument. I have records to prove it. Now, as Willie mentioned, you are in no trouble. You just need to assist us and make a statement. We are trying to track down Harris' whereabouts and when we do, with the information you confirm here, then we will have a case against him. There are no repercussions to you or any of your loved ones. You have your own uncle here-why would he be assisting me if you were to come to any harm?"

I looked at Willie and he nodded in agreement. "Listen to the man, John-Paul."

I shook my head. "And what about Quinn, the notorious fuckin' scumbag of the area? Does he get away Scot free and poor Frankie takes all the blame?"

Again, O'Halloran smiled.

"He really has got inside your head, hasn't he? We have no records of any wrongdoings. It makes me laugh this. Harris comes down to the community centre preaching Bible passages and pouring scorn onto men of the cloth and then has the worst word in his belly to say about his own step-father."

I laughed aloud.

"*Step-father?* Is that what he is. Do you know the way he treats Frankie in that house? You know rightly he is the one who is dealing drugs in the area- not Frankie. Now, let's cut the shit here and speak some truths."

O'Halloran leaned forward in his seat and stared at me.

"That is a very serious accusation. If I know rightly, as you say, why on earth would I be protecting him?"

"Why? Because you are in love with Frankie's mother. You were having an affair with her you scumbag."

O'Halloran thumped his fist on the table. He sat for a moment before another smile dawned upon his features.

"Another vile and dangerous accusation that has come from Harris. Total lies. And, answer me this. If I was so in love with her as you say, then why would I be protecting the man who's with her? It's completely ludicrous and doesn't even make any sense."

I sat in silence contemplating his rhetorical response. Once again, check mated.

Willie broke the silence after a few seconds.

"Mr O'Halloran makes a very good point John-Paul. I think there's only one person who can answer that question. Wolfe, will you do the honours?"

I sat in further confusion until Wolfe headed towards the door. After a minute, he re-entered and left the door open behind him.

Then he entered the room a few seconds later.

Checkmate.

As We Sat Amongst the Sleeping Swans

CHAPTER 18

I had always thought it was merely a figure of speech until I saw it happen in front of my own eyes. The colour had drained from O'Halloran's face, turning from a pinkish hue to an ashen white in less than a second. The smirk he had worn, literally wiped off his face.

Frankie had entered the room, followed by two men I had never seen before.

I'm sure the colour had drained from my face too.

We had literally just seen a ghost.

He looked like one too. He had two black eyes, his face was puffed and pale (not as pale as O'Halloran's was at that moment) and he walked with a bad limp.

As I stood frozen, staring at him in a daze, a commotion behind me was beginning. O'Halloran had the same idea as I had initially when I saw *him*-fight or flight syndrome. He had made a move to the door and Wolfe had stood in front of him. O'Halloran stood back and read Wolfe's intentions before hitting him square on the jaw. He hit him with the same force he had hit poor Frankie, but Wolfe stood his ground and didn't flinch. Wolfe hit him back as hard as he had been hit and the two stood trading blows one by one with no defence on either side. I had never seen anything like it. Two giants hitting each other with blows that could kill or at least severely damage a normal human being. They kept it up until they had worn themselves out, both men bleeding

As We Sat Amongst the Sleeping Swans

profusely. None backed down until O'Halloran sat back down in the seat at the desk. Willie went out to another room, disappearing for a minute or so before coming back in with a roll of kitchen paper. He gave it to Wolfe who took a few pieces, wiped his face, and then threw it to O'Halloran who did the same.

Frankie walked past me like an old man, giving me a friendly wink, the twinkle in his eye inspirational. He sat down in front of O'Halloran, the body language of the two men now putting Frankie into the interrogation seat.

Frankie paused for a few seconds, obviously enjoying the situation.

"Ach, what's up Pat-Joe? You look like you've seen a ghost."

O'Halloran sat like a wounded animal, patting his mouth and nose with the tissue, his knuckles bleeding too. He didn't speak.

Frankie looked around at Wolfe who stood, dressing his wounds too. He laughed and shook his head.

"Well, well, well…the great Pat-Joe. The man-mountain, the hardest man in all the land. Ye didn't put Wolfe down did ye? But sure, look at the size of him, how could ye? And then there's little old me. I'm only a kid who took your best, and sure I'm still here, still alive and kicking. You certainly didn't expect that, did ye Pat-Joe?"

O'Halloran sat glaring at him, before glancing away. He shook his head and sombrely replied; "It never should have come to this. What the fuck are ye playing at? There was no harm done, people were getting on with their lives and your past convictions were never gonna be made known...well only to this thick cunt to warn him off ye.", he finished pointing towards me.

Frankie rolled his eyes and laughed bitterly.

"No harm done, eh? Some fuckin' cop you are." He leaned forward and stared at O'Halloran for a few moments before continuing; "What about the poor kid lying up in hospital fighting for his life? What about his parents? What if it was one of *your* kids in his position?"

It was now O'Halloran's turn to let out a bitter laugh; "Don't make me laugh. My children have been reared right, they have sense and intelligence...they would never put that shit in their bodies...never."

"Unlike the rest of the stupid fucks in the country, eh?", Frankie asked. He turned to the rest of us; "Ye see what this arrogant prick thinks of the rest of us, eh?"

"Listen fuckhead", O'Halloran replied, "I've been trying to put the kids in the country on the straight and narrow. Pointing those kids to football, hurling and sports...instilling discipline and self-control."

Frankie howled with laughter and it was so infectious we followed suit.

"What about your own self-control? Sitting up there, condemning kids who have fuck all in their lives only to go out at the weekend and make stupid mistakes. Harmless kids who have a lot of growing up to do. We all make mistakes, that kid in the hospital…it might be the last one he ever makes. But when it comes to you and keeping that cock in your trousers, self-control goes out the window…you self-righteous pig"

His words had been laced with venom and genuine hurt. O'Halloran sat contemplative. Frankie once more leaned forward; "O'Halloran. Tell the truth and shame the devil. You and my ma. Why?"

O'Halloran sat back and stared at Frankie. The silence was deafening for a few seconds.

"She was…is, a very beautiful woman. There was an infatuation, on both our parts. It only happened the once, one night."

Frankie stood and clapped his hands in mock applause. "Finally. The truth. Well, partial truth. One night…my hole."

"It was one fucking night", O'Halloran shouted. "A mistake…a *big* mistake."

"Don't give me that shit. A mistake is a mistake. You pursued her for a long time, courted her. Ye knew what ye were doing. Did you ever think of your wife and kids…or my poor aul da?"

"Don't you even mention my wife and children. You're not fit to utter their names ye piece of shit."

"Is that right?", Frankie replied.

"Yeah, it is. And as for your father, he was an even bigger waste of space than you."

Frankie laughed bitterly; "Is that right? I would be very fuckin' careful what you say over the next few minutes motherfucker."

"Really? I'm just telling the truth when home truths are being spun. The man was a drunkard, a waste of space."

Frankie paced over to one of the men he came in with. "Give me it...give me *it*", he demanded. He paced back over to where O'Halloran sat.

"Frankie", I roared in horror. Willie grabbed me and told me to be quiet. I wasn't and he put his hand over my mouth to stop me.

Horror rose in O'Halloran's eyes, but he tried with all his might to maintain the tough guy façade. Frankie stood over him, a large metal gun in his hand. I had never seen a gun before and the sight of it was terrifying. I could see Frankie's fingers turn white from the pressure he was applying. No one in the room said anything to dissuade him. His eyes finally found mine and I shook my head and glared at him, my eyes roaring not to do it.

One pull of that trigger made him a murderer. A life lost and another ruined. The magnitude of what was happening made my head swirl so much I thought I was going to lose consciousness.

Frankie put down the gun and walked towards us. He shook his head.

"No, I won't do it. You'll get it tonight, but it won't come from *me*. I won't give you the satisfaction."

As We Sat Amongst the Sleeping Swans

To my surprise, O'Halloran laughed; "I knew ye didn't have it in ye. Like your father...completely ballless."

What was O'Halloran playing at? Did he have a death wish?

Frankie rose above it.

"You can say whatever you want dickhead...but everyone knows my father was a top man. Far better than what you could ever dream of. Your words mean nothing to me. The only words that mean anything is the truth. I want you to tell everyone here the truth about me...the truth about the set-up that night. I want you to clear my name in front of my friends."

O'Halloran sat and shook his head. He ran his fingers through his hair and tiredly rubbed his eyes; "If you hadn't gotten involved in it then, you would have at some stage. I was just doing what was right for the community.", he sombrely responded.

Frankie sat at the table and put his head in his hands. O'Halloran sat wiping his wounds. Nobody spoke for a few seconds, until Frankie broke the silence.

"You despise me so much you cannot admit it. Even facing imminent death, you can't tell the truth. Boys meet super cop here. The cop who can predict future criminals and nail them before they have even committed a crime. What was your training in Guard school? What is your evidence for bringing in this man, Sergeant O'Halloran? Well, I didn't like the head on him."

There was a nervous laugh from everyone in the room from Frankie's remark, everyone apart from O'Halloran who sat defiantly staring at him.

"Have ye ever heard the likes of it boys?"

Frankie sat for a few seconds in further silence. He stood, shaking his head.

"Ye had your chance for redemption, O'Halloran. After all you have done to me, I was willing to give ye a chance, but you just couldn't tell the truth. Boys do what yis have to do.", he concluded as he walked towards the door. O'Halloran spat after him but missed by a few feet. Frankie turned before he left the room, calling for me to come with him.

"I was gonna ask that ye say hello to my da where you are going, O'Halloran. But I doubt your paths will cross, as yis will surely be in two very different places."

I followed him out through the door. From inside the room I could hear much commotion and shouting. Wolfe and Willie followed us out of the room and Willie grabbed my arm and guided me out into the night air.

"What's happening in there?", I asked. I didn't want to know but felt I had to ask.

"Nothing, the boys are just having a word with him.", Willie answered. When I looked over my shoulder, I noticed Wolfe helping Frankie walk out of the building like a frail, elderly person. Willie told me to get into the back of the car and left the door open for Frankie. He got in beside me and patted me on the leg and smiled. Just before Willie closed the back door, the noise from inside the building resonated across the yard and into the metal of the car.

The unmistakeable sound of a single gunshot.

I put my head in my hands and broke down in tears. The shock and magnitude of a man losing his life a few feet away, too much for my senses. Frankie put an arm on my shoulder and consoled me as best he could, but I just couldn't stop.

Wolfe turned on the headlights and put the car into gear. We drove up that quiet country lane like the first car in a funeral procession.

We drove for another half hour or so before Wolfe stopped the car and got out; "Come on in boys"

We got out and went into his house. Wolfe made each of us coffee with a generous shot of whiskey in each one. We drank them down quickly before he disappeared into the kitchen and came back seconds later with a full bottle and four glasses. I drank a few and didn't feel at all drunk. In fact, they seemed to settle and sober me. We sat in silence for half an hour, all of us seemingly enjoying the stillness of the early morning in contrast to the violence of the late night's activities. After another few drinks, Willie stood in front of the fireplace.

"Sorry about the deception John-Paul. You are in no trouble and you don't need to worry about a thing. We had to play you to get O'Halloran where we wanted him."

I shook my head; "So, you fuckin' used me as a pawn in another man's murder?", I replied, anger rising in me.

"Cool it Moz.", Frankie interrupted; "He's not a man, he's a snake...a rat. Did he or did he not leave me for dead and threaten to kill your family? He's getting what's coming to him, so don't give me that shit."

I sat and took another sip, it only fuelling the anger in me.

"I've been used as bait. If O'Halloran's a snake or a rat as you say, what does that make me...a worm?"

Willie paced across the room; "John-Paul see the bigger picture here. He was a dangerous bastard. You saw what he did to Frankie, what he *tried* to do."

I looked over at Frankie who sat in contemplation with his drink. I nodded in agreement; "What happened that night? How did you survive, Frankie?"

He looked haunted, and before he could reply, Willie put a hand on his shoulder and spoke for him; "That night Wolfe and I were in the pub in Ballymoy having a drink after work. We sure weren't gonna waste our time listening to them shower of bastards down in that community centre. Anyway, the crowds began pouring in afterwards and the whole talk was about Frankie barnstorming the meeting. Surprisingly you had a lot of support for what ye said.", he stopped to turn and address Frankie. Frankie nodded his head in acknowledgement.

As We Sat Amongst the Sleeping Swans

"Anyway", Willie continued; "When we heard your man here had bolted after his argument with O'Halloran, alarm bells were raised. We phoned his house and when there was no answer, we headed towards the lake."

"The lake?", I interrupted; "How did you know to go there?"

"Come on now John-Paul.", Willie responded with a tinge of irritability as I was interrupting his flow; "How long do we know Frankie now? We all know that lake has special significance to him because of what happened his...". He stopped and looked over at Frankie; "Sorry"

Frankie waved him away in dismissal and told him it was OK.

"So, we headed towards the lake and when we got there, we could see movement ahead of us. We ran towards it and saw a large figure running away, into the woods. We called for Frankie with no reply. We walked towards the lake and called out again. Then Wolfe spotted something in the water."

Wolfe took over the story; "It was dark, but the water was lighter than the surroundings. About ten feet in front of us, I could see something darker than the lake jutting out from it. I asked Willie did he see it and it was only then did we realise it was a body floating face down in the water. We waded in and turned the body around. It was your man here. We were sure he was..."

Wolfe was one of the biggest and hardest men I knew, but he struggled to finish the last sentence, the emotions in him running so high. He composed himself before continuing; "We dragged him out of the water and over to the grass. He wasn't breathing. We were scared shitless and didn't know what to do. Luckily for us all, your man here, young Willie, had first aid training when he had started the job in the factory. We got him into position and Willie gave him the kiss of life. You must have worked on him for a few minutes, right, before we could see Frankie was breathing for himself."

Willie nodded in agreement, before taking over the story once more; "That's right. Your face was a mess, Frankie. I could taste your blood in my mouth. I'm sure some of your blood runs in my veins now brother, and I'm fuckin' proud of that."

Frankie nodded. "Ye saved my life the pair of ye. We're all brothers here, every one of us. Believe me, John-Paul, what that dog O'Halloran is getting is too good for him...too good. He's a murderer in his heart."

We sat in silence for a few seconds. I was the first to speak; "So what happened afterwards?"

Willie continued the story; "We put Frankie in Wolfes van and took him back here. He's been here all week, mostly in bed. We didn't think there was any major damage, broken jaw or anything, so we kept an eye on him and tried to feed him liquids."

I shook my head in confusion. "Why not bring him to the hospital-get him medical help?"

"I heard them discussing it.", Frankie said, "But I kicked off, even though I was half dead. I knew I just needed to recover on my own and knew if O'Halloran got word he hadn't finished the job, he would certainly try again. I wasn't safe lying up in a hospital."

"So, we put the word around the next morning that Frankie had been spotted around the town. Nosey, who had seen you that morning, told people the both of you were in his house that morning. That meant there would be no missing person report for Frankie, and it would keep O'Halloran guessing and sweating that he hadn't finished the job. We saw the big cunt through the week, and he looked as white as a ghost with worry.", Willie continued.

"God love him.", Wolfe sarcastically replied, and it was the first time we all had a small chuckle.

"Anyway.", Willie continued; "As the week went on, Wolfe and I approached him in the street one night as he came out of the chippy in Ballymoy. At first, he was hard to break down and talk to, obviously not wanting to associate with "low-lives" like us. But, when we mentioned we had been watching Frankie over the past few months and had a fair idea of where he was, and had plans to "deal with him", we had piqued his interest."

"We knew we had him hook line and sinker when we mentioned we knew where *you* were. We told him we planned to use you to smoke out Frankie.", Wolfe continued; "His eyes lit up with blood lust."

I scratched my head in bewilderment; "What I don't understand is how you knew I would make an appearance at some stage. You bided your time knowing I would come back to fulfil your plan. For all you knew I could have been in England, the US...Australia?"

It was the first time that night a genuine laugh was raised from the three of them.

"The fuck's so funny?", I asked petulantly.

"Well", continued Willie, looking around at the other two; "You're not exactly the most...streetwise of fellas."

They all let out another belt of laughter. I didn't see the funny side. I had endured the week from hell. It depressed me further that my closest friends, who knew me so well, had no confidence in me.

"Anyhow.", continued Willie, "We all kept a low profile and awaited your call. Don't get me wrong now, we were worried about ye, very worried. Frankie was more worried about *you* than his own personal health."

I looked over at Frankie who sat staring at the ground.

"Thanks boys. I'm so sorry. I had the week from hell. Literally fuckin' been to hell and back...and my poor family.", I had to stop as my voice was beginning to crack with emotion.

Willie sat beside me and put his arm around me. Having someone I loved doing that, melted my heart, after living amongst strangers for a week.

"It's OK, John-Paul. You've had a hard time boy. We're here for ye. You're safe. Every one of us love

As We Sat Amongst the Sleeping Swans

you and you're gonna get home soon to your family. We just have to get the word soon…and it's all over."

We sat for another while, the air heavy with emotion; "What are we waiting for word on?", I asked.

"Well.", answered Willie; "There's a plan in place to put things right. As the man says, "Say nothin' til ye hear more.". Listen, your home, Frankie's alive and well and things are good. We'll soon have ye home, so let's have a few drinks and enjoy ourselves…for fuck sake. Wolfe, get some tunes on."

At that, Wolfe put his record player on, and we drank together and forgot as best we could the nights activities.

Just as we were about to open another bottle of whiskey, at around 7.30 in the morning, Wolfe's phone rang. He turned the music down and answered. He didn't say anything, simply nodding before thanking the person and hanging up. He turned to Frankie.

"It's done."

Frankie sat and nodded his head. He didn't say anything, but I could see he was emotional. Willie and Wolfe shook his hand and patted him on the back; "You're a free man. Finally, free.", Willie said to him, kneeling to look into his eyes.

Willie turned to me and smiled; "Now as promised.", he spoke.

He lifted the phone and dialled.

As We Sat Amongst the Sleeping Swans

"It's me. He's here. Yes, he's OK."

Those were the only words he spoke. I didn't even need to ask him who he had spoken to. He simply turned to me, winked and said reassuringly; "Ye have nothing to worry about. It's OK."

I nodded.

He stood in front of the fireplace, took a drink and then spoke; "You two boys, Frankie and John-Paul have been to hell and back. For two young lads you have had to endure some horrible truths…and lies. It should never have happened, but it did and ye got through it in your own ways. The fallout of tonight will hit the community and the greater area like a bomb. You boys were instrumental in the justice served. Whatever happens in life, us four have an unbreakable bond and Wolfe and I want you to know that we will always be here for ye. Call it a big brother role. We are all fuckin' brothers here tonight…and always will be."

"Here, here.", Wolfe boomed, and we all raised a glass to that.

Ten minutes later, the door knocked. My dad entered the room. At first, I barely recognised him. He had shrunk in size and had aged ten years. He stood and looked at me. Tears stood in his eyes, but he managed to hold them rather than letting them drop. I walked to him and we embraced. I could feel his heartbeat in his chest, like a homecoming drum. We broke off and he grabbed my shoulders, the strength in his body still very evident.

As We Sat Amongst the Sleeping Swans

"Thank God we have ye back son...thank God."

We drove home in silence. When we arrived, my three siblings rushed out of the door and almost knocked me over with their embraces. We stood in the front garden and group hugged, the sobs of joy rocking us back and forward like the most beautiful tidal wave.

"Where's mum?", I asked.

They led me by the hand up the stairs to my parents' room. The room was dark, and my mother lay in bed. I sat at the edge and took her hand.

"Mum. It's me. John-Paul. I'm home."

Her eyes opened for a few seconds and she smiled sweetly at me, squeezing my hand before going back to sleep.

"It's the first time she's smiled in over a week.", my dad whispered before instructing us all to go downstairs.

Downstairs, Susan rustled up the most delicious breakfast of sausages, bacon, white pudding and fried tomatoes. We sat eating and made our way through three pots of tea between us. There was no judgement, no harsh words telling me off, questioning my motives. Tea, food, and love existed at that table for an hour or so and it was the happiest I had been in a very long time.

I had a fresh start, we all had. Life seemed fresh and new, full of possibilities. I had witnessed the futility of life, experienced the hopelessness of the hopeless and finally realised how lucky I was to be embedded in the bosom of a loving family and a good community.

Once we had eaten our fill, Susan told me to go to bed for a sleep. I didn't argue. When in bed I fell asleep within a minute and slept for a few hours. I was awoken by my mum. She sat at my bedside stroking my hair, wearing a white nightdress, and looking every inch the angel she was to me. A large teardrop fell onto her cheek and she wiped it away. She looked tired but was a sight for sore eyes. We embraced and she told me to go back to sleep. I slept until morning.

When I awoke, I washed, dressed, and went down to the kitchen. My mum stood and cooked breakfast and sang along to the radio. She looked fresh and healthy...and happy. My father came in and hugged her from behind singing along to the song. They began dancing around the room and the twins sat cringing. Susan came back from the shop and I grabbed her, put the bag down and danced around the kitchen with her, until the twins sat and laughed at us all, thinking we had lost our minds.

We *had* lost our minds but had found them all together on that joyous morning.

We sat and ate breakfast, my poor mum making a fuss and everyone else joking why I was getting all the special attention. It was nice...blissful. When breakfast was finished, my mum and Susan told my dad and I to go into the living room. My dad looked nervous, and in turn I fed off the nervous energy. He closed the door behind us.

"What's wrong dad? You look nervous, everything OK?"

He nodded and hesitated before speaking; "Listen, I just wanted to show you this before anyone else mentioned it. After all you've been through, I don't know what you're goin' to think about this but take your time and read it."

I was totally confused as he went to the unit where the TV sat and produced a newspaper from the drawer. He gave it to me and asked me to read the front page. It read;

O'HALLORAN TACKLES DRUG GANG

Amid dramatic scenes early yesterday, a drug gang who had operated in the area, causing much heartache and worry among local families, were taken down by Sergeant Pat Joe O'Halloran and his team.

O'Halloran, a two-time All-Ireland hurling winner in his heyday and a prominent member of the local community, sustained a bullet wound to the leg and is currently recovering in St. Matthews Hospital.

A gang of eight men, led by the notorious Dublin criminal living in the border area, Sean Redmond, were arrested yesterday morning with over a million punts worth of various Class A drugs seized in the process. A local resident in the area, George Quinn, has also been arrested and is under investigation. There have been no further arrests or suspects made known.

As We Sat Amongst the Sleeping Swans

From his hospital bed, Sergeant O'Halloran made the following statement;

"It is with a great sense of pride and honour that we have seized the drugs that were causing so much heartache and worry to the people of the local community. I had been working hard with the team on this case over the last few months and ironically it was a tip-off from one of my former colleagues, Ger Mulligan, that helped us finally solve the case."

Asked by our local reporter what he plans to do next, O'Halloran surprisingly answered he is contemplating retirement; "Listen, I've had a hard paper round over the years. There were a lot of injuries with the hurling and now this leg injury doesn't help things. I'm sure the great medical staff here will patch me up, but I think the Garda business is a young man's game. My employers have offered me a generous early retirement package and my family, and I are considering a permanent move back home, where we own a small farm and I could do a bit of farming. Growing up my passions were always hurling, helping others less fortunate and farming. I have completed the former two with my careers as both a hurler and a Guard, now I'd like to move onto my third passion and live in a bit of peace."

Well, what more can we say? Hurling and societies loss will surely be to the farming industries gain. More to follow on this story in the next few days.

Pat Joe O'Halloran…a true Irish hero!

As We Sat Amongst the Sleeping Swans

My dad put a steady hand on my shoulder. Reading my thoughts, he spoke; "Jeez son, you're as white as a ghost. You have a lot of questions I'm sure. They'll be answered in due course. You've had a lot to deal with. O'Halloran has caused a lot of trouble and pulled the wool over a lot of people's eyes. In fact, I only found out about all this last week after ye left. Broke our hearts son, but I don't want you to feel bad or guilty about any of this. What you did ye did for all our benefit and we won't forget this."

I sat and tried as best I could not to cry. I would cry in front of my mum but couldn't in front of him. We sat for a further minute in silence.

"But, dad, what the hell's all this about O'Halloran...Irish hero? What?"

He shook his head solemnly; "I don't know, John-Paul. I don't agree with it. The one person you need to speak to is young Harris. He masterminded the whole thing."

Then, he finished his sentence with the one thing I had hoped he would say, but never believed he ever could, considering the recent events.

"He's a good fella that. A real good fella."

Those words were the only validation I needed. O'Halloran may have gotten away Scot free once more, but the main thing was Frankie had been completely acquitted.

Before my dad left the room, he told me to take as long as I needed to get back to normal. As he was about to walk out the door, he turned and raised his arms. I stood and we hugged.

When he left the room, I sat and let it all out, the tears flowing more from joy and relief rather than sadness.

I think he knew from outside the room what I was doing.

But it was OK.

Everything was OK.

CHAPTER 19

I slept most of the weekend when I got home. There had been nightmares, but at least they evaporated when I woke, instead of distilling further like they had in Dublin.

St. Patrick's Day fell on the Tuesday, so there was no point in going back to school on the Monday, for one day only. The holiday couldn't have come at a better time for me, so I went back on the Wednesday. There had been a few awkward conversations on the bus and to my friends in class, but by lunchtime everyone seemed to have moved on.

Life was funny. It turned upside down and back again in the space of two weeks. Although they had been horrific, they weirdly had the same effect a good holiday had on a person. I was focused, rejuvenated, and would never take my family and friends for granted ever again.

I hadn't celebrated St. Patricks day; everything was still so raw. Frankie, Willie, Wolfe, or any of the gang didn't make a fuss of it either. The dust was still settling.

On the Thursday night, Willie arrived at our house when we were having dinner. I almost had to rub my eyes when my dad stood and shook his hand, patting him on the back. I had to do an actual double take when my mum hugged him, telling him to sit and eat something with us.

As We Sat Amongst the Sleeping Swans

To say they hadn't gotten along in recent years would have been more than an understatement!

Willie didn't eat anything, instead sitting drinking tea. The talk was light-hearted and good natured. He made my mum laugh like no one before had, including even my dad. After an hour or so he let us know the reason for his visit. He was throwing a belated St. Patrick's party at his house and he was inviting us all. To my surprise, my mum and dad accepted and went straight to the phone to organise a babysitter for the twins.

I studied hard that night and worked hard in school the day after, the promise of a big party once more a great motivator.

Saturday arrived and my dad was still in work at five o'clock. My mum was getting herself ready and cursed him, albeit good naturedly, for working late on a Saturday as usual. At that moment, the old beaten up Nissan pulled up outside and tooted the horn. I shouted upstairs to my mum that I was going to Frankie's first and would see her at the party. I jumped into the car, Frankie had some good tunes on, Bowie...as usual.

We drove to his house and we popped in for a minute to say hello to his mother. She looked amazing, far better than I had seen her before...and happy...very happy.

She gave me a hug. She hugged Frankie and told us to be careful but to have a good night. It was like another person had taken over her body. As usual we headed to the off-licence. Unlike when I was in Dublin, using alcohol as a sedative, a painkiller, we were once more like children in a sweet shop. He had a glint in his eye once more.

"Right.", he said. "Because there are a few "proper" adults coming to this party tonight, I think I'll get a few bottles of wine and a good few cans. Everyone can drink away at those. But, for our island adventures beforehand, let me introduce you to my new friend; "The Black Russian", I think you'll like him."

We went to the counter and bought the beers and wine alongside a bottle of vodka, Tia-Maria and coke. We bought a couple of Screwball ice creams and ate them on the way to the lake, so we would have at least a receptacle to drink our cocktails from. When we got there the sun was beginning to set. The lake reflected the sun like a mirror of peace. It was stunning in its beauty, truly stunning.

We sat on the grass and Frankie made up the cocktails. As usual, he waited until I took a sip, gauging my reaction. I smiled and gave him the thumbs up; "Very nice, very nice. Tastes a bit like coffee but a good bit of sweetness to it. Think this is actually my favourite."

He laughed and drank his too; "Good stuff that.", he replied, licking his lips, and sitting back to admire the scenery in front of us. Spring was bursting into life around us, soon the evenings would grow longer, the futility of winter disappearing for another year.

As We Sat Amongst the Sleeping Swans

We drank one or two of the cocktails and I braced myself to ask the question that had been on my mind the past week. In my brash and rash way, I blurted it out of the blue; "How come you set O'Halloran up as the hero of the hour? Bit weird. Thought you hated him?"

Frankie sat back in his cool and collected way, absorbing the question, and taking a sip of his drink. I wished at that moment I could have been a little bit more like him in his mannerisms.

"Moz, we both know he had to be stopped."

Again, without thinking, I blurted out; "A good way to stop him would have been to put a bullet in the fucker...like I thought we had."

I regretted it immediately and he looked at me as if I had went mad, before continuing; "When you thought we had done exactly that, did you not sit in Wolfe's car and cry like a baby?"

It was my turn to sit and say nothing. I had no response to that. Good naturedly as always, he patted me on the shoulder and apologised.

"Listen Moz, because of my views a lot of people think I can't back them up. I'm all mouth and a hypocrite. The one thing I despise more than anything is hypocrisy. If I had gotten O'Halloran killed, which I could very easily have done by the way, it would have made me no better than him. Leaving a wife without a husband, his children without a father. He's a dog, but they don't know that...he's their world, who am I to take that away from them? I know what it's like to grow up without a father, I wouldn't want to put anyone else through that."

"It never done you any harm though Frankie. You are one of the best dudes I know…sorry *the* best dude."

Frankie laughed; "OK fuckin' Michelangelo dude. No, I appreciate your sentiments, but you don't live inside my head. You don't feel the way I feel about my da, the loss and inadequacy I feel. The jealousy I have when I see others with their fathers, including you, to be honest. Not a jealousy, a yearning for something that I had, loved, and lost. I couldn't live with myself doing that to other kids…innocent kids."

I understood what he said and sat back thinking about it for a while.

"OK, fair point. But why the whole hero deal with O'Halloran? My dad reckons you masterminded the whole thing."

Frankie laughed; "Mastermind-more masturbate. The thing is, we had to do something about Quinn…and O'Halloran. How about killing two birds, or snakes, with one stone?"

I considered his response and sat nodding my head; "True, true. But how did ye do it?"

"Well", he continued; "Living with the enemy, although fucking horrific, can have its benefits if one's objective is to bring the enemy down. Recon is made pretty easy. I don't think I ever told you the story of how O'Halloran nailed me for drugs, did I?"

As We Sat Amongst the Sleeping Swans

I sat upright in anticipation of the story, as he had never disclosed it to me. It had always been a very touchy and sometimes explosive subject; we had rarely visited it.

"It happened one night when we were coming home from one of Quinn's "business meetings" after we had been out for dinner for my ma's birthday. We knew Quinn was carrying some heavy shit. For fuck sake, my ma and I helped him carry the bags into the boot, nestling them in beside the spare wheel. Anyhow, there was a Garda checkpoint in front of us just as we crossed the border. Moz, you know how little faith I, and everyone around here come to mention it, has in the Guards or the cops. But at that moment in time, they fuckin' seemed like Guardian Angels to me. The excitement that ran through my body was electric. The cops were gonna nail that fucker and in turn free my ma and I. Moz, the shit he used to do to me in that house."

At that, he took a swig of his drink and looked out upon the lake and all its tranquillity for a moment. I put a hand on his shoulder.

Now I could understand life and its hopelessness at times, empathy was borne in me.

"Anyway, as we neared the checkpoint, my heart soared and then suddenly sunk. Who was the main man in charge? The one and only "great" Pat Joe O'Halloran. I could have been sick. The only ray of sunshine was he was accompanied by another colleague. At that moment that man was my saviour. I put every hope I had in him and his integrity. So, when it came to our turn, Quinn wound down the window. Bear in mind the cunt also had a shit load of drink in him too, if they had of bothered breathalysing him, he would have been in deep shit. But they didn't. O'Halloran shone the light into the car. I could see his eyes light up, even in the darkness when he seen it was my mum sitting in the passenger seat."

He sat and took another swig of the Black Russian. Then he produced two cigarettes, handing me one and lighting both before continuing; "The encounter was fairly straightforward, O'Halloran checking Quinn's licence and insurance papers and all that stuff, but his colleague was walking around the car checking the tyres and number plate when he took O'Halloran to one side. Quinn and my mum began to panic…big time. O'Halloran came back to the car and asked us to step out. He instructed his colleague to open the door for my mum as Quinn and I got out from the driver's side of the car. His colleague spoke; "The reason why we are asking you to vacate the vehicle is because we suspect illegal substances are somewhere in this car or on someone's person."

O'Halloran took charge, showing his seniority; "I'll take it from here. I have a fair idea of where the substances are. He brushed past Quinn and walked straight to me, opened my jacket and took two bags of pills and a large bag of cannabis magically from my inside pocket. I protested and shouted, telling the other Guard the drugs had been planted on me. He seemed to believe me, but O'Halloran had me rammed up against the bonnet of the car before I could say anything else in my defence. The other Guard wanted to open the boot and check the rest of the car, but O'Halloran snapped; "Ger, we have our man. I've been keeping an eye on this boy for a while now. We've got him, let's get him to the station."

Ger? That name. I recognised it but couldn't remember from where. I looked over at Frankie who wore a knowing smirk; "Ger Mulligan. One of the two men I walked in with last week, when we scared the shite out of O'Halloran. I don't know who he was more scared of to be honest."

I sat and laughed, shaking my head; "Holy shit. How did you get *him* involved? And who was the other boy?"

"I will answer your first question in a bit. The answer to the second question is a friend...acquaintance of Wolfe and Willies.", he shook his head, before continuing; "Ye don't want to know...one of the boys, let's just say."

I asked no further questions.

"So, that night O'Halloran took me in and charged me for possession with intent to supply. They couldn't really do much only take the drugs off me and give me a slap on the wrists because of my age...but I still have a record. The next day my ma came into my room, crying her eyes out at what happened. I calmed her down and told her it was OK. That's when she told me about this Dublin scumbag who was running the whole operation."

"This Redmond fucker?", I asked.

He nodded his head; "Yes. He was a dangerous bastard. O'Halloran knew all about him and Quinn, but he wouldn't bust Quinn because of my ma. She had pleaded with him a few times to turn a blind eye to Quinn, as she would be in danger from Redmond and his crew if he was caught. These fuckers will go to extreme lengths to get people to shut their mouths. My ma was worried sick, and she used her "relationship" with O'Halloran to help cover things up. And sure, who do ye think was driving her to do it? Quinn himself. He used to kick the shit out of me relentlessly and abuse my mum verbally. He was a bad egg, man...fuckin' bad egg."

He stopped and took a sip of his drink to compose himself. I patted him on the back to reassure him; "He's gone now Frankie. Ye got rid of the fucker finally. So, tell me the rest, how did ye manage it?"

He took a deep breath before continuing; "That night I was set-up, Mulligan smelt a rat. He knew something wasn't right. He could smell the grass in the boot, you know how pungent that shit is, and the boot was packed with it. There was worse shit in the boot than grass. Pills, powder, and other bad shit, but Mulligan wasn't stupid. He knew rightly that the smell wasn't coming from a wee bag of grass O'Halloran *found* in my pocket. Anyway, he must have been shouting his mouth off about it round the station, because he fell afoul of his superior, who was also in the O'Halloran fan club, and was eventually given a few warnings before being dispatched to some shit hole in the middle of nowhere...Craggy Island or some fuckin' place"

I laughed; "Down with that sort of thing." and Frankie laughed too.

As We Sat Amongst the Sleeping Swans

"So", he continued; "Mulligan came to my house one day before he left. He took me for a drive in his car, bought me a chippy."

"Sounds like a paedo", I joked. He shook his head in disapproval at my inappropriateness.

"You know my thoughts on the pigs, but this guy was decent. He was young and did things by the book. He seemed to be in the force for the right reasons, to do good...fight for justice and all that shite. He seemed to feel bad about me being set up by O'Halloran. He took my number and we agreed to keep in contact. Our friendship was borne by our hatred of O'Halloran. Imagine that, me having a Guard as a friend. You would never have guessed that, would ye?

I shook my head.

"Having Mulligan in my corner who was quietly working away on the case meant I could bide my time in nailing both O'Halloran and Quinn. Mulligan was building a good case, mostly in his spare time. You see, O'Halloran and Quinn were secondary characters in the whole thing. To nail both them, we needed to weed out the root, Redmond. He was the kingpin, take him down and everything else fell down around him."

I nodded in agreement. "Easier said than done though."

He took a sip of his drink; "Damn right. It wasn't really until I met Willie that I began to extend the net. Willie, as you know, has a "unique" set of friends and contacts. So, Mulligan made great strides in mounting the evidence against Redmond and it was a few days before the community meeting that he rang and told me he was planning to bust Redmond and his gang during the week. Well, I was beside myself with joy. That's one of the reasons I kicked off at the meeting, kind of a way to let O'Halloran know I was on to him, as Mulligan was also preparing to hang him in the process along with the gang. I didn't think the bastard would mention my past conviction in front of everyone though, he had promised my ma he never would. His pride obviously couldn't take being made a mug of by a spotty kid."

"But how did you get everyone nailed at the same time. I don't get that?", I asked.

"Well, after being saved by Willie and Wolfe that night, I rang Mulligan a few days later. I was nervous as I didn't know whether he had done it yet. Luckily, he hadn't. I told the boys the whole story from start to finish. Willie then came up with the plan, to use both you and I to smoke out O'Halloran and nail Redmond and Quinn in the process. It was him who masterminded it, not me."

I sat for a few moments thinking. "So, how was it all co-ordinated then? And why did O'Halloran agree to retire and fuck off back from where he came from?"

Frankie lay back on the grass and propped himself up on his elbows; "Well, this is how we used Mulligans expertise and technology skills he had utilised in the Guards. Firstly, he had been carrying out surveillance on Redmond's base for months, a fuckin' silo in the middle of nowhere where he ran the operations from. Mulligan could sit hundreds of yards away and snap photos with this powerful camera he had...like a fuckin' sniper. He had photos of the whole gang making their dispatches. He had a mountain of photos of Quinn, so we had him nailed. Secondly, Willie was convinced that you would reach out to us at some stage very soon."

He stopped to look at me and gave me an apologetic smile. I didn't react and gave him the cue to continue.

"So, knowing how keen O'Halloran would be to finish the job with me, Willie put the word out that I'd been seen around the town the next morning. He approached O'Halloran saying he would wait for your call and then they could smoke me out. It was as simple as that. When you called, Willie got on the phone to him and got everything arranged. He set up the location which was the home of the man who walked in with Mulligan. That was that. A pretty easy plan and the big fucker fell for it. So then after we left, the gunshot we heard was directed to O'Halloran's thigh. They took him straight to hospital; he wasn't even part of the sting at the end of it."

I was still confused; "So who did the sting then? And why did O'Halloran get all the credit?"

"Mulligan and the second man hit Redmond's base...hard. Mulligan didn't have much firepower on him, but the other boy certainly did. They raided the base and called for support. When the backup got there, Mulligan told them O'Halloran had been shot in the fracas and had been taken to hospital.

As We Sat Amongst the Sleeping Swans

Redmond had been alone and had been, let's just say, getting high on his own supply. He didn't know what day of the week it was, never mind being able to remember if he shot someone or not. He had been alone, but with the information and photographic evidence Mulligan had, the homes of the other gang members, including my own, were raided and all culprits were arrested. In the meantime, Mulligan's wife was driving O'Halloran to hospital. According to her, he was lying in the back seat of the car running his mouth off that we were all going to jail because of what happened, laughing at us. She told him the plan of what was going to happen. He was to take credit for the siege, and he was then expected to resign and fuck off back home. According to her, he howled with laughter for about a minute. Then she dropped the bombshell that wiped the smile off his face."

"And what was that?", I asked confused.

"The one thing O'Halloran loves as much as himself, is his family and reputation for being a top man. Top men and good family men don't go around fucking other men's wives though. She told him that he was going to be exposed for his affair with my ma. Again, he howled with laughter, although it was tinged with a certain nervousness. It was her turn to play the trump card. She explained that her very clever husband had been recording the whole event on a camera set-up in the corner of the room. He didn't believe her but when she told him she had been sitting in another room, watching everything on a monitor, and could quote word for word what he said, especially the crucial part of him admitting to being with my ma, he knew he was, well...fucked. He knew Mulligan was a talented photographer, the new breed of Guard embracing modern technologies. She told him the plan there and then in the car. He was going to get the credit, along with Mulligan, for arresting the gang, but he was going to have to ride off into the sunset. Any funny business out of him, the tapes would be released to the Guards...and to his wife. We had him bang to rights. He had admitted setting me up and crucially having an affair with my ma...and there was evidence to prove it"

"Check-mate", I thought aloud.

"Check-mate", he confirmed smiling, seemingly liking my analogy.

"But what I don't understand is, we have him on tape admitting all this shit. Why don't we just release it. Hang the fucker and strip him of everything. Mulligan will get all the credit and O'Halloran will get sacked and exposed for the rat he is. He's a bad bastard, a dangerous bastard and he needs stopping...right?"

Frankie sat thoughtfully before replying; "When dealing with a character like O'Halloran ye have to remember the ego and pride involved. As I said, I don't want to ruin another family. His wife and children are innocent, why should they suffer? Its plain to be seen he loves them deeply. Yes, he's a monster, but there is humanity there too...somewhere. If we had released the tape and hung him out to dry, it ruins his family and makes him an even more dangerous adversary. He wouldn't quit until he got his revenge…and don't we know what he's capable of?"

He stopped to gauge my reaction and I agreed with him. We both took another drink before he continued; "So, dealing with that monstrous ego, we have given him the bulk of the credit. That drug gang is gone, they're not coming back. The drugs in the area will now dry up and the crisis will die, thanks be to God. O'Halloran gets to ride off in a trail of glory, knowing the firm deal put in place-any shit out of him and those tapes will be released. He won't step out of line, believe me. Mulligan will get a deserved promotion and we have a good, decent guy in the Guards calling the shots. My name is cleared, and my ma is free from Quinn. We will get her addiction cured and get her back to normal. Yes, it would have been so satisfying to nail O'Halloran, but the bigger picture shows a lot more good coming from the plan we have in place…everyone's a winner apart from the true scumbags who were the root of all the trouble."

I couldn't help but admire his maturity and broad thinking. I vowed then I would be more like him, rather than thinking about myself and my own circumstances in a very narrow-minded way. His maturity was way beyond his years.

The evening grew darker and once more the swans made their way from the lake onto the grassy bank. They sat in a small group intermingled with a flock of ducks. The peace and serenity made it the most natural scene I had ever encountered, but ironically having a very otherworldly feel to it.

"So", I finally broke the silence, "When are ye movin' back to England?"

He stood and walked out towards the lake, motioning for me to come with him.

"I'm not goin'"

"*What?*", I replied barely able to hide my glee.

He smiled and continued; "Now my chief tormentors are out of the picture I have decided to stick around for my ma. I'm gonna try and get my shit together and make something of myself. I've decided to become...a Guard."

My jaw almost hit the ground.

"A...Guard?"

He laughed; "Course not. Didn't realise you were so gullible. No, only joking, I want to train as a teacher. Do something good with my life. Ironically, it was O'Halloran's words that struck me when he mentioned his work with the kids in the country, taking time to teach them football and hurling, instilling discipline and giving them a direction in life. Its easy for people to criticise someone like him, me more than anyone, but he gave up his time for those kids when others are sitting up in the pub or watching tv at home."

"What is this? Are you campaigning to be the new president of the O'Halloran fan club? Thought you hated him?", I exclaimed.

He looked at me, a little irritation creeping in; "Easy Moz for fuck sake. You do say the most inappropriate things sometimes."

I didn't reply. He was right.

"Anyway, to answer your question, of course I hate him. He's a piece of shit, but at least he tried to make a difference in kids lives. It may have been all show to make himself look good, but at least he did it. I know fuck all about football, but to become a teacher and help kids to excel would be a great way to make a living. I'm gonna keep my job and go to night school. It will take me a while, but time is something I have on my side."

I high fived him. After having lost my best friend and family a few weeks before, I had regained them all with interest on top. Frankie was staying, all my friends and family were well. I looked to heaven and thanked God.

We stood at the lakes stony shore. The evening was dark but there was a warmth that hadn't been around in months. New beginnings, new growth. Life was good again.

Frankie got on his haunches and said a little prayer. He took a stone before skimming it across the dark lake. Under his breath I could hear him speak to his dad across the water.

I put my hand on his shoulder.

"He'd be proud of ye...*is* proud of ye. You done it. You've put the bad guys away once and for all. Now, let's get our asses up to this party. It's gonna be one crazy night."

The swans and ducks sat peacefully on the ground as we made our way quietly past them, afraid of awakening them from their slumber. I wondered if they remembered us, remembered the violence of the previous night we were there. I wondered if through their ethereal presence, they indeed had brought a certain peace to the troubles they had seen.

I couldn't help but wonder.

Printed in Dunstable, United Kingdom